Royal REBEL

By JJ Knight

USA Today bestselling author of

Single Dad on Top

Big Pickle

Hot Pickle

Spicy Pickle

Royal Pickle

Royal Rebel

Tasty Mango

Second Chance Santa

The Accidental Harem

Uncaged Love

Fight for Her

Reckless Attraction

Want to make sure you don't miss a release?
Join JJ's email or text list.

About the Royal Series

★★★★★ From the moment Prince Leopold literally lunged onto the first page, I was hooked. Sunny and Leopold are a study in contrasts, and Royal Pickle charms you from the moment they meet, through their unorthodox relationship, and leaves you laughing. **Swoony, flirty, rom com fun!** ~ New York Times best-selling author Julia Kent

★★★★★ Endearingly witty and delightfully clever yet brimming with poignant heart, Leo and Sunny's story will take you through every emotion on **a laugh-out-loud, touching, enchanting ride.** ~ Bookaddict

★★★★★ Royal Pickle is at the very top as my favorite as **I LOVED IT SO HARD!** ~ Power of Three Readers Book Blog

★★★★★ Royal Pickle is **absolutely charming!** ~ Sunny Shelly Reads

Royal Rebel
You've never made a mistake like mine.
It's bad enough being a bloomin' princess.
It's not all cake and tiaras.

There's rules. Expectations.

Your internet is censored. Your cell phones are tapped.

And your father is literally king.

Mine made a law that no man between the age of seven and thirty is allowed to work inside the palace.

Which means I'm surrounded by kitchen staff, female guards, and a dusty old tutor named Maurice.

Now I'm twenty-three with zero experience around men. I've never even texted one.

But on the castle lawn, there are dozens of hunky new guards working out below the tower. I spy on them every day.

I've chosen one.

Kind. Beautiful. Strong.

I sneak through the underground tunnels to surprise him in the rose garden and tell him how I feel.

Except when I finally confess my love through the trellis, and we walk to the end of the hedge to begin our forbidden romance...

I realize I've accidentally propositioned the biggest playboy the palace has ever seen.

Royal Rebel is a standalone romantic comedy about a princess who breaks all the rules, overzealous donkeys that interrupt make-out sessions, and a hunky guard who thinks he'll never, ever, limit himself to one woman — until he does.

Edition 1.0

Casey Shay Press
PO Box 160116
Austin, TX 78716
www.jjknight.com

Also available in paperback: ISBN 9781938150968

CHAPTER 1

Octavia

My sister Lili grabs my hand as we rush down the long stone tunnel beneath the palace.

Two princesses on the run.

"This is exciting," Lili says. She's three years younger than me, just turned twenty. We've only escaped our guards one other time in our lives, when we helped our older brother Leo avoid his wedding a few months ago.

The wall sconces light up as we approach each one, reacting with motion sensors. We go so fast I almost lose a shoe. I borrowed these silver flats from Lili, and we had to stuff tissues in the toes to make them fit.

But they looked perfect with my jeans and silver sweater. Lili and I spent hours deciding on my look for this big day.

Now, we only have to get there.

"What are you going to say to him?" Her voice drops to a whisper. We're in the part of the tunnels that branch near Mother's office. That woman can pick up the sound of her daughters through a wall of steel.

"I don't know! Hello? I love you?"

She shakes her head, her long brown hair settling on her shoulders. She's definitely the prettier princess, so I had to be the wild one, streaking my black hair with blue and pink. I'm also freakishly tall, even if my feet are smaller than hers. I tighten my toes to avoid the shoes falling off. We should have used two tissues.

"Octavia, you barely know him. Keep it simple. Tell him you'd like to meet."

"But we *will* be meeting!"

"You know what I mean. At night, some other moment when you can spend some time together."

Right. Like that will be easy. We're risking life and limb and our father's wrath to do this.

Meet a man.

A guard, in fact.

When I was born twenty-three years ago, my father took one look at me and decided that no boys between the ages of seven and thirty would be allowed to work inside the palace walls. No man would ever compromise his daughter.

But this year my big brother Leo defied him and hired a new set of young guards. They've been training for weeks on the palace grounds, and I immediately spotted the one I wanted.

Gregor Lisbon.

He's 1.99 meters tall (six-foot-six to you Americans and Brits). Twenty-four years old. Played rugby in high school. Strong. Huge. The sort of man who can sweep you up and carry you away.

And he's single. At least according to the serving girls who know these things. So I've fallen madly in love.

But here's the thing.

We've never actually *spoken*. He has no idea I am pining for him.

I'm going to fix that today.

"Flashlight ready?" Lili asks.

We're coming up on the part of the tunnels where the lights have stopped working. We can't report it, or our guards will know we've been here. They think we're taking a nap.

It's a tremendous risk.

This better be worth it.

The next lamp fails, so I click on the flashlight. The final part is tricky, because we have to exit into an old mop room, make sure no one is there to see us, and pop into the hall to dash to the gardens.

That's where he'll be.

Not waiting for me. No, he has no idea I'm coming.

But because he always takes a walk in the gardens after lunch.

And this time, I'll be there to meet him.

I ease the tunnel door open and peer out. No one uses this closet, and stacks of deteriorating mops are there solely to hide the tunnel entrance.

"It smells so bad in here," Lili says.

"Shhh."

We leave our flashlights in a bucket inside the tunnel by the door. I'm careful as I pass through the mops to avoid making noise.

Lili almost knocks one over, but I catch it. "Careful!" I hiss.

I pause outside the door to listen.

"Anyone out there?" she whispers.

"I don't think so."

We slip into the hall. It's empty.

"Here we go!" Lili says. We exit a side door to the herb garden.

No one has seen us. We hustle past the raised beds, mostly barren since we've only just started to see signs of spring this early in March.

Soon, we're out the rear gate to the back side of the rose garden.

"I'll stay here and keep watch," Lili says, dropping onto a bench under the cover of a trellis. "Remember the signal."

I hoot like an owl, which is probably ridiculous since we've never seen an owl in Avalonia. But it's what we agreed to.

"Perfect," Lili says. She looks me over, spreading my hair on my shoulders. There's a chill in the air, but we didn't think about coats. It doesn't matter. I'm practically sweating with anxiety.

She puts her hands on my shoulders. "Go get your man."

I give her a squeeze and hurry through the maze of rose bushes to the front entrance of the garden. Everything will go perfectly. I'll confess my undying love. Gregor will take me in his arms.

And we'll live happily ever after.

That's what happens to princesses, right?

My mind tries to butt in with a list of all the princesses

with divorces, scandals, and tragedies, but I shove them away. This is the Disney version of the story, and I'm the lead.

I smile down at my silver slippers. Even the shoes are right.

The roses are barely budding, but the high trellis arches over the spindly vines, providing protection from anyone looking down.

I hear male voices and duck behind the evergreen hedges that line the path to the entrance. This is a great place to wait. I can stay hidden until I'm ready to make my presence known.

Footsteps arrive. A ton of them. There are many voices, plus the occasional hollow bounce of a ball on the path. Most of the guards head to the basketball courts after lunch.

"I'm taking you down today, Sendrick."

"Not a chance."

"You couldn't make a basket if we lowered it to the ground!"

There are others. It doesn't matter. Gregor is a man of routine, and his routine is to enter the rose gardens every day.

The crowd moves on. It's quiet for a moment.

A single set of footsteps gets closer, walking along the hedge.

It's him! It has to be! This is how it's happened each time I've watched from the tower.

He gets closer, the clop of his guard boots firm and sure. He's on the other side of these bushes! A few more steps and I'll see him!

I'm supposed to wait until we get to the roses, when we'll be face to face.

But I panic. What was I going to say again? I can't remember. I blurt, "I might be in love with you."

The footsteps stop. I should walk around the tall hedge so I can see him.

But this is nice. The leafy wall between us makes it easier. I'm so wild with emotion that I probably look like a crazy apple, all red cheeks and shine.

No response.

I push on. "It's Princess Octavia. I'm not very experienced with these things, but I've been watching you." Oh, gross. I sound like a stalker. I quickly add, "You're amazing."

Gregor says nothing, so I drop to my hands and knees. The base of the hedge is only a twist of branches you can see through.

His palace-issued guard shoes are still there.

I stand back up so my voice won't be coming from the ground. "I understand that there's a risk to meeting me. My dad is a little overbearing." I let out a shaky laugh. "But I'd like to see you. There are ways."

More silence. Maybe he's not interested. My heart falls.

"If you don't want to, I understand. Go on to the courts with your friends. But if you are, I'll meet you under the cover of the rose arch."

I wait, my heart pounding. I can't hear him moving.

I drop to the ground again. He's tapping his foot.

Then a step! Toward the entrance of the gardens!

Oh, God. He's coming.

I crawl along the ground, watching his feet.

Another step. Another.

I stand back up.

Here it is.

The beginning of Octavia and Gregor.

We first met in the rose gardens. It's what we'll tell our children.

We walk side-by-side, separated by the hedge. Only a few steps until it ends, and we will see each other beneath the arch.

Will he take my hands? Will we kiss?

My heart hammers. This is happening!

Three more steps.

Two.

One.

I turn to face my great love.

And gasp.

It's not Gregor at all!

I've confessed to another guard!

And this one is the worst! I've seen him flirting with the girls on staff, stealing away with them for trysts. Rumor has it he was caught with his face between someone's legs on the back stairs!

He's the biggest manwhore of the guards!

I suck in a breath, sure I'm going to pass out from fright.

He shifts his mirrored sunglasses to the top of his thick, dark hair and gives me a slow grin. "Hello, Princess. Thrilled to do anything you like." His eyes drink me in. "To the bench, then?" He peers up at the trellis that hides us. "Looks private."

What have I done?

CHAPTER 2

Finley

This is certainly a surprise.

Octavia, Her Royal Highness, Princess of Avalonia, crushing on me.

She's adorable. Her black hair is sleek and striped with pink and blue. Her silver sweater glints in the afternoon sun.

She looks shocked, her eyes wide. I'm sure she's terrified of being caught. I had no idea she was into me. I'm sailing with the thrill of it. I can already feel her in my arms.

This is going to be an afternoon she will never forget.

I reach for her and pull her close. "I didn't think you remembered me." I'm about to lower my face to hers when she wrestles away and steps back.

"Wait. I know you?"

Huh. She's forgotten. No matter. "Everyone calls me Finley now. Nobody says Dory like you used to. Finlandorio was a mouthful." I grin at her. "Although I like mouthfuls." I lean in again.

8

She takes another step back. "Dory?" Her jaw drops, and I see a glimpse of the small girl I once knew before I was ousted from the palace for getting too old. We played together most every day.

I might have had a young boy's crush on her, but it was hard not to. She was a princess, and I was the son of a laundry worker. No longer getting to see her every day was the worst birthday present of my life when I aged out of her company. It took years to recover.

I filled those years with every willing woman on the palace grounds.

Except her.

And here she is.

But as her shock continues, I realize something's wrong.

She starts to pace, her fist in her mouth.

That's not how a woman looks when she's into you.

Understanding dawns. "That speech wasn't for me, was it?"

She opens her mouth to say something, then closes it again.

I get it. I shake off the disappointment. The Princess was always a pipe dream, anyway. "So, who were you planning to meet?" I take a step forward, but she takes yet another back.

"Don't come any closer!" she says. "I know about you! You — you seduce women! You — you're crazy!"

So my reputation has preceded me. But she didn't know who I was when she heard those stories.

"Hey. It's me. Dory. Fuzzball and Blockhead forever?" These were the names of our Webkinz.

"Oh!" She presses her hand to her chest. "I forgot about Fuzzball and Blockhead."

"They got deleted in 2019."

Now her brow lifts. "You were still playing Webkinz in 2019?"

"No. Naw. Okay, so I get nostalgic."

She taps her foot, and I swear parts of her haven't aged a day.

I glance around. "You slipped your guards. I'm guessing Big Daddy doesn't know?"

Her foot stills. "Are you going to tell him?"

"No. I would never—"

"Oh, like that time you said you would never tell your mother we were sneaking into the bakery fridge and stealing frosting?"

"I didn't know that blue frosting would come out the other end in the same color!"

Her face screws up. "Ugh! What?"

"I thought I was dying!"

"You…pooped blue?" Her eyes fix on mine, then she laughs so hard and deep that she doubles over, her arms over her belly, sucking in air until she's hiccupping.

Yeah, I remember that, too.

I bang on her back. "You're going to get hiccups of doom," I warn her.

"Noo—" Hiccup. "Ooooooh."

"It's happening!"

"It's—" Hiccup. "Not!"

"Only one cure!" I haven't done this since we were both six years old, but I step behind her, wrap both arms around her waist, and squeeze her against me as I turn in a circle.

Her legs whip out, her arms flying. It's different now, with long limbs and her woman's body.

But I spin her. It was the only way to get rid of her hiccups back in the day.

I realize after two turns that in trying to hold her tight, I somehow got two handfuls of breast.

Very nice breasts.

But even so, I stop and let go abruptly. She's lost a shoe in the whirl. I go to fetch it.

She doesn't seem to think anything of my accidental manhandling of her, bending over, hands on her knees, her hair falling in a cascade of black, pink, and blue.

She's really something.

She stills, then holds up a hand. "Wait," she says.

I pick up the shoe. It's silver and flat.

She rises to stand. "I think they're gone."

She's glorious, her hair wild, her face pinked up, sweater askew.

I'm in love with her all over again. All the women I've known, in all the years since I had to leave her, disappear completely. "You all right?"

"You were the cure, but you were also the cause," she says.

My grin is so big. I haven't felt a smile like that in forever. "Guilty."

I kneel in front of her and tap my knee so that she can put her foot on it. She lifts her bare toes and I slide the silver shoe back on.

"It doesn't fit," she says.

"What?"

"Don't get any Cinderella vibes. I had to stuff tissue into the toes."

"I guess no happily ever after for us then."

She pushes her hair off her face. Her eyes glitter, golden-brown and mischievous. "Nope. What are you doing in the rose garden, anyway?"

"You lured me here."

She takes a step back. "Right."

We're back to the original problem. "So you said that speech was for somebody else."

Her throat bobs as she swallows. "Yeah."

"One of the guards?"

She turns. "I've gotta go."

I take hold of her arm. "Hey." I have to stop her from leaving. She was the biggest loss of my life. Now I have this chance to see her again. Forget those other women. They are nothing compared to her.

Nobody ever compared to her.

"If he's a guard, I probably know him. I could, I don't know, give him a message or something."

Her face swivels back to me, our gazes locking. "You'd do that for me?"

I'd do anything for her. Literally anything. But I have to tuck that thought away. "Sure."

She presses her thumb into her palm, a gesture so familiar to me that my heart squeezes from seeing it again. She's anxious. She used to do that when she'd tell me about how she wished she could go to regular school, and that her father was scary, and, in the end, that the stupid age rule meant we couldn't see each other anymore.

I press my thumb into her palm, right next to hers. That was something else I used to do. Touching her is like starting an engine. Everything in my body roars to life. That's the Finley all the women know and love.

I shake it off. "You can trust me. You always could."

She wraps her fingers around mine, and her smile makes me feel like the sun has invaded my body. "Unless it involves blue frosting."

"If we get that for dessert tomorrow, I'm going to know what you did."

She laughs, a normal one this time that won't set off the hiccups. "How is your mom, anyway? I never see her."

She wouldn't. Mom does laundry in a separate wing. "Good. Now that I'm not banished, we got to move into palace quarters again. It's nice."

Her eyebrows shoot up. "So you live here? In the palace?"

"Just the staff wing."

She bites her lip. "Do all the guards live there?"

She's thinking of a tryst with this other guy.

I stuff the disappointment down one more time. "No. Only the ones who have families working inside the walls. The rest of the guards are in the barracks beyond the south gate."

"I've never been beyond the south gate."

"You're not missing much."

"So, that's where Gregor would be?"

His name makes my brain temporarily go white, like my memory is an old digital cartridge erased by a magnet. "That's him? Gregor?"

She won't meet my gaze. "Maybe."

"How did you even meet him?"

She hesitates, but finally says, "I watch from the bridal tower. It looks down on the fields."

So, she's been spying. "I'm guessing based on your speech that you haven't hooked up?"

She smacks my chest. "Dory!"

"It's Finley now. If you call me Dory, I'll end up doing extra push-ups to prove my manliness."

"Good. I think I'll make a big banner that says 'Make Dory do more push-ups to be manly!'" She swings her leg out, and I forget her signature move until my knees are knocked out from under me. She's whacked in just the right spot to shift me off balance.

"I'm going to get you for that!" I swing her up and over my shoulder, hanging on to her legs.

She pummels my back with her fists. "Dory! Put me down!"

"Promise to call me Finley?"

"No!"

I jog through the rose gardens, causing her to bounce.

"Dory!"

"Finley!"

"Stop!"

"Nope!" I head for a bench, where I plan to deposit her.

"Okay! Finley! Finley the Great! Finley the Destroyer! Finley the Almighty!"

"That's more like it!" I plant her feet on the concrete bench. We're in the farthest corner of the garden.

She finds her footing and stands way above me, my face at her belly. I have to fight the urge to bite the swath of skin that's exposed before her sweater falls to cover it.

I want to seduce the hell out of her. Use every ounce of my knowledge on her. Turn her inside out. Make her scream.

But this is impossible. She wants Gregor. Of course she'd pick him. The tallest, the strongest, the best leader. Compared to him, I'm a chump. He's a fourth generation palace guard. My mother washes bedsheets.

But he's a good guy. Still a guard, and a big-ass scandal if they're found out. But a good guy. I can't fault her choice.

Octavia leans her elbow on my head like I'm a fence post. "Just like when we were kids. You were always a pipsqueak."

"Not anymore." If she's thinking of dallying with a lowly guard, I'll give her something to think about. I grasp her waist and lift her, holding her close as she slides down my body. When she's back on the ground, I tilt her chin so she has to look up at me. She's tall, but I have her beat.

Her brown eyes are bright with challenge, but something else, too. She liked what I did. I can see it in the flush in her cheeks, the way her hands clutch my shoulders.

But there's a shout from beyond the hedges, the Sergeant calling the guards back to training. Damn.

Her arms fall slowly, her fingers grazing my chest before dangling at her side. I let her linger, let her think about it. Finally, she steps back.

"So, what's your message to Gregor?" I ask.

She looks around. "He was supposed to be here."

"You were meeting?"

"No, he's always here."

"Oh. He's been named squad leader of the trainees. He was called away after lunch."

"Oh."

"You want me to tell him something?"

It takes a second before she answers. "Meet me here, I guess? Tomorrow? After lunch?"

"Sure." I want to say something else. Anything else. But I simply repeat, "Sure."

And then I have to go. Sergeant doesn't make any allowances for being late.

But before I turn the corner to exit the rose garden, I take a quick glance back at the Princess. She's sitting on the bench, her hands in her lap, staring at the ground.

Beautiful. Solitary.

And if I'm guessing right, terribly lonely.

CHAPTER 3

Octavia

I stay in the rose garden as long as I dare, trying to recover from what has happened.

A thousand confused and conflicting thoughts bounce through my head.

I told the wrong guard I loved him! But then it was Dory? Or, I guess, Finley. That name does suit him better.

And then Finley offered to send the message to Gregor.

What a mess I've made of the whole thing.

And yet, it worked out.

So weird to see him all grown up. Finlandorio Bulgari.

I adored him back in our day. He was my primary playmate. When I was five, Leo had been thirteen and already traveling with Father. Lili was only two and the absolute worst toddler.

But Dory — Finley — had filled in that gap perfectly. We were born only a couple months apart, him to a laundress. He was such a charming, clever little thing that none of the palace staff minded him running about the rooms. We became fast friends.

Our meeting in the rose garden was a trip through the greatest hits of our relationship. Hide and seek. Webkinz. Laughing till I hiccuped. Stealing treats from the palace kitchen.

When he and his mother were moved out of the palace on his seventh birthday, a whole different era of my life began.

I was never the same. The pain didn't only stem from losing my friend. It was also the first time I realized I could completely, absolutely, want something, and my father could arbitrarily take it away.

And when I protested, he said it was for *my own good*.

Through all those years, Finley hadn't been that far away, living in the cottages beyond the stables. But for a princess living under a royal decree that no male over the age of seven be near her, he might as well have been on the moon. I never got so much as a glimpse of him. Despite all his cleverness, he never made his way to the palace.

It had hurt. I thought for sure he'd try to sneak his way in to find me. We'd been stealing frosting from the cake fridge, after all. Only now, looking back on those years with adult eyes, do I realize he couldn't take that risk. It wasn't only his. It was his mother's, who needed the work, raising Finley alone.

And, sixteen years later, he's my confidante once more, taking my secret message to one of his fellow guards.

My heart speeds up. Regardless of my mistake with Finley, my mission was a success. At exactly this time tomorrow, I will be alone with the object of my desire, my dream man, Gregor Lisbon.

There's so much to do!

What will I wear? It took forever to choose this outfit, and now I need another?

I cut back through the herb garden. Lili remains on the bench. "I heard voices! What happened?"

"I'll tell you when we get back. Let's go!"

We hurry to the storage room and race through the tunnels to our wing. At the last fork, Lili heads to her room and I go to mine.

I shove my flashlight in the bucket by my secret door and push it open, knocking the wall tapestry askew.

And uh, oh.

My guard, Valloria, sits waiting on the end of my bed.

I'm so busted.

I feel sick.

Valloria stands, short and stout, more muscular than half the male guards doing push-ups in the yard. Her gray uniform is impeccable, and, for a moment, my eyes rest on her shoes. I've done a lot of staring at guard shoes today.

Her voice is firm and low. "You were in the tunnels."

I have no idea what to say. If she doesn't let me nap tomorrow, I won't be able to meet Gregor! I picture that beautiful tall man pacing the rose garden, wondering where I am, and despair fills me.

Valloria follows the rules like her life depends on it. And it might. I don't know what Father does with guards who fail their duty.

When I don't speak, she does. "Your Grace, I have to report this to your family."

I need to come up with something to tell her that won't endanger my ability to sneak out again tomorrow. But I'm not sneaky like Leo or a quick thinker like Lili. I stammer,

19

trying to come up with some explanation for my tunnel excursion.

Lili pops in through the open door. "Octavia! Did you steal that paint like I asked you to?" She comes up short when she sees Valloria. "Oh no. I'm so sorry. I didn't want to get you in trouble. And your guard is here."

I get it. She's saving me.

I follow her lead, trying to think quickly. "I didn't make it. Some of the lamps are out, and I freaked out and came back."

Lili walks to the end of the bed. "Some lights are out in the tunnels?" She turns to Valloria. "Isn't it the job of our personal guards, the only people who *know* about tunnels, to keep them safe for the royal family? Should we report this?" She presses her hand to her heart dramatically, and I hide a smile.

Now that the story is formed, I can add to it. "You might as well report the light problem to Grisholm. Valloria will no doubt tell our parents that I took the tunnels to get that spray paint you wanted. And then, of course, we'll have to explain about her failure to keep the lights working."

Valloria taps her guard boot, arms crossed over her uniform. She knows something about our story is off. "Why couldn't you get this paint by asking?"

Lili's face brightens. She loves the nitty-gritty details of a lie. She's an expert at social media and has real-world practice at fabricating entire personas.

She's also wearing a smuggled outfit. The royal stylist would never have approved her short cropped top, beaded bolero jacket, and jeans so tight she can barely bend.

But Lili has ways.

She's in performance mode. "If you must know, there's a group of very talented painters in town looking to become graffiti artists. With Father's ban on spray paint, they can't get it themselves. I've been helping them. You may have stopped us today, but you won't in the future." She raises a fist.

I have to resist clapping. Lili has not only made up a fantastic story, she's covered the current crime while simultaneously creating a cover for future crimes. I am in awe of her.

Valloria lets out a long exhale. "You two are going to be the death of me."

Lili smiles. "This whole thing can be easily solved if you provide me with four cans of spray paint in black, blue, red, and green. Then this whole problem goes away."

Valloria stands. "Put in a proper request to Madam Mariam. If she denies it, let me know, and I will put in a word. But nobody should support graffiti artists. They are a scourge, defacing our town."

"You are misinformed," Lili says. "They are brave, bold, and avant-garde. And I assure you, they enjoy their status as miscreants and outsiders."

Valloria shakes her head. "Enough on this. I'll fix the lights. What are your plans for the afternoon?"

Lili threads her arm through mine. "Sister talk. We're going to paint our nails and braid our hair." She drags me to the door. "We'll be in my room. Don't worry."

"No tunnels," Valloria says.

"No need for them if you get my paint!" Lili calls.

We race down the hall to her room, past her own guard

outside her door, and into her bedroom, where it's harder to be heard from the hallway.

"Tell me what happened." Lili kicks off her shoes and sits on her window seat, pulling me beside her. "Did you meet him?"

"No. Gregor didn't come to the garden today."

"What? I thought he did that every day! Oh, Octavia." She squeezes my arm. "I'm so sorry."

"But I ran into Dory. Do you remember him?"

She shakes her head.

"He played with me when you were little. He was in the gardens. He's going to tell Gregor to meet me tomorrow."

Lili drops her arms. "Really? You're trusting him with that secret?"

"He's good. We were so close as kids. It will be okay."

Lili looks doubtful. "If you say so. What are you going to wear?"

I let out a sigh. We're past the hard part. "I don't know. You can help me decide."

"It can't be anything from your official wardrobe." She hops off the seat and drags me with her. "Let's head back to the secret part of my closet."

As we move to the secondary room that serves as Lili's dressing space, the mixed emotions flood me again. I don't like leaving out so much of my story. How he spun me around. That moment on the bench when our bodies slid against each other.

But there's no easy way to explain about Finley.

He's a secret I have to keep to myself.

CHAPTER 4

Finley

I pay close attention to Gregor the rest of the afternoon.

It's not like I don't know him. We've been guard trainees for two months, and everybody knows everybody.

But I'm seeing him through Octavia's eyes. And I get it. Tall, strong. Basically, the pinnacle of the species. And nice, too. You can't even hate him. He's not arrogant or a blowhard.

Sergeant has called for a run through the donkey fields, and, of course, Gregor is out in front. He's not even showing off. He never takes a deep lead, even though he could. He cheers the others on, sometimes slowing down to run beside an exhausted guard to help motivate him to keep trudging.

He's the guy everybody wishes they could be, if they could get over themselves.

Maybe I run faster to keep up with him today. Maybe I don't.

I can step up when properly motivated. I've been shoveling donkey manure and working the fields since I was twelve. So, I'm not too shabby in the exercise department.

But we have a subset of guards who struggle at the comic level. They must be legacies, or their rich families got them these positions. They are soft, struggling to complete the obstacle course, and quickly losing at the sparring matches. It's unlikely they'll pass their guard challenge when it's time to earn their stripes.

Even so, Gregor slows down to encourage one of them, Marcell, who is stumbling, wheezing in and out.

"Come on, bloke," Gregor says. "The donkeys are beating you!" He gestures to the left, where a herd has seen us running and taken up a merry chase, their hooves knocking dirt clods into the air.

Their herder tries to get ahead of them to cut them off, but one of them is determined to reach us.

He's extra tiny, a mere foal among the already miniature breed. He ducks his head and tears across the field to intercept Gregor and the faltering man.

Marcell is clearly unfamiliar with the beasts in the wild. A townie, for sure, and never one to work the herd. His face goes bright red as if he expects the tiny donkey, barely bigger than a large dog, to butt his head and send him flying.

"That's more like it," Gregor shouts as Marcell puts on a burst of speed.

The donkey takes chase, loving the game, and soon the two of them are crossing the line of guards, darting in and out of the thick of the runners.

"Townie," someone says and the others laugh.

But the herder has lost control of the dozen donkeys in

his charge. They race across the path of the guards, tossing up dirt, forcing us to dodge them.

I slow down and aim left to go behind the frenzy. I know exactly how they'll behave. After a moment of jogging in place, I'm able to continue on the path, unlike the others who have run laterally to get away from the clomping, braying herd.

One donkey begins its signature laugh, the one we breed for in Avalonia, and the other donkeys take up the sound. Soon it's a chaos of men and laughing donkeys, other than Marcell, who is well afield, trying to outpace the foal.

I slow down. It will be a while before the runners can regroup. I don't need to be killing myself over this. I have nothing to prove. There was only one race that mattered. A princess had observed our training from a tower, planning to choose among us.

I hadn't even known it was happening. And Octavia made her choice.

I haven't delivered her message yet. I'm not stalling, not really. Okay, maybe a little.

But there hasn't been much of a chance. After the rose garden escapade, we had hand-to-hand combat training, a primer on how to disarm a shooter, and now, endurance running.

Gregor has called back the recruits, leaving the herders to manage the loose donkeys. He's taking his leadership role seriously. I head toward our mark in the field, and my shoe sinks in a soft spot. The hills are showing hints of spring.

The snow is completely gone from the ground,

remaining only in the mountains. Occasionally I shift my footfall to avoid a sprig of new grass. If I were still tending the donkeys, I'd be out there somewhere, whistling and corralling the herds. I definitely wouldn't have allowed them so close to the recruits.

Prince Leo recruiting young guards was a boon for me, for sure.

It's a big step up. Unlike Gregor and many of the others, I'm not a legacy. I don't have a father of record, much less one who served as a palace guard after *his* father served as guard.

I'm lucky. And grateful. Normally, a washing woman's kid does one of two things. Accept a similar job after coming of age, or get the heck out of the palace to try their luck in college or working in the shops. Some leave Avalonia all together, disgruntled by the whole idea of monarchy.

I stayed for Mom. I'm all she's got, and I wasn't sure what I would do, anyway. The palace is all I've known.

But being a guard? That's a big deal.

Sergeant blows a whistle, indicating we should be at the halfway point and heading toward the palace grounds. The lines are a mess after the donkey escapade, and a lot of the recruits make a circle where they are.

But Gregor doesn't do that. He continues to the fence post that marks the turnaround and begins the route back. His honesty puts him near the end of the line, but that's how he likes it.

I figure I better talk to him while I can. Otherwise, I might miss him for the rest of the day. After endurance, we often break down into smaller groups to concentrate on specialties. There's no guarantee I'll see him again if I don't make a point of it.

And Octavia will expect him after lunch tomorrow.

I jog over so our paths will intercept. When he's in earshot, I say, "Hey, Gregor, got a sec?"

He closes the gap. "What's up?"

"I have a message for you."

"All right."

"You need to be in the rose gardens tomorrow after lunch. There's an arch in the far corner with a bench."

"What for?"

"A girl."

His eyebrows shoot up. "Someone wants to meet with me?"

"Yep."

We come up on a struggling recruit. Gregor smacks him on the back. "You can do it, Phillipe."

I wait until we're clear of him to say more. "So, you'll be there?"

"Who's the girl?"

Suddenly, I realize something critical. Gregor plays by the rules. If he knows he's meeting Octavia, he might not show. He won't violate the oath of the guards. Not when he's already working his way up.

Damn.

I think quickly. "She wanted to make the introductions herself."

Gregor's lips press together. "I guess I can do with the mystery. Is she someone I'd be interested in?"

"Most definitely."

"Pretty?"

"The most beautiful."

"Engaging and sweet?"

"Absolutely."

He nods. "All right then."

I dislike that he'd question Octavia's perfection, but of course, he doesn't know it's her. "Good. She'll be waiting. Don't screw this up."

He nods. "Got it." And, in a burst of speed, he takes off ahead of me again.

I swear he's a machine.

But I've set this thing in motion. I'll do right by Octavia, despite the utter craziness of her plan. Fraternizing with a guard? She can get him fired. It *would* get him fired. There might be more punishment awaiting a guard sworn to protect the Princess, banging her instead.

Oh, that is not a pretty picture for me. I might have messed with her head a little, sliding her down my body, but the one who got the full effect of the contact was me. She's as innocent as she always was. She might not understand what she's in for.

But then, I have no doubt Gregor is a gentleman to the core. I'm the rogue. Damn. That woman has seriously put me between a rock and a hard place.

One thing is for damn sure — I'm also going to show up to the rose garden. Because if Gregor is going to break her heart when he realizes who he's meeting, I am absolutely going to be there for her, in whatever capacity she'll have me.

CHAPTER 5

Octavia

Valloria watches our every move after the tunnel escapade. She keeps all the doors open and an eye directly on us. We don't get a moment's peace and resort to hiding in Lili's cavernous overstuffed dressing room to muffle the sound of our planning. We have to get me back to the gardens tomorrow.

The next morning, I pretend to have a headache, thinking I can be alone in my room to get ready and then slip through the tunnels.

Valloria listens to my complaint and calls the palace nurse to sit with me.

I'm forced to have a miraculous recovery and escape to Lili's room to try something else. We sit half-hidden among her dresses, heads pressed together.

"I don't know," Lili says. "Normally I'm full of ideas, but until our guards chill out, we might be stuck."

This can't be happening. "But Gregor will be waiting for me in the rose garden! I have to get there!"

Lili falls back onto a pile of discarded clothing. "I wish

Leo was here. He could've sent the guards away and wandered the gardens with us. You know he's a sucker for love."

I wish he was here, too. "What if we go for a walk, anyway? Lose the guards in the hedge maze?"

Lili shakes her head. "I don't think they can leave our side once we're outdoors. If we take a walk, they have to be five steps behind us."

"We have to figure something out. We have to!" I check my phone. Ten-thirty. What will Gregor think if I don't show? That I'm not interested after all? Or that it was Finley's idea of a joke?

Tears well up.

"Don't do that," Lili says. "If I add any more makeup to your face, they're going to get tipped off."

She's right. I'm not much of a makeup wearer ordinarily, so two makeovers on the same day will stick out to our guards as suspicious.

"Oh, why did I have to get caught yesterday?" My wailing gets too loud, and Lili shushes me.

"Water under the bridge. Let's think."

She sits cross-legged, elbows on her knees, bracing her chin on her palm.

I'm dressed and ready, hoping for an opportunity to slip out. We've chosen an outfit that we think strikes a proper balance between, *yes, I'm interested*, and not tipping off the guards that I'm doing something I shouldn't.

They're all smuggled clothes. Lili is shorter than I am, but we found a pair of purple jeans that were miles too long for her, and a heavenly lavender sweater that might be too snug for me. Lili has assured me it sets off my assets.

I pluck at the neckline. "Are you sure this isn't too much?"

"Only if you want him to think of you as some little girl princess who should be in a tiara drinking tea. Show him you're all grown up. That you're ready to do something adult with a capital *A*."

"I'm not sure I want to get that adult. Not that fast."

Lili shrugs. "It won't happen that fast. Besides, you're in the rose gardens. How far can you possibly get in the rose gardens?"

I flash to Finley sliding me down his body from the bench. That felt pretty private. And he's notorious for getting it on wherever he feels like it.

It felt like a lot more could've gone on. But I only say, "Right."

"It doesn't need to be a long meeting," Lili says. "You just have to get there and make the first connection." She sits up straight. "What if I can get you to the gardens, and you can take off running, and I can distract our guards long enough for you to say hello? You can give him your phone number and then you two can text."

"Aren't they monitoring our texts?" I wave my hand randomly at the palace walls. I don't know who would be watching, but I have no doubt somebody is.

Lili's eyes narrow. "You think I don't have a burner phone for that? I'll get it for you. I have one I used for Instagram before I found a way to hack my current one. It'll be your Gregor phone."

She crawls to a corner and unburies a pink shoe box. Inside are a half-dozen older-model phones.

"Where did you get those?"

"Same way I get the clothes. You might underestimate my Instagram following."

"Father could stop you if he wanted."

"Maybe." Her eyes glint for a moment, and I wonder what she's thinking, but she changes the subject. "Okay, about Gregor. Once you can contact him directly, it'll be easy. When you have a moment away from the guards, you'll text him to meet. All the guards live near the palace grounds. As long as he's not in training, he should be at your beck and call."

Gregor at my beck and call. That sounds amazing. "So we wait until it's close to meeting time."

Lili nods.

"Then we get close to the spot, you distract the guard, and I rush into the gardens. I find him and give him my phone number. And then we find a more advantageous time to meet."

"Exactly. It's not our best plan, but it's all we can do on short notice. And if it completely falls apart, find another way to send a message. Surely one of the servers will do it."

But they might blab.

Finley would do it again. In fact, Finley probably has Gregor's number or could get it. But I would have to get to Finley. If I can get to Finley, I can get to Gregor.

"We'll get this done," Lili says. "I have confidence."

Lili puts the secret phone on a charger, and we head into the bedroom to pretend everything is normal.

When it's time for our lunch, I'm far too nervous to go

to the dining room with Mother and Father. Besides, it's way less fun with Leo and Sunny away from the palace. Four royals alone at a giant table isn't a good time.

So Lili and I eat in her room, my nerves jangling the whole time. I can scarcely swallow a bite, but Lili makes a big show of finishing everything. Her bedroom door stands open, with both Valloria and Lili's guard, Botania, waiting outside.

"I ate way too much," Lili complains. "I think I want to take a walk in the gardens. You want to come?" She shakes her head at me to say no.

What is she doing?

"I don't think so," I say uncertainly.

"Oh, come on. It's almost spring. I want to see if the rosebuds have started coming out." She shakes her head no again.

I get it. She wants it to appear like she's dragging me there, so they won't suspect that I have any motive in going.

"Lili, you're always trying to make me go to the gardens. It's not my favorite place."

"Well, where do you want to go?" Her nod tells me this is a good conversation for the guards to overhear.

"I don't know. We could play billiards or something."

"How about I promise you a game of billiards if you will take a walk with me in the gardens?"

"Fine. I'll get my shoes."

I brush past the two guards to head into my room for a pair of soft leather flats that go nicely with the purple outfit. Neither of them look my way.

So far, so good.

Lili waits for me in the hall. "Botania, would you mind letting the kitchen know we will want some drinks and snacks when we get back? I'm sure Valloria can handle our walk. We'll be in the billiards parlor in about half an hour."

I marvel at her calmness. I'm practically quaking. I don't even trust my voice anymore.

Botania turns to Valloria, who nods. "That'll be fine. A short walk then?"

"The shortest," Lili says. "I'm practically having to drag Octavia out there."

She's good.

Botania heads toward the kitchen while Lili, Valloria, and I peel off toward the back exit for the gardens. We're slightly too early. As we pass the Great Hall, I can hear the rumble of the guards talking as they eat.

I glance back through the doorway. None of them have left yet.

How long will he wait? How long can I safely be out there?

Lili steps close to butt her shoulder against mine. "It's all right. You're fine."

I nod. My instincts tell me to delay a while. Gregor will wait, but I can't.

There are so many ways this can go wrong.

We head to the hyacinth garden first, so Gregor has time to finish eating. This early in the season, only the tiniest shoots are poking through the mulch. We wander about, exclaiming over the tender green bits until I sense that I should head to the rose gardens. The feeling suddenly becomes strong, like a heartbeat.

"Let's go to the roses," I tell Lily. "I bet they are starting to bud."

"Okay!"

We cross the grand promenade to the other side, where the tall hedges lead into the rose garden. I immediately think of Finley, his rugged face popping around the hedge. Those mirrored sunglasses! That scruffy face!

He absolutely looked like a man who seduces every woman in his path. And I can see why they'd fall for him. Handsome and sexy, with a wicked charm. Their panties probably fly right off when he flashes that killer grin.

But there's another side to him, the one I knew when I was young and saw again yesterday. He was kind. He immediately smoothed over my mistake in thinking he was Gregor, as if it was nothing at all. And even offered to help.

I'm lost in thought, walking deeper into the garden, when Lili grabs my arm. "We shouldn't go too far before we take a look for new blooms," she says.

Right. I can't lead Valloria straight to my secret meeting spot. "Do you see some?"

We pause by a spindly bush that honestly looks totally dead. Lili reaches out to grab a branch and immediately shrieks. She pulls back, blood oozing from her finger.

"Oh no! Oh no! Ouch!" She whirls around to show Valloria. And I get it. This is the diversion. As Valloria bends over to examine Lili's finger, I inch away from them. When I come to a corner in the hedge, I run.

CHAPTER 6
Finley

Where is Gregor?

I wait on the bench near the arch I told him about on our run yesterday. But he hasn't shown.

Light footsteps flutter up the path. They can't possibly be a guard. It must be Octavia.

I move behind a hedge, so I can't be seen. She appears by the bench and wanders the space, talking to herself. "Oh, no! He has to be here. I can't stay!"

She rushes from one section of the arch to the other, but all the rose garden paths lead to this bench.

She looks amazing in a purple outfit. Her black hair shines, the pink and blue strands bright with color. She circles the space once more. "Well, that's it. I have to go." Her voice is heavy with despair.

I can't bear it.

"Octavia?" I step out.

"Finley? What are you doing here?" Her voice is shrill.

"I wanted to make sure Gregor could find the spot."

"Well, he's not here. And I have to go. My guard is looking for me."

"Try again tomorrow?"

She shakes her head. "This was hard. I was hoping to exchange numbers." Her face lights up. "Do you have Gregor's number?"

I wish I did. "No, but I can give him yours."

"Oh! Yes! Give me your phone! Quick!"

"I'll memorize it."

She rattles off the digits. "Don't forget!"

A voice calls out. "Octavia? Where are you?"

It's a female guard. I recognize the training in her voice.

Octavia gives me a fierce hug, and my whole body flames. "Thank you." Then she's gone.

I sit on the bench and tap her number into my contacts. I can't believe I have it. Just like when we were little, I can talk to her anytime I want.

If that's okay with her. I'm not sure.

Heavy footsteps enter the gardens next.

About time.

Gregor enters the arch and looks around. His face is serious, and he slicks back his hair as if he's concerned the lady might not approve of his appearance.

He spots me. "You? Was this a prank?"

"You missed her."

"Really? How close?"

"She just passed by."

"She couldn't wait?"

"No."

Gregor turns back toward the entrance. "But the only

people I saw leaving the garden were a palace guard and the Princesses."

"Bingo."

His jaw drops. "No."

I nod. If I'm giving him her number, he has to know who she is. "It was Octavia who wanted to meet you."

He sinks onto the bench. "Princess Octavia?"

"The one and only."

Gregor stares at his hands. "The Princess. Damn."

I wait him out. This is the moment. Maybe it's better he wrestles with it away from her. I can shield her from any rejection, even an honorable one.

His shoes tap on the ground. He stares down. "I can't be with her."

Before I can comment, he adds, "Can I?"

Yeah, that's the issue. He can, but it's risky. "It's possible."

"Should I?"

"She's pretty smitten."

"Really?" His gaze catches mine. "How do you know?"

"I saw her yesterday."

"You…talk to her?"

"She's a person."

"A royal person!"

I slap him on the back. "A royal person who wants to meet with you."

"Me." His eyes turn back to his feet. "I'm not worthy of a princess."

"She's already into you."

"Me?"

I sigh. Here we go again.

"She gave me her number to give to you."

His head pops up. "I'm supposed to call her?"

"Text, probably. Where's your phone? You can put it in."

"Oh, no. I couldn't possibly take something as private as the Princess's phone number."

Oh, boy. "She's expecting to hear from you. Do you want to disappoint her?"

"No."

"So, where's your phone?"

He digs around in his uniform pocket and passes it to me. "Here."

"Unlock it, you numskull."

He shoots me a look for the insult, but keys in the code.

I create a new contact. I'm not so dumb as to use her actual name. "I'm going to call her Rose Garden."

"Okay."

I punch in the numbers and pass it back.

He stares at his phone like it's a foreign object.

"What are you going to say?" I ask.

"I don't know. What should I say?"

"Just tell her it's Gregor. She'll need to know it's you."

"Okay." His fingers hover over the keys, but don't press anything.

"Jesus. Here." I take the phone again and tap out a message.

This is Gregor. Missed you in the garden. Finley gave me your number. Sorry I was late.

I pass it back without sending. Gregor stares at it. He's totally lost his mojo. He's nothing like the star trainee he is on the field.

"You have to press send," I tell him, like he's an idiot. Because he's being one.

"I know. I will." But he doesn't.

I blow out a long gust of air. This is way more involvement than I wanted. Am I going to have to stand behind him and tell him to take her hand? To kiss her?

Ain't gonna happen.

But the vision of her pacing the gardens rises up. She likes him. She wants to see what happens. If I help her, I get to see her, talk to her.

"I'll help you."

His head pops up again. "Help me talk to her?"

"Sure. I've known her since we were young. My mom works in the palace. I used to play with her before I turned seven."

"You played with her. All the time? Like you were ordinary kids?"

"Just like that."

"I can't imagine."

I hold back a sigh. "Hit send."

"All right." He presses the green button, and the message goes off with a ding.

"First step, accomplished." I clap his back. "We should get back to training. You'll need your head in the game."

"That I can do." He tucks his phone into his pocket. "You up for some sparring after training? You had some moves."

Yeah, throwing some punches at his perfect mug sounds like a great way to work out my frustration. "Sure."

We walk out of the gardens together. "You're not going to tell anyone about this, right?" he says.

"Hell, no. And you shouldn't either. It might play out. Just give it a go."

"Play out. Right. It's probably some game to her."

My anger rises up that he could think Octavia would act like other girls, but I stuff it down. "See how it goes."

We head past the courts to the training field. "Thanks for seeing me through this," Gregor says.

"No problem, man."

"If she writes me, can you help me figure out what to say back?"

"Sure."

"Thanks."

We part ways at the equipment benches. He slides on his chest pad for sparring. He's preoccupied, a frown on his face that isn't like him. He's wrestling with this whole thing.

I pull on my pad and tighten it around my waist.

This situation is a nightmare. But, at least if I'm telling him what to say, I can make sure Octavia doesn't get hurt.

CHAPTER 7

Octavia

I'm barely back in Lili's dressing room when the first text comes.

This is Gregor. Missed you in the garden. Finley gave me your number. Sorry I was late.

I let out a loud *squee* that makes Lili jump. She snatches my phone. "Let me see!"

She scans the words, and I lean over her shoulder to look at them again.

"He wrote you!" She clasps my neck, dragging me down on the rug amongst her wild piles of clothes.

We squeal together a moment more, then lie on our bellies side by side. "What do I say back to him?" I ask.

"Ask when you can meet!"

"Already? I can't be sure I'll be able to go for a while." My heart pounds painfully in my ears. "Maybe I should take it back a notch until we figure things out."

"Ugh. The safe route. Fine." Lili rolls on her back. "I don't know. Ask him about him."

I glance at the upper corner of the phone to catch the

time. "There's no hurry. He'll be back at training. They have sparring on Wednesdays after lunch."

Lili jumps to her feet. "Let's go to the tower, then!"

"Won't that tip-off Valloria?"

She grabs my arm to drag me to stand. "You've been going there for months. She got tipped-off ages ago."

We hurry through her bedroom, past Botania and Valloria, who are quick to follow.

Their closeness isn't unusual. It's their job to go about the palace in our wake. But since yesterday's disaster of getting caught, then Lili's theatrics in the gardens today, they are paying close attention.

By the time I made it back to the scene of her bleeding finger, having failed to meet Gregor, Valloria was quite put out with our antics. "Don't think I don't know you're up to something," she said. "And don't think I won't report it."

Lili had sucked her wound and looked between us with concern. It's not many a sister who'll sacrifice herself for the cause. At some point, though, I expect to hear from Mother. I feel sixteen, not twenty-three.

"Where are you going?" Valloria asks, as she tails us across the main foyer.

"The tower," Lili says. "It's got the best view as spring takes over the fields."

My sister always has an answer. I wish I were half as clever. We dash up the spiraling steps to the bridal tower, which will be empty again for decades. Neither Lili nor I will ever stay in it. It's solely for the brides who come from outside the royal family. Sunny spent a week up there before marrying Leo.

Normally it would be locked up, but we've spent so

much time in the sitting room of the tower, the cleaning staff has left it open.

We reach the padded window bench overlooking the training field. The guards are putting on their pads to spar. I might not stay. It's hard for me to watch them punch each other, even if they are striking pads. I've never been one to manage violence well.

"You're right," Lili whispers, her gaze on the door where our two guards are choosing their spots to stand and wait. "He's going to be busy until the end of the day. We have plenty of time to decide what to say."

I scan the trainees. Despite the helmets and oversized pads, I easily spot Gregor. He's the tallest by far.

But I also know which one is Finley. His loose, laid-back stride reminds me of the boy I once knew. He jokes with another guard, moving his feet in a quick pattern and faking jabs.

I watch both Gregor and Finley as they line up to be paired off. When everyone turns to the instructor, who calls them forward from a list on a clipboard, only one face turns up to the tower, as if he knows I'm there.

It's Finley. He's watching for me.

And, although it's Gregor I'm after, a thrill zips through my body.

"You should pick one out," I tell Lili. "There are so many."

She shrugs and turns away from the window, her finger racing over the keyboard on her phone. "I've got my sights set on other things."

"You don't want to have a love affair?"

"Eventually."

"What's more important?"

She holds up her phone. "My ticket out of here."

Lili often says things like that. I don't know how she can escape. We're the royal family. It's our duty to be here. "What's the current plan?"

"Biding my time. I've started a second Insta account. Everyone wants to follow a princess, but it's a real test of your skill if you can build without relying on celebrity."

"What will that do for you?"

"I'll be a normal human. Someone like them. I'll make friends who won't expect things from me, who invite me to regular events."

"You still have guards and parents and zero control over where you go."

She shrugs. "Maybe."

She's crazy. There's no escaping this, at least not for any longer than Leo did, a few months of racing ahead of guards in random cities for parties and wild living.

But they got him eventually. They always do.

I focus back on Gregor. He's been paired with a much smaller guard, and he places his hand on the other man's shoulder as if to assure him that he means him no harm.

My heart warms. That's the behavior that drew me to him. I slide my finger across the screen over his words.

Missed you in the garden.

I know he means that in the literal sense. We weren't able to meet.

But it's nice to think he might miss me. Even though we didn't see each other in person, my plan worked. I can write to him now. We can get to know each other. And hopefully, someday soon, we'll get to meet face-to-face.

And maybe even mouth-to-mouth.

CHAPTER 8

Finley

Octavia's got it bad. She sat up in the tower watching us until we left the fields. I could only make out the shadow of her in the window, but I'd know her shape anywhere. I see how this happened. She spotted us, watched, saw Gregor being the leader, and figured out a way to meet him.

After training, Gregor jogs up to me, eyes on his phone. I remember he wanted to spar. The light has faded in the fields, and his sweaty mug is mostly lit by the screen. But he says, "She wrote me."

Jealousy stabs me. "What did she say?"

"She wants to know what music I like."

"That's easy. Just tell her."

"What if she hates it?"

"So it's not something you have in common. There will be other things."

"Nah. This is the first question. I need a slam dunk. You know her. What does she like?"

I can't admit that the last time I listened to music with

the Princess, it was Kidz Bop. "You want me to find out for you?"

He smacks my back. "That would be terrific."

I guess we're doing this instead of sparring. "I'm heading in for a shower, but I'll see what she says and forward you some ideas."

His face shifts into relief. "Thanks, man. I don't have any idea how to talk to her."

I nod. "Give me your number. I'll text you later." I hesitate. "You're not seeing anybody, are you?" That would complicate things.

He sniffs. "Nope. Not really."

"Is that a no?"

"Yes. It's a no."

"Good." I stop short of threatening him and hurry across the darkening lawn of the palace to the side entrance of the staff wing. Mom will be holding dinner for me. She likes to finish it up while I shower.

Sure enough, she's at the kitchen counter when I enter our rooms, cutting up chicken in her favorite blue velour sweats, her unruly brown hair twisted into a loose knot.

It's nice to be back in a staff suite rather than sharing a cottage way out in the fields. It was a long walk for Mom to get to the palace, plus we were pretty cramped with only one bedroom. I had to sleep on a mattress behind the sofa.

Here we each have a bedroom connected by an open space with a living area and kitchen.

The palace rooms are lush, even in our wing, with stucco walls, soaring ceilings, and tile floors. It's never too hot or too cold, and you never have donkeys poking their laughing snouts through the open windows, sniffing out your supper.

"Chicken and dumplings tonight," she says. "Go on and get cleaned up."

"Yes, Mom." I hurry past her to the bathroom we share. While the water heats, I quickly tap out a message to Octavia. I use the name I called her when we were kids.

Vi, it's Fin. Lover boy wants a playlist of your faves to pump iron to. Watcha got?

Only after I've sent it do I realize I've practically told her I'm working with Gregor to help him talk to her. As the water spills over my face, I have to shrug. I'm not beholden to anyone's secrets.

Besides, it's only getting them started. I'm sure when they get serious I won't want anything to do with it. Imagining Gregor holding Octavia in his arms makes me crazy.

But picturing that sends my thoughts to when I held her myself. Spinning her around to cure her hiccups, her body grown and lush. Then when I took her down off the bench, every scintillating inch of her sliding down mine.

And now I've done it. My cock throbs. I shouldn't, but I drop into the fantasy. This time, I kiss that strip of exposed skin, pushing her soft sweater up and away. The breasts that briefly brushed my hands are mine again, molded to my palms.

This is my lane. What's gotten me called a manwhore around the palace. I love women. Sex. The whole thing. One after another after another. I rarely circle back around.

The real Octavia is off limits. But not the one in my head.

Our kiss goes on and on in the rose garden, a breeze ruffling our hair. I taste her, kissing her neck. My hands slip into her jeans, and she sighs in my ear.

I fist my length in the shower, pumping it. I don't even have to get very far before I've unleashed into the flow of water.

I press my hands against the tile wall, shaking my head so that droplets fly. Damn. I've got it bad. And here I've handed her off to someone else.

I rinse off and step out, running the towel over my head. When I pick up my phone, I have a whole series of messages from Vi.

Octavia: *Did he ask you for that?*

Octavia: *I asked him for his taste in music.*

Octavia: *Lili thinks he will only tell me what I want to hear.*

Octavia: *This is the problem Leo had with his brides!*

Octavia: *Don't give him anything! Don't!*

Huh. I can see her point. Everybody knows about the women who tried to unseat Prince Leopold's chosen bride. They were born and raised to follow the Prince's every preference, hoping they'd have an advantage when it was time for him to marry.

I'm torn between my devotion to her and helping Gregor.

No, I'm Team Vi, for sure. Gregor can piss off.

But I wouldn't mind listening to something she loves. So I ask anyway.

Me: *What if I'd like to know one? Just one?*

I towel off while I wait. I'm curious if she'll tell me anything. I don't have a dog in this hunt. She's clearly hot for this other guy.

My phone buzzes.

Octavia: *Lady Gaga. I'll Always Remember Us This Way. But DO. NOT. TELL. HIM.*

Huh. Sentimental. I know the song, roughly, but to get it full on, I play it while I dress in jeans and a sweatshirt.

And, partway through, I have to sit down. I'm flooded with what she's feeling, thinking. It's so emotional that when it ends and the phone goes quiet, I can't quite pull myself together. The song could be about us, her and me. We were terribly young, but isn't that when the strongest attachments are made?

Finally, I tap out, *Thanks for that. I like it a lot. Makes me think of you. Vi and Dory.*

That was too much, but I send it anyway.

She responds. *It does.*

I definitely won't tell Gregor about the Gaga song. I want to keep it for myself.

But I text him.

Hey, she likes female singer songwriters. Send her something off the beaten path.

He writes back.

Like what? I'm clueless here.

I hear the clink of Mom setting plates on the table. I have to go. I remember a song Mom loves, one she often listens to at night. Before I can think better of it, I send it to him.

Amy Winehouse. Wake Up Alone.

Only after I've sent it do some of the lyrics rise up. Oh, that's going to put gasoline on the fire. It's a song of longing. Of wishing you were with someone.

I might have overachieved on his behalf.

Gregor buzzes me back.

Great! Thanks!

Mom is placing the dish of dumplings on the table when I come out. "You don't usually listen to music after a shower. You okay?"

"Yeah. Someone mentioned that song today, and I wanted to check it out."

"It's from that sad movie. I saw it with Arlenia in housekeeping."

"Is that so?" I plunk down on a chair and snatch up a piece of garlic bread. I'm starved. The workouts have gotten increasingly intense.

She sits opposite me. "Oh, yes. I've seen *A Star Is Born* in every iteration. The Lady Gaga one might be the best, although I did like the original."

"You like that sad stuff?" I spoon a hefty amount of the thick broth laden with chicken, carrots, and dough into my bowl.

"Sometimes." Her gaze takes on that faraway look she's always had. When I was little, I called it her "dog eyes" because she'd look so woebegone. But even then, I never dared ask her what it was about.

I'm not about to start now. I assume it has to do with my father, and I don't want to get bogged down by that asshole, whoever he is. Mom might have some sweet nostalgic story about him, and if she told it to me, I would surely say something boneheaded in anger at how he left her in a lurch.

"Has your training gotten more rigorous?" she asks.

"It has. It was always challenging, but it's like they flipped a switch this week and decided to torture us."

She blows on her spoonful of broth. "I'm not surprised. You only have a month to go."

"Then I'll be assigned." My jaw tightens. I wonder if I'll be placed far from the palace.

I immediately think of Vi. I might not get a chance to see her anymore once training ends.

Mom reaches across the table to squeeze my fisted hand. "You will get a great assignment. Now eat."

Gregor and I might be the top of our recruiting class. If the two of us can lead the others, even the townies who get chased by donkeys, then we'll create a young, strong addition to the palace staff.

And I will make sure nothing will ever happen to my Vi, even if I have to witness her love affair with another guard.

CHAPTER 9

Octavia

I run my finger over the screen as if it's big, strong Gregor's cheek. He sent me a song to listen to. It's perfect.

I press play again.

Amy Winehouse's voice soars. Tears squeeze from my eyes. He's got me exactly. He didn't say it was his favorite, but that he thought I should take a listen. And he was right. He's nailed my feelings so completely. This huge stone-walled room. The silence echoing. The aching loneliness.

It's exactly what got me pining in the tower over men I'd never been allowed to see before. It's time for me to be with someone, even if it becomes my first broken heart. I know all about it. I have access to music and movies.

It ends and I press play again. I could listen to it all night, pine until dawn. But I fall asleep, and the dreams are poignant and sharp. Gregor, coming up to me, his face serious.

Dancing in the Great Hall, the tinny music echoing off empty walls.

Then, I'm in the rose garden, wearing a short dress that lifts when I twirl. I've forgotten panties. I'm too exposed. I panic, wanting to push the skirt down, but then I'm in powerful arms, and a firm hand slides up my thigh and into that swollen place.

But it's not Gregor.

It's Finley.

I awake with a start. An earbud falls out, rolling along the blanket. The music player has moved forward on the playlist. It's R&B, sexy, sultry, and I can tell this is what discolored my dreams. I fumble with my phone and shut it off.

I try to settle back in bed to sleep, but the moonlight is bright, casting shadows on my bed through the slats of the blinds. I should get up and close them, but I can't let go of the dream.

Finley in the rose garden, touching me. My whole body trembles. I squeeze my thighs together. It was intense.

I try to shift my focus back to Gregor, but the edges of the dream are already melting into nothing. Soon, all that is left is the ache between my legs.

I force myself to think of Gregor again, feeling disgruntled that my childhood friend has invaded my perfect dream. But sleep eludes me until I put on the sounds of a thunderstorm on my phone and finally, I drift back away to the heavy pounding of artificial rain.

I feel terribly unsettled about the dream, even when I wake up at a proper hour. I immediately want to plan a meeting with Gregor. Finley has some unexpected hold over me after our time alone in the gardens.

I need to meet with Gregor, and this strange spell will be broken. It's only because I haven't had any contact with men before now that I've oddly latched onto those moments with Finley. I can fix it.

I hear a heated exchange in the hallway and slip on a robe to move closer to the antechamber outside my bedroom.

It's Valloria, dressing down the night guard. She must have just come on shift.

"You can't trust her alone in her room," Valloria says. "She's slippery as an eel."

"I'm not authorized to enter the Princess's chambers while she sleeps," Tyson says, his voice a bit warbly. He's seventy-two, but he knows about the tunnels, and Father tries to keep those who know to a minimum. The tougher guards are at the end of the halls.

"Then we need a female night guard," Valloria says. "The Princess has been—"

"You will not speak ill of the Princess!" Tyson shouts with surprising force. "I'm here to keep peace in the hall, and you are making it sour with your negative tone."

Valloria sighs. "Go on, Tyson. I'm on shift now."

The knob turns, and I race back to my bedroom and snatch up a brush.

Valloria raps on the door only once she's already got it half open. "Your Grace?"

I lean back. "I'm brushing my hair!"

She sighs in relief. "I'm on duty, Your Grace. Let me know if you need anything."

"Thank you, Val!" I use the shortened form out of spite. I despise my lack of privacy. I'm twenty-three!

But I don't know how to take it up with Mother. If I make waves, Valloria might tell her about the tunnel trip.

I have to bide my time.

When Valloria has settled outside the still-open door, I move to my bathroom. I turn on the shower and sit on the floor with the burner phone.

First, I text Gregor.

Fell asleep to your song. Love it.

He won't get it any time soon. Training is well underway for the day.

Then I text Finley.

Any ideas about how I can meet Gregor? My personal guard is ridiculous right now.

My life is already so different since yesterday morning! I have *two* men to talk to!

I won't hear from them for hours. I hide the phone in my basket of soaps and step into the shower. As the spray falls over me, I find myself humming Gregor's song. "Wake Up Alone."

If only I actually did, and not with guards nosing in my business.

If only there was a tunnel access point in the bathroom. I'd be out of here.

If only.

I massage in a dab of shampoo, trying to calm myself. This is working. I will meet Gregor. I will have something — and someone — for myself.

I begin to rinse, but when I open my eyes, I gasp. A trail of blue and pink color flows down the drain. No! I can't lose too much color from my hair. Mother dislikes my streaks and only authorizes the royal hairdresser to refresh it every two months.

This is no time to lose my one bit of style rebellion! I pick up the shampoo bottle. It's not my usual color-safe one, but something new. I toss it toward the trash. Who bought a different brand?

I stamp my foot, then nearly slip. I clutch at the tile, clamoring for balance. Finally, my heels brace against the edges of the tub and I right myself. Good grief. Look at me!

The tears start falling then. This is so ridiculous! I'm one of the most envied people in Avalonia, and I can't even choose my own shampoo.

I double check the conditioner before applying it to my hair. It's safe. By the time I'm back out, I've calmed myself.

And just in time. When I extract my phone from the basket, I have a message from Finley.

Finley: *What's your guard situation? That's the hard part.*

He's right.

Me: *Day shift is a nightmare. She doesn't even let me close my door.*

Finley: *And the night shift?*

Me: *An elderly gentleman. But he's after supper, when I'm either with family or expected to stay in my rooms.*

Finley: *Let me try to arrange something for then. I know the donkey herders well. A stroll to the stables?*

That's not very romantic, but I'll take anything at this point.

Me: *I'll be happy with whatever you can arrange.*

Finley: *I'll get back to you.*

I rub my head with a towel. Progress!

But, as I comb out my hair in the half-fogged mirror, I wonder one thing.

If Finley can text me, why isn't Gregor?

CHAPTER 10

Finley

This is, without a doubt, the most awkward situation I've ever been in.

I'm sneaking a royal princess out of the palace to meet with a fellow guard, when I'm the one who would prefer to be the object of her rebellion.

But I have promised myself that I will not get in the way of Octavia and Gregor. And in doing that, I've turned myself into the reluctant wingman.

Every step of the actions I've taken to help them can get me fired. Or worse. It might be treason. I don't know. I'm not well versed in Avalonian law when you aid and abet a member of the royal family escaping their security detail.

But I'm doing it.

For Vi.

The sun is setting over the donkey fields as I hurry toward the palace gardens. Gregor is waiting on the back side of the birthing stable, where the latest newborn foals have arrived.

It's not unusual for members of the royal family to visit the stables during foal season, so no one who is inadvertently part of this scheme will be found at fault if we are caught.

No, the trouble will lie solely at my own traitorous guard boots.

It should be no different from all the times Vi and I sneaked into the kitchen to eat secret cake, but the stakes are much higher now that the Princess has come of age. The whole reason for the King's rule about males seven to thirty was to keep rapscallions like myself away from the young ladies of the royal family.

And with good cause. I have definitely not been a saint. It is well-known that the donkey herders and the young women of the palace staff hook up in the fields. There's one patch of trees surrounding a pond not too far from the castle grounds that has become a favorite spot for clandestine encounters. Many a party has been held there, away from the watchful eyes of the palace guards.

Certainly, the occasional couple comes out of it. Signed, sealed, and delivered into marriage.

But I have always chosen women for the good time we are both seeking, and nothing more. I can spot the ones looking for a husband at one hundred paces.

Octavia is definitely one of those.

And her eyes are set correctly on wholesome, good-guy Gregor.

There's nothing I can do about that. Even if she had recognized me from the tower as she got herself emotionally attached to our alpha trainee, it might not have changed a thing. She treats me the same way we behaved when we were six, with laughter and silliness. Nothing romantic. Not for her.

Perhaps that's what comes from knowing someone since they were in diapers.

Or maybe from knowing my reputation.

I might have lived a different life if I'd suspected for a moment she could ever have been mine.

Too late now.

I reach the outer wall that surrounds the palace and give a quick nod to the guard there. I don't know all of their names, although I'm sure I'll meet more of them once I officially enter the guard regiment.

Still, we recognize each other's garb and training. All guards curl their fingers a certain way and take a specific length of stride, much like a marching band. This is how we recognize each other, whether in uniform or not, and how we can spot someone who might have tried to play the old movie trick of knocking out a guard and stealing their clothes.

That won't work here. The stance, the speaking voice, the stride, the pose. It's all trained into us.

I pass the courts, then the hyacinth garden, and slow down at the entrance to the rose garden. My vision of Octavia there is no longer of a young girl laughing and dashing between the bushes. It's the woman, appearing at the end of the tall hedge, shocked and surprised that she has confessed to the wrong man.

And her laughter as I spun her around. Her hiccups. Lifting her off the bench.

Everything about her is imprinted on my memory.

And even though I'm coming for her so that she might meet with Gregor, I get to spend time with her.

It will have to be enough.

I stop short when I hear her voice. "Oh, do tell me more about the vintage roses. No one knows as much as you."

The warbling voice speaking next is undoubtedly the elderly guard. He must be an amateur gardener, because he explains in great detail about the heritage of the plants they must be standing near.

We were originally to meet at the back door, but I assume this was the measure Octavia had to take to lure him outdoors, and probably also away from other family who weren't up for listening to the old man's lengthy lecture.

"And the yellow ones?" Octavia asks. "Are they also from that era?"

I enter the rose garden and spot the pair at the end of the hedge. My breath catches. Octavia is glorious in a tawny gold gown that sparkles in the light. She's still dressed for their formal dinners. Her hair is caught up in a knot that hides the color streaks.

Her long neck is adorned with a gold chain dripping with pale yellow gems. Matching ones dangle from her ears. I can already imagine kissing that neck, feeling the contrast between her warm skin and the cool stones.

I shake myself out of the thought.

The old guard is in full uniform, and, despite his age, commands the guard demeanor. Only his voice is missing the old training, although the slight trill of his *r* belies the speech adjustment we must use when revealing ourselves to each other, another security tactic.

"Oh no, those were brought in by your grandmother. She spent a lot of time in the gardens. In fact, she was the one who had the trellises erected."

Most likely to hide her indiscretions. Everyone knows about the former queen's infamous line of lovers.

I walk up to them, scraping my foot along the ground as they come together, followed by a quick click of the metal heel of our boots, another of our many quirks that prove our station. "Your Grace," I say with a small bow. "The new foals are prepared for your viewing as you requested. The breeders and herders are delighted for you to convey your blessing."

Her guard frowns. "I was not briefed that you were to visit the stables tonight."

"It was meant to happen before supper, so Valloria was told," Octavia says easily. She's good. "We will only be a minute. It will be no more than if we'd spent the time here in the gardens."

"All right," the old guard says. "We will have to continue your instruction another night."

"Oh, let's do."

Perfect. Now she has set up a second escape later on. She's cunning.

Her big wide eyes meet mine as she walks ahead of her guard toward the back gate. She's ridiculously beautiful, bathed in twinkling light as the lamps hit the sparkle of her gown.

Her personal guard follows her at five paces, and I

follow him at five additional more in deference to his superior position.

"Aren't you a trainee?" he asks.

I acutely feel my lack of finished uniform, arm stripes, and cap. "I am. And I am also a former herder, so I was the perfect person to fetch the Princess."

He nods. The length of his gait is well-defined, and he has to adjust his speed to stay on pace with the Princess. But he is quite spry and easily traverses the path out the back gate to the stables.

Octavia slows down as we approach the buildings. "Which one is the foaling stable?"

"The third one on the left," I say. This will be the tricky bit. I will need to distract her guard while she steals away with Gregor.

I kind of hate this.

"Why don't you lead the way?" she asks.

"No problem." I catch up to her and take her in through the front gate of the foaling stable. The smell of hay takes over as we walk deeper into the facility.

Gregor is waiting at the other gate. He's not visible, but I double checked that he was there before I went to fetch Octavia.

A donkey tender is ready to meet her, an apprentice vet tech as noted by the pale green of his vest. "Your Grace," he says with a bow. "We are grateful you're here to bestow your blessing on the foals."

The high partitions of the stalls are solid so that the donkeys aren't distracted by visitors. The man opens the upper partition of the door, so that Octavia can peek inside.

"Oh!" she squeals. "They're so adorable."

I stand aside, but I can still see into the pens. In the four narrow partitions are four full-grown, female miniature donkeys, or jennies. Three of them have a single foal, and one of them has twins. They are all standing, although one of the foals is quite wobbly and is repeatedly nudged under the belly by his mother.

"They're standing so well!" Octavia cries.

"They are strong ones," the man says. His hands are shaking. He's nervous to be in the presence of the Princess.

I turn to watch her guard. He hangs back the proper distance.

"There are several other mothers who are coming up on their time," I tell her.

She blows kisses at all the foals. "The blessings of the Royal Family of Avalonia are upon you all. Good job, mamas!"

The man leads her to the next stall. Here are the mothers almost due, their round bellies hanging low as they graze on hay. They are held overnight to avoid the foals being born in the open pens, or for them to bed down in the fields to labor.

I hang back with her guard. It's my turn to distract him while Octavia enters the next stall. This one is wide and long with an exit to the pens from the inside. This will put her near where Gregor waits.

My gut twists.

"I don't think I quite got your name," I say to the guard.

"Tyson McFellow."

"Have you been Her Grace's guard for long?"

"Since she was born. I've been the night guard of the

children's wing since the King himself was a boy. I like to be up all night and then tend to my rose bushes in the morning before the heat sets in. It has been a good system for me all my life."

"I heard you talking about the roses." I hesitate. Vi better appreciate me for what I'm about to put myself through. "So, what kind of roses do you grow?"

Tyson launches into a long detailed accounting of his flowers. I smile and nod. Out of the corner of my eye, I watch Octavia enter the maternity stall. It will be up to her to lose the man tending them and leave out the back, but he seems so nervous he certainly won't question anything she does.

She disappears inside the walls.

As the old man drones on, my anxiety rises faster and faster. What are they doing? Did she make it to Gregor? Are they talking?

Doing more? I can picture that hulk of a man leaning down to kiss her.

I feel like I will explode. Another herder I used to know, one who seemed to take an interest in the flora and fauna in the fields, passes by. I grab his arm.

"Didn't you notice once that there was a new breed of daisies or something on the far hillside?"

His eyes light up. "I did."

"That's impossible," Tyson says.

"Tell him all about it," I say. "I'll check on the Princess for you."

I leave the two of them, chuffed at my own scheme.

I approach the maternity stall, saying, "Aren't they lovely?" as if I'm speaking to the Princess. I glance back at

Tyson and give him a nod. He catches my eye with the nod of his own.

I enter the space. Octavia is gone. The vet apprentice walks amongst the fat-bellied donkeys, then kneels by one. She's breathing heavily.

"Is she okay?" I ask.

He nods. "Looks like labor is starting. The Princess was overcome with concern, so she stepped outside the door for some air."

Perfect. "I'll handle her, thank you. Good luck with the jennies."

I pass through the back gate. I was counting on the fact that the elderly guard wouldn't know that there was a second way out of this stall.

The air is cool and sweet as I step into a holding pen filled with roaming donkeys. This group brays with a normal *hee haw*, no signature Avalonian laugh. They are likely here to be gelded so that they don't pass on their disappointing traits to any offspring.

"Sorry, fellas," I tell them as I scan the area. No Princess. No Gregor.

I exit the pen. The sun is fully down, and the moon shines over the hills. A breeze stirs up, sending a chill through me, and the grasses, long dead from winter, rustle in the fields.

I walk farther out for a better view. At last, I spot their silhouettes, perhaps a hundred yards away. They're walking too close together for my taste. I move along the length of the pen, blending in with the fence posts. When I reach the end, I'm not within hearing distance, but I can see them more clearly.

I know I shouldn't spy. I know it.

But I can't help it. This is my Vi. And she's with this other man.

Vi is tall, but Gregor towers over her. They face each other, like a prom picture, or wedding vows.

My heart beats mercilessly in my chest. I can't stand it.

Donkeys approach from the other side of the pen wall. I reach through the metal bars and pet them. "What do you think, guys? Are they going to fall in love right here under the moonlight while I'm watching?"

A few of them bray softly, and I'm relieved that they are not the laughing kind. I don't think I could handle that kind of commentary at the shattering of my heart.

Gregor's holding both of her hands. She's looking up at him. They're having a moment. This is it. The point where my princess falls in love with someone else.

They're going to kiss.

And I can't seem to stop myself.

I pull the pin to the gate and open it wide, sending the donkeys their way.

CHAPTER 11

Octavia

What in the world just happened?

Gregor and I jump apart as half a dozen donkeys rush between us.

A couple of them take off running, but the others circle around us, hoping for treats.

I hold up my hands to show that they are empty. "Sorry, donkeys."

Gregor's brows furrow. "Why aren't they laughing? All the donkeys I've ever seen always laugh."

"Not all of them do." Has he never paid attention to the donkey breeding? Maybe not. His family has always been guards. "Our signature donkeys laugh, but there are plenty that don't." I pet one's head. "They are still important and adored, just not sold at the high prices the laughing ones get."

Gregor frowns. "I admit I've never been a big fan of livestock."

I almost take a step back, but catch myself. I've never met an Avalonian who didn't respect the royal flocks.

But that's okay. There's no reason why he has to like them. In fact, Lili was afraid of them when she was young.

I ring my fingers between my lips and whistle, harkening back to the days when I roamed the fields with Finley and learned the call of the herders.

The two wayward donkeys return, and I flop my arms to shoo them all back toward the pens. "Where is your herder?" I ask, as if they could answer.

Shouts ring out, and two young men in gray herder vests run toward us.

One of them, very young, barely eighteen, calls out, "Your Grace, Your Grace! I'm so sorry. I don't know how they got out." Another herder arrives, and they push the donkeys back toward the pen.

"It's all right," I tell him. "I love them. I've always loved the donkeys."

Gregor frowns at that. "I didn't mean offense. Of course, I like donkeys. They are important to Avalonia."

I wave him off. "It's fine. They're not for everyone."

But the mood is definitely broken. I could've sworn he was about to kiss me.

But, admittedly, I wasn't sure I was ready. I've never been kissed. And doing it only ten minutes into meeting Gregor face-to-face seems almost rash.

So, I'm grateful for the donkeys, however they may have arrived.

We walk with the herders back to the stables. I see the figure of Finley, and then of my official guard, at the back gate.

"You should probably go with the herders," I tell

Gregor. "I'll text you later. My guard is ahead. He'll be on to us."

Gregor bows. "Of course, Your Grace."

I laugh. "Please call me Octavia. I don't think I can stand it if you call me anything else."

"Of course, Octavia." He says the syllables slowly, and I admit, I love the sound of my name coming from his lips.

This is going well. We only talked of his guard training and the weather. But it was enough. No gaffes. No accidental confessions. A perfect start.

Gregor walks with the wayward donkeys until they reach the corner of another stable, where he disappears.

Tyson rushes forward. "Are you all right, Your Grace? I'm sorry. I did not realize you had left the stable."

"I'm fine. I saw these little rascals get away and helped bring them back. I love walking among the donkeys like I did as a child."

"We best get back," Tyson says, his face etched with worry. He's not used to going anywhere with me or Lili, so he doesn't know how slippery we can be.

"You're right. We wouldn't want anyone to worry." I glance around for Finley, but like Gregor, he has wisely melted into the shadows. My step is light as I head back to the palace. We successfully got a meeting completed.

Gregor was the kind, thoughtful gentleman I knew he would be. I've studied him for too long to have doubted it.

And I almost had my first kiss. Before we meet a second time, I'll be ready. No chickening out. And no donkeys.

My sister is sitting on my bed when I return to my chambers. She's always out of her dinner gown the moment she makes it back to our wing, so, predictably, she's wearing jeans and a smuggled off-the-shoulder top.

She practically bounces on the mattress as I kick off my shoes.

"Leave nothing out," she says. "Wait. First, did you kiss him?"

I shake my head. "It was a short meeting. We were beset by donkeys." I relate the story to her, recounting our conversation as well as our near miss when the donkeys arrived.

"I find that curious," she says. "So near to that first romantic gesture, and all hell breaks loose."

"Don't take any meaning from it," I tell her, unclasping my heavy necklace. "I was near the pens. I'm sure moments like that happen all the time to the regular herders."

"I wonder. Where did you say that Finley went?"

"Once he had safely passed me off to Gregor, he simply disappeared. He was quite instrumental in our being able to meet at all. I couldn't have done it without him. And Tyson is none the wiser."

Lili stretches out on the bed. "I'm glad you're getting what you want. When are you going to do it again?"

"I think I have to give it a few days to avoid pressing my luck. But I'll think of something."

The night maid enters. "Time to get you ladies out of your gowns." She spots Lili. "Where did you leave yours?"

"I'll show you." Lili hops from the bed. "I'll be back."

I sit at the window to wait, thinking of Gregor. The maid returns to put away the jewels and my gown. Lili and

I hang out in my bedroom to watch TV together. Only hours later do I get another text from Gregor.

You were entrancing tonight. I was completely transfixed. I will move heaven and earth to find another moment to spend with you.

I see actual sparks in my vision as I re-read the lines.

Entrancing. Transfixed.

Lili looks over my shoulder. "Those are some pretty words."

"I know."

"What are you going to say back?"

"I don't know. What should I do?"

"Send him a song like he did you."

"Ooooh. Good idea."

We spend an hour searching for the right message, finally settling on Meghan Trainor's "After You."

When Lili heads back to her own room, I write Finley.

I didn't get a chance to thank you for putting your neck on the line for me. I have forgiven you for the blue frosting betrayal.

I get a response almost immediately.

I hope you know by now that I will do anything for you.

I have to look at the contact name twice. It was Finley who said it. Not Gregor.

Finley.

It's incredibly romantic, and I don't know how to respond. He's helping me meet another man.

But I hold the phone to my chest as I change for bed.

And strangely enough, once again, it's not Gregor who invades my thoughts as I fall asleep.

But Finley.

CHAPTER 12

Finley

When I arrive at the training yard early the next morning, Gregor sits on the bench, staring at his hands. He's in ideal form otherwise — immaculate guard training uniform, polished boots, his dark hair combed in perfect waves.

But he looks like someone stole his ice cream.

We're the first trainees to arrive, other than the staff who sets out equipment for us to use throughout the day. They're at a decent distance to avoid hearing us, so I plunk down beside him. "You all right? Did the Princess like the message you sent her?"

He nods, but his eyes remain on his hands.

I smack his shoulder. "What's up, bro? I don't think I've ever seen you like this."

He only grunts. I've never heard Gregor grunt.

For a moment, my heart leaps that Octavia broke up with him. Maybe he did something dumb he didn't tell me about. I was close, but I didn't see everything, and I couldn't hear what he said. It might have been awkward.

Every text message that has gone to Octavia was

written by me. Even the one last night about her being entrancing. I came up with that on our walk from the stables.

But I wasn't beside him when he was with her. He could have botched it.

"Did something go wrong?"

He sighs. "It's not right."

"What's not right?"

"Me. The Princess. If this goes south, I could jeopardize my family. Second, the King only recently allowed guards our age again. And already, one of us is coming for his daughter. That's exactly what he was trying to protect them from. People like you and me. We could screw over all our fellow trainees if he kills the program after what I've done."

My inclination is to make a joke about not including me in that number, but I know better. He's struggling with this.

"I hear what you're saying. But you have to remember, this wasn't your doing. The Princess came for you. You're kind of stuck."

"I know. I know."

"You don't know how the King will react if it turns out his little girl is madly in love." I pause, trying not to choke on the words. Will she fall in love with him? Is she already?

"She's not. Well, she shouldn't be. It was, like, ten minutes."

"Do you have a reason to think it's going too fast?" I have to stuff down my rising fear. Octavia isn't experienced, not in the least. She could easily rush in, head over heels.

He pulls out his phone and starts a song. Within two lines, I get his point. It's a lot.

"She sent it to you?"

He nods.

Yeah. She's caught up in the fervor of it all.

"Hey. The King married who he wanted. So did the Crown Prince."

"But we're guards. It's different. I'm sworn to protect her. Not seduce her."

This makes my veins turn to ice. "So you're seducing her now?"

He sits up straight at that. "Hell no! In fact, those donkeys saved me last night. She looked like she was expecting me to kiss her. We'd only been talking for ten minutes! I don't move that fast with a regular girl, much less the Princess."

That makes me feel better. Considerably.

"You don't want to kiss her?" I don't like this conversation, but I'm already knee-deep in this. I might as well wade in a little farther.

"Of course I want to kiss the Princess. Who wouldn't want to kiss the Princess? Who wouldn't want to do a lot more?"

I hold up my hands. "Whoa, whoa. That's a whole different matter. Definitely bring me in to chaperone if you're getting close to that. I guarantee you knocking-up the Princess can get you in a world of hurt."

Gregor shoves me hard enough that I nearly fall off the bench. "Shut up about that, man. Of course not. No way."

I scoot aside, mainly to avoid him knocking me into next week. "Okay. So, what do you want to do?"

Other guards arrive for training, so he lowers his voice. "I don't know when I'll see her again. It's apparently difficult for her."

"Definitely. But tomorrow, there's the monthly inspection of the guard. We'll be in it this time." It's a tradition, the palace guards suiting up in lines for inspection and going through drills to ensure the precision and look of the entire legion is up to standard.

"The royal family never shows up for that," Gregor says. But I raise my eyebrows, so he adds, "She's going to come, isn't she?"

"If there is an official way to get her eyes on you, I bet she'll take it."

"Should I discourage her?"

"I don't think you could."

"What if the King sees her looking at me?"

Wisling, one of the whiny townie guards, comes up from behind us. "Who's looking at you?"

Gregor meets my eyes with concern. This conversation needs to end.

"All the women who skip right over you." I tilt my head toward Sergeant, who strides toward the benches. "Time to line up."

Wisling moves on. Gregor's voice falls low. "Should I text her about it?"

"Sure."

"Can you help me at the break?"

"No problem."

He nods. "Thanks for being my sounding board on this."

Sergeant calls us over for our first drills of the day. I

glance up at the tower window, but there is no shape there this morning.

On the whistle, we all drop to the ground for push-ups. Gregor knocks them out like each one is necessary to save someone's life.

I know the feeling. I match his pace to get my frustration out.

Sergeant towers over us. "The rest of you knuckleheads need to keep up with these two."

There are collective groans, but Sergeant silences them with a whistle.

I should slow down. I have nothing to prove. But damn it all, if I'm not worked up over how all this is turning out. I want to give Octavia what she wants.

But, I'd vastly prefer that it be me.

CHAPTER 13

Octavia

When the text comes through from Gregor, I can't quite hold back my squeal.

The manicurist painting my toenails bright blue sits back with a pained but practiced smile. "Your Grace? Is everything all right?"

Shoot. I can't draw attention to myself. I swear everyone is reporting to Valloria these days. The mean ol' guard warns everyone who comes into the room with me that I've been feeling off and should be watched closely.

I feel *fine*.

Very fine, actually.

"Everything is perfect. I love the color."

I shove the older phone into the cushion of the armchair. I've tried to avoid flashing it around the staff any more than I have to. I never know who's going to recognize it as an older model and make some comment that gets back to our parents or the guards, or even one of the heads of staff.

If they knew I had an illegal phone, they might search

my things. And I often leave it behind. I can't carry the burner phone to meals with my family. The gowns don't have pockets, for one. And two, I would be way too tempted to take it out and look.

Like now.

Because Gregor's written to me!

The manicurist continues with her work, but I don't dare peek at the message again. I got the basics. Tomorrow afternoon, there is an event with the palace guards. It's something the royal family is welcome to attend, even though they haven't lately.

I need to learn more about this.

But who can I safely ask? Lili has never talked about it once.

Leo might know, but he's not here. He's very iffy about replying to texts, too. He's having too much fun with Sunny before their baby comes.

Will I have as much fun when I'm married and can leave the palace at will?

I can't wait.

I watch the manicurist, Caralinda. She's mid-forties with an elegant twist of black hair and nails to die for. She always covers them with little wraps to protect them when she works on me.

She's been on staff for several years. She might know, and, if I ask her casually enough, she probably won't report the conversation to anyone.

"Have you ever been to the monthly guard inspection?" I ask.

"No, Your Grace. I've never attended. But that would not be unusual. The only staff that might be summoned to that event would be servers for the refreshments and families of the guards."

Families of the guards. So, I might get a glimpse of Gregor's family. We didn't talk about that last night. I want to know everything about him. His mother. His father. Does he have a bunch of brothers and sisters?

"Do you have any friends on staff who are family of guards?" I ask.

"Of course. Your father is most generous with employment when guards are hired."

I recognize her patronizing smile. Caralinda is saying what she thinks will keep her in my good graces, as if I'm some sort of tyrant. I wish things were different, and I could have an easy time with members of the palace staff. And that I could date guards without worrying about it.

Or that I could even walk about without being followed.

That won't change until I'm married. I know this.

But I will ask this woman all my questions. She leans down to apply a top coat.

I tap my already-dry fingers against the plush blue fabric of the chair. "With the new contingent of guards, it seems there should be more fanfare at the event this time."

"Perhaps."

"Has my mother asked for anything special to be done with her nails or appearance for it?"

When the woman hesitates to provide information, I wonder if she's not allowed to provide me even basic information about my own parents. I quickly add, "I only thought to possibly coordinate colors with her. But it's fine."

Caralinda smiles. "But of course, your mother sticks with her pale neutrals always. Your Grace prefers bright colors."

She's got me. I have no more information about whether or not my family intends to attend this shindig. We usually don't get our daily schedule until the morning.

But I want to know now. If I'm going to lay eyes on Gregor, I want to prepare. And, if I need to control my expressions so that no one suspects, I should practice. People will see us eyeballing each other.

Valloria raps on the door and steps in. Even when I'm with staff members, she doesn't allow the door to go completely shut. I wonder if that would change if I got something super private, like a bikini wax. If I did that, could I then ask the staff member to sit and wait while I ran through the tunnels to meet Gregor, even for only a moment?

Maybe.

I weigh the pain of the wax with the moment alone.

Valloria bows. "Your Grace, I've gotten word that your parents have requested you attend lunch with them today."

Rats. Most days we can lunch on our own. "Thank you," I tell her.

Valloria glances down at the manicurist. "There is half an hour."

Caralinda's pink mouth pinches. "Let me apply a quick dry coat," she says. "But I wouldn't wear closed-toe shoes. It will smudge."

I lean back to let her finish, and my hip buzzes from the phone.

Oooh. I want to see. It might be another text from Gregor!

I glance at her. She seems occupied, applying another clear coat. Valloria is gone.

I sneak the phone out of the crack of the cushion by my thigh.

This time, it's Finley.

Inspection of the guard is tomorrow. The royal family hasn't come lately, but, because of the new recruits, you might make a case for attending. Just FYI.

He's told me more than Gregor. And he's right. Members of the family *should* be there. I know what I'll be saying at lunch.

Or maybe I'll make Lili do it.

Yes, she'll be better.

Caralinda gathers her bottles and tucks them into her bag. "Anything else, Your Grace?"

"Can you ask the guard if Lili can come in?"

"Of course." She bows.

As I wait for my sister, my excitement grows. This is going to be perfect.

I'm here.

I don't know what this event normally looks like, but the field before us is resplendent with banners and flags.

Pure-white stands have been erected on the opposite side of the field for the families. They are filled with mothers and fathers, sisters and brothers, all waving handkerchiefs and waiting for the guards to arrive.

A raised platform with two chairs has been prepared for me and my sister.

We're the only two here.

Turns out my parents are gone for three glorious days. Lili gave a heartfelt speech about us becoming a part of the new traditions of a more modernized palace life.

Father recounted some of his favorite inspection memories with his own father, walking amongst the troops all lined up in their uniforms. He decided that our attendance at the event was a smart idea.

Mother assured us that the entire family would be present at next month's festivities, which would be even larger and grander since the guard trainees would be presented with their official stripes.

The thrill in my heart is unmatched by anything other than almost-kissing Gregor. Everything happening right now is new and exciting, such a huge divergence from my ordinary days.

Today, it might be *good* to be a princess.

Valloria and Botania stand behind our chairs in guard position, but even their proximity cannot temper my enthusiasm.

To the far right of the field, an entire banquet of refreshments has been set up. This includes cupcakes with blue frosting. I had the kitchen staff arrange it.

I have to bite back my smile. I can't wait for Finley to see them.

The wind whips through the banners, filling the air with sharp cracks as they flap overhead. I draw my coat around me more tightly, although I can't possibly be cold. I'm warmed through with the idea of seeing Gregor on the field. I know he will be the most perfect recruit of them all. He's so tall and strong and broad. Quite possibly the most handsome, although Finley's roguish good looks are a close second.

Or maybe they're equal in their own way.

Regardless, I can't be any more overcome to be sitting outside on a cold March afternoon.

A bugle plays from across the yard.

I grasp Lili's hand. "They're coming!"

Lili looks me over, adjusting the sleeve of my bright red wool coat and fluffing the fake fur at the collar. She smoothes my hair, twisted in a tight updo that hides the color. That wasn't my choice, but my parents always instruct the hairdresser to minimize my rebellious streaks at official events.

Mostly, I obey. I always keep in my back pocket the idea that I could pull the pins and let my hair fall in all its multicolored glory if I wanted to.

But, I have more important things to think about.

The guards are approaching.

A drummer's quick cadence drives the steps of the first row of marchers. The sun glints off the shiny silver accents at the bases of their fuzzy hats. Dark gray brims partially obscure their eyes.

The first three rows are decked in ceremonial blue, silver buttons angling across their chests. They carry long rifles against their shoulders. These are the most highly decorated palace guards, the king's regiment. At least the ones who aren't with the King at his engagement in Belgium.

I glance up at Valloria. "Are you upset you don't get to

march?"

It has only just occurred to me that because of our presence, they must remain on the podium. Although, had we not gone, they would've had to stay inside and miss it entirely.

"We are pleased to serve in whatever manner our King wishes," Valloria says.

Lili shakes her head. "That's an official line if I've ever heard one."

"Well, I'm glad you at least get to see it," I tell my guard. "You too, Botania. Maybe for the next one, we can arrange for someone else to sit by the royal family, and you can take part in the presentation."

The two of them give a brisk nod.

The blue palace guards have crossed the field and march in place in their arrow-straight lines. The next segment wears gray. They vary in age from young thirties to Tyson's proud seventy-two. I wave at the old guard, but his vision does not stray from his formation. I may not have to worry about my eyes meeting Gregor's. Most likely, he will not even look into the stands.

"Here they come," Lili says, her hand clutching mine.

She's right. Three more lines of gray uniforms, these without hats. They wear the same gray uniform and black boots, but their shoulders are bare of stripes and they carry no weapons.

Even so, they have been training for two months, so their gaits are in sync, and their postures are good.

Lili leans in very close. "Do you see him?"

I scan the rows, quickly noting the tallest of the group. "Yes," I whisper. Gregor is in the center of the first line.

Even though he is right in step with the others, it's clear he is a leader. He stands straighter, and his march is more crisp. His chin is set precisely like the guards before him. He could easily fit in with the experienced regiment.

The drums change their cadence, and a voice yells out a command. All the guards turn to face our podium and halt in unison.

I'm so overcome by the view of them facing me I almost leap to my feet to scream my excitement. But Lili knows me and holds me in my chair. "A nod of approval is the official protocol."

Of course, she would look this up. I should have. We both nod our heads to acknowledge their performance, and another shout goes up, then another cadence.

The entire brigade turns right to face the tall stone wall. Another shout. The entire regiment spins to face the other direction.

It's breathtaking. They move so smoothly and with such precision that I forget to watch for Gregor, enthralled with the spectacle. They're so beautiful. So perfect. So aligned and poised and still.

They continue to make more movements, sometimes turning, sometimes taking several steps forward or back. Finally, they face the family stands, and these fans have no official protocol to follow. They jump to their feet and cheer and shout the names of their favorite people.

There's no way to know which family belongs to Gregor, but I scan the stands for Finley's mother. I met her many times when she came to fetch Finley from my chambers or the rose garden. Although it has been sixteen years since I last saw her, I feel certain I will recognize her.

But I'm quick to realize the laundress is not in attendance. They are distinctive by their beige aprons over the blue base uniform.

Did her superior not let her off to watch her own son in his first event?

This will not stand. I turn in my seat. "Valloria, please run to the laundry women and make sure Finlandorio Bulgari's mother, Atraya, is brought down to the field immediately. She should be here."

Valloria frowns. "But, Your Grace, I'm here for your protection."

My face blooms hot. "That is an official request. I could not be more well guarded than I am. The entire regiment is down below. Please go immediately before she misses the whole thing!"

Botania steps forward. "I'll go. I know where the washing women work."

She takes off in a quick walk.

I settle back in my chair. I'm angry. Is this only for the staff who happen to be off? How important can washing be that it can't wait a single hour?

I wonder if Finley is upset his mother couldn't be here. I scan the line until I find him. He turns with the same precision as the others, his shoulders thrown back.

My eyes linger on his chest and the uniform. I remember how it felt to slide down it in the rose garden.

I shake my head. I have to put that from my mind.

I force myself to look at Gregor instead. Watching him is like witnessing the gears of a clock. There is no error in his movement. Only incredible accuracy.

I move back to Finley. While his motions match his line

89

precisely, there is more character to him. Something about his stance as a guard is still uniquely him.

"Your eyes betray you, O," Lili says.

"What do you mean?"

"Gregor is over here." She gestures to the first line. "But you're watching the last line. Is that where Finley is, or has some other guard caught your interest?"

"I'm just looking about."

"Sure." She kicks out her legs in thick white stockings and matching fur-lined boots. We're both in white and gold, outfits brought to us by the stylist. It's common to be told what to wear when we're out among large groups. But I swapped out the sterile white coat for my red one. I wanted to stand out. And I definitely do, given the white stage, gold chairs, and my sister's compliance in her white coat.

I hope Gregor spots me from the corner of his eye.

Botania reappears from the side exit of the building, followed by a stout woman drying her hands on her apron.

It's Atraya. They stop short when they reach the edge of our podium, as they can't easily cross the yard to the family stands. There are lines of guards in their way.

I leap from my chair. "Come here and sit with us," I tell Atraya.

Her eyes open wide as she bows.

"Come on, then. We have the best seat." I bend down and reach out a hand to lead her up the steps.

Reluctantly, she comes up. I try to give her my chair, but she stands firm next to Valloria.

I point to the back row. "He's right there."

Atraya grips the decorative arm of my chair, her eyes

glistening. I want to apologize for her missing part of it, but realize I should leave her be to watch what is left.

The regiment splits, fans out, then comes back together. They expand their movements, no longer always moving together, but shifting in sections, creating an undulating wave of blue and gray.

"It's breathtaking," Atraya says. "I've heard about it, but I've never seen it before."

"Me, too," I tell her. "It's wonderful. Finley looks so great."

"Have you spoken to him?" she asks.

My heart falls that Finley hasn't mentioned me to his mother. I'm sure he has his reasons. Perhaps she would worry about him getting in trouble for talking to me, even losing his guard position.

"Not really. But I've watched quite a lot of the trainings. I recognized him." A lie, but there's no easy explanation otherwise.

My sister's face is turned to the guards, but I know she's willing me to shut up. I can see it in the tension in her jaw.

"Please stay for refreshments. I will personally send word to Madam Mariam to ensure there is no misunderstanding that I took you away from your work."

"Thank you, Your Grace," she says.

I would like her to call me Vi, like she did when I was small and she'd wash out my spills so that Mother wouldn't know how I'd crawled through the mud with Dory or gotten into the frosting.

But, I know things are different. I'm not a little girl.

And she's staff. There are protocols, and they exist for a reason.

But, right now, they stink.

The drum cadence begins to speed up, and the movements of the guards become more staccato, more mesmerizing.

The blue uniforms flow through the gray like fish swimming in a stream. Then, somehow, miraculously, the pattern resolves into the original rows. They all turn to our podium once more, and in an incredible moment of unison, all shout, "Halt."

Forget bowing. I leap to my feet, clapping. The families erupt as well, and the yard is filled with happy shouts and cheers.

Lili stands next to me. She's good like that, making sure we are a unified front. We're here alone, so we can do what feels natural. It's only right that we react as our generation would.

We are the next round of royals.

As the guards are put at ease, their legs slightly apart, one arm behind their backs, they seem to see us. I wave instead of bowing, high from the amazing show of skill.

Gregor's face is a mask of concentration and reserve, the same expression I see on all the experienced guards.

But Finley's is not. He's spotted me in my red coat, gripping his mother's hand.

And his grin is big and wide.

I like that.

Yes, I like it very, very much.

CHAPTER 14

Finley

Sunday is the only day off for guards, and I mostly spend it with Mom. We clean our rooms and bake bread for the week. In the afternoon, we walk around town and spend a little money on a cake to celebrate the guard inspection.

"I was so proud to see you down there!" she says as we enter the bakery.

"Thanks, Mom."

We peer into the glass case. Mom being there was Octavia's doing. I know that. I sent my thanks to Vi last night as well as helped Gregor respond to her exuberant texts about how dashing he looked. She'd forgotten to take pictures, but the royal photographer had some she would forward.

I'm glad he came to me. His draft messages were all curt and clumsy — *Thanks for coming. You had a big chair.*

We changed them to *Seeing you in your bright coat was like finding a bloom in winter.* And *I was so grateful to have the honor of the attention of the most prominent woman on the field.*

And he sent her another song. I know she pined over it

because she wrote me late that night, wondering if I'd heard it. Strange, to be sure, to get sent the link I'd made myself and passed to Gregor.

This awkward threesome has to end sometime. I'm not sure how much I can take.

"How about the red velvet?" Mom asks, snapping me back to the display of cakes. "It's your favorite."

"That would be great."

"A shame the guards didn't get to partake in the banquet."

"We're the laborers, not the revelers."

"The cupcakes had blue frosting, just like that time you and Vi—"

"I remember." I glance up at the curious bakery worker, a teen boy.

"Wasn't that a cute coincidence?"

"They matched the uniforms." Of course I know Octavia requested the color. She told me. But since the Princess ensured my mother made the event, saying so might suggest to her we have a relationship that we don't.

"The small red velvet, please," Mom says to the teen. As she waits for it to be boxed, she turns to adjust my jacket collar. "Some of the other trainees wear their uniforms on Sunday to ensure they command the respect they deserve from the townfolk."

I know she's proud of me. Palace guard is one of the best ranks someone like me can achieve. But I say, "I like to be me at least one day each week."

She nods, smoothing the coat over my shoulder. "I could never see you being some stuffy businessman. But I'm glad you're no longer out in the fields."

"I liked the fields just fine." I don't mean to argue with her. But I'm good with where I come from, where I'm going. There's a lot more to a person than their occupation.

She takes the cake box, and I pay for it. She tries to protest, but I remind her that I'm living rent-free in her rooms and guards are paid more than staff, even during training.

Mom lets me do it, and we walk along the square, arm in arm, to witness the early signs of spring. Sprigs of iris and tulip leaves pop up in the flower beds, and tiny buds show their green on the tree branches. The first early showing of birds flit about, looking for sheltered spots to weather the last vestiges of winter.

It's a fine life. I don't need to be anything more than I am.

I've done a good job of getting Octavia out of my head until I enter the Great Hall on Monday for lunch, and there she is, standing behind the serving line in an apron and plastic gloves.

I stop short. Her hair is in one of the updos that hides her color streaks. She's in a plain blue dress. She looks sort of — official?

And gorgeous. Her hair is silky black, her eyelashes fringed and heavy. And those lips. They're pink and glossy, and I don't think I can tear my gaze from them.

Until some punk guard stands in front of her to be served, blocking my view.

But it breaks the spell, so I glance around the room for Gregor.

He sits at the back table as always, choosing to go last. That's the kind of guy he is. Everyone else gets served first.

Could he be slightly less perfect?

But his gaze is not on the Princess or the serving table, not anywhere near that direction. He's watching out a side window, and he looks pained, like someone has kicked him in the balls.

I'm about to, if he doesn't do right by Vi.

I slide into a chair opposite him. No one else is at the table, so we have a moment. "Who peed in your chili?"

His jaw goes tight. "She's here."

"For you. Looks like she's official. She got this set up."

"We're going to be seen. Figured out. I'll be thrown in the brig."

"There's no brig, Gregor."

"There is. You just don't know about it yet. You have to be a certain rank."

Right. His dad is the head guard.

I rap my knuckles on the table. "Look, it's lunch. She's dropping bread on a plate. Don't maul her, and you'll be fine."

"It's not me I'm worried about. It's her. She's so happy. It's going to be obvious."

I turn in my seat to look. Sure enough, Octavia's watching us both with shining eyes, like a kid who got a puppy.

"Point taken. How about I go up with you and draw the foul? I'll chat her up, and she won't be able to make goo-goo eyes at you."

"You say the weirdest things."

"Come on. It'll work. You have to eat."

I stand up and, thankfully, he follows. He needs to do normal things. Get food. Sit down to eat it. Vi's personal guard is standing at the door, and she's watching the room. She'll have already noted the direction of the Princess's interest.

This might not have been Vi's best idea.

But I'm the one whose mother she summoned. The guard is already aware we have a connection, and, by now, she's asked around and knows we were playmates as kids. That should hold us at least for a while to keep the heat off Gregor.

We arrive at the beginning of the serving line and accept our trays from the first server. Sweat is beading on Gregor's head. I've never seen him this uncomfortable. It's wild.

We're served thick slices of ham, sweet potatoes, green beans with almonds, and grisulu, a traditional Avalonian dish of lentils and cream.

Then we arrive at the end to receive a chunk of bread from Octavia.

She asks me, "One piece or two?"

"Two," I say.

She drops two on my plate.

"You look official."

"The royal family was impressed by the inspection and wants to show their support."

She's working angles. Nice.

Octavia keeps her expression neutral as she turns to

Gregor, although her eyes do take on a new sparkle. "Is having only one enough for you?"

Now, that wasn't official. Damn. She knew how to make the most of the moment. I wonder if she practiced.

If only she was flirting with me.

But Gregor doesn't lift his gaze, his hair sticking to his damp forehead. "One is good."

"Coming right up." She drops a large hunk of bread on his plate.

"Thank you very much," Gregor says.

We move on from the line. She places bread on another plate, and we are clean away.

I cut my eyes toward her guard. She isn't even looking at us, watching the serving line with narrowed eyes.

Totally passed.

But something's amiss. The guard is stiffening, shifting her weight. I know that stance. It's the one where we're about to pounce.

I look back at the serving line. It's Manning, one of the townies. I've missed whatever he said at first, but I clearly hear him say, "I'll take whatever you're offering."

And that's it. The guard is on the move. I set my plate at an empty spot right as she halts next to the Princess. "Take care with your tone with Her Grace," she says, her voice so full of menace that a lion would back down.

"It's all right," Octavia says. "He meant no harm by it."

"I'll be the judge of that," the guard says.

Manning backs away without his bread. It's still suspended in Octavia's tongs. "I'm good. So sorry. I meant no offense."

Gregor sits next to me. "He's risking it."

"He heard her flirting with you and thought it was an open invitation." I drop into the chair. "His ignorance is our cover."

Octavia meets my gaze with a nervous glance. Her guard is behind her, so she can't see where her charge is looking. I give her a small smile and a wink.

She returns the smile and focuses on the next uplifted plate. The line is almost at an end, and the first server packs up her stack of trays.

"Do you think she'll be here tomorrow?" Gregor asks. He's only picking at his meal. The stress is affecting his appetite, but he better eat. It's hard enough to get through training without having food as fuel.

"It won't matter. We're fine. She wants to see you."

He grunts. This relationship is clearly wearing on him. And given that Vi went this far to make sure she could see him, she's not giving up any time soon.

All I can do is to be here for the inevitable explosion.

CHAPTER 15

Octavia

I drop my stupid dress on the bed and kick off the sparkling flats.

"Don't do it," Lili warns.

"I'm going to." I snatch up black yoga pants and a white sweatshirt.

"You're pushing your luck."

Gah. Sisters. "This is the last day Mother and Father are gone. I'm going to do everything I can get away with."

Lili drops onto my bed on her belly, her feet in rainbow socks kicking back and forth. It was her idea to go to Rosenthal, our cultural director, to ask ways to show support of the new guard trainees.

He thought he was so clever to come up with the lunch line. And once the Cultural Director has placed something on the calendar, only my parents can stop it. He's one of the highest ranking members of staff, even if his duties are all about ceremony and pomp.

I'm to serve this week, and Lili next week. Except, I'll be taking her turn, of course.

Gregor guaranteed, each and every day.

But today? Lunch is done, and I'm headed out to the yard. I've arranged for one of the fight trainers to give me self-defense lessons. Leo got them when he was eighteen, but Mother said it wasn't princess-like to knock about with our fists.

But she isn't here. The trainer has no one to ask about my lesson request other than Rosenthal, who would probably say it's fine. My guard Valloria could kibosh them, I guess, but honestly, I plan to send her on an errand while I'm with the instructor.

So, I'll be on the training field at the same time the guards are.

"It's a good thing I like you," Lili says, her fingers flying over the phone screen. "Or I could bust you more often than Phineas and Ferb."

"Their sister never busted them."

"You're way much more bustable."

I shove my feet into sneakers. "You're good to me, Lil. Don't worry. I'm living for right now. Tomorrow can work itself out."

She rolls on her back, phone in the air, swiping through screens so fast that I'm not sure how she can see what's on them. "Seize the day."

"I intend to."

I cross the antechamber to the open door of the hall. Valloria stands outside.

"I'm taking a lesson with Horitus today."

"All right."

That was easy.

Too easy.

But I'm going with it.

Nothing's going to bring me down.

I take care to exit the palace far from the guard training so that Valloria won't realize I'm insinuating myself into their vicinity.

Horitus waits by the courts. His dark skin is bold in the afternoon sun, a sharp contrast with the white of his loose karate uniform. He bows. "Your Grace, I was so glad to hear of your interest in the arts."

"Thank you for seeing me." I turn to Valloria. "Can you locate some small weights that are suitable for me?"

She looks between me and Horitus for a moment, then around the perimeter. There is a guard station just above us at the fence. She nods. "I'll be back shortly."

"Thank you!" Yes. Got her out of the way.

While she walks back to the palace, I ask Horitus, "What now?"

"First, we must clear our minds."

"Okay."

Horitus stands, feet slightly apart, hands pressed together in front of his chest, head bowed.

I follow his lead, eager to make my excuse to move to the other yard. I'll never clear my mind if it's full of Gregor!

He seemed so nervous at lunch. Did that have to do with me? Fin was fine. Maybe it was something else entirely. Something having to do with training, I bet. I can picture him sitting by the window, staring out onto the grounds.

"Breathe in through your nose, then out through your nose." Horitus startles me completely. I'd forgotten he was there. "Focus on slowing down the breath."

I think about my breath for a nanosecond, then it's back on Gregor. I need to get over there! If I wait too long, Valloria will make it back.

A cloud passes over the sun, and a stiff wind picks up. I shiver.

Perfect.

"Can we move to the sunny side of the palace?" I ask. "It's warmer there."

"You should clear your mind of your discomfort." Horitus hasn't moved positions in the least.

Oh, boo. I bow my head and try to slow down my breathing. Soon, I *am* shivering. I almost say, "I should have brought a jacket," but stop myself.

"If you find your mind wandering," Horitus says, "Just draw it back to your breath."

But I want my mind to wander! To the training yard. To Gregor. In the warmest part of the day, they often take their shirts off. I want to see this from the ground, not the tower. The idea of it sends such a sharp jolt of electricity through me that I suck in a breath.

"Return your mind to your breath," Horitus admonishes. "Note what is making you stray, then let it go."

Oh, I'm straying all right. To shoulders. Chest. Abs.

Yeah, I'm done here.

"That was a great first lesson. Thank you so much!"

I don't so much as glance back at Horitus before I take off in a dead sprint. I'm a woman with a mission, and my mission is shirtless Gregor.

Sometimes a girl has got to do what a girl has got to do.

It's a lot farther than I thought past the gardens to the side yard. I'm out of breath, my hair all askew. I stop, my hands on my knees. Now I'm focusing on my breath. Or lack of it.

"Your Grace!" It's Horitus, sounding alarmed. "You're supposed to be with me!"

"Then, come on then. This princess needs some sun." I take off again.

Horitus has no trouble keeping up with me. "Getting in shape can certainly include cardio. We can rearrange the lessons."

"Oh...I'm sure...I'll want...to practice my breath." I wheeze in and out, but suddenly, we're there. The trainees fan out across the yard, working out at various stations. I can't see well enough to spot Gregor with the sweat in my eyes.

I put on a burst of speed like I'm crossing the finish line. Horitus keeps up with me. "Keep going, Your Grace. You're doing great!"

Perfect. I should have switched my updo for something more secure, though. By the time we reach the side entrance to the palace, my hair has half-fallen. I shove a blue hunk off my face, wipe my eyes, and look for Gregor.

So much muscled-man glory. For the first time, I understand what swoon means. Seeing it from down here is an entirely different experience than up above.

I spot Finley, who runs through a set of tires, catching sight of me on the last row and almost tripping. He's the one who helps me find Gregor by looking off to his left.

And I spot him, so tall, glistening in the sun like an oiled god. He leaps several feet in the air to clasp a set of rings, swiftly moving hand-over-hand to cross over the mud pit that runs beside the climbing wall.

His muscles undulate, pulling, flexing, shifting like ocean water. I'm transfixed until Horitus clears his throat. "Ready for another run?"

I wave my hand at him. "No. We can do that breathing thing now."

"This is the wrong place for you."

"I was hoping to go up that rope." I point to a guard moving into the air.

His face goes tight. "I don't think it would be appropriate for the Princess to work out with the guards."

"Why? Because it's never been done before?" I feel bold, *so* bold. I'm changed. Gregor has made me a better woman. I'm fearless. Willing to try anything. I head straight for the rope.

Gregor drops to the ground at the end of the line of rings. He hasn't spotted me yet. The recruit on the rope reaches the top and starts sliding back down. He's pretty stringy, actually. I can't be any worse than him.

"Your Grace," Horitus says, but I hold up a hand.

"I can do this."

I stand at the base of the rope and wait for the skinny guard to leave it. He almost trips over himself to get out of my way.

Several of the guards pause to watch. I notice their commander out of the corner of my eye. He doesn't order them back to their stations.

Gregor turns to me from across the yard. This is my moment.

Have I ever climbed a rope before? No.

Am I confident I can do it? Also, no.

But I'm going in.

"Any tips?" I ask the bystanders as I approach the dangling length.

A few men cough, but no one speaks up.

It's gone awfully quiet on the training course.

I realize I know nothing. Not how to grab it. Not where to put my feet. I try to picture the last guy. Nothing useful comes to mind other than his hands were above his head.

I can do that.

I reach up and grasp the rope. It's rougher than it looks, and as soon as I grip it tight, something sharp bites my skin.

I can't let go, though. I have to be tough.

I smile at the guards. "I'm sure I'll appreciate you all even more after this."

Now that I have the rope, I'm not sure what goes next. Am I supposed to let go with one hand and make it go higher? I'm as high as I can go already. My face burns.

I lift my knees, trying to catch the rope with my feet. It swings unsteadily, and I start to go diagonal.

My arm muscles are already screaming, and I haven't moved up at all! I could set my feet down and nothing will have changed.

This was a terrible idea.

"Reset!" I call out and drop my feet. I shake out my arms.

Horitus stands aside, his face pinched. I can't look at the trainees, and definitely not Gregor.

I want to melt into the ground.

But this time, I jump, grasping the rope much higher. Somehow, my dangling ankle ensnares the rope so I can stand up. And my arm has space to move up!

I did it!

I mean, I'm only a foot off the ground, but I moved!

The guards clap for me, and I'm determined to go farther. Unfortunately, the lucky twist of the rope has me stuck rather than helping. I kick my leg free, but then I'm dangling again.

Uh, oh.

My arms are on fire when I hear a familiar voice. "You're doing great, Your Grace. Lift your knees to your belly."

It's Finley. I don't dare look down. I'm afraid to move, or I might lose my grip on the rope.

"Lift your knees!" he says again.

It's not easy, but I bring them up.

"Now you have to trap the rope between your feet and create a step."

What does he mean by that?

"Look down," he says.

God! I can't! I'm aimed at the sky!

"Lean forward."

Oh, I get it. I manage to shift forward enough to look down.

He takes the rope and moves it between my shoes so that it bends between them. "Clamp it tight!" He braces my feet together.

"Okay."

"Stand up like the rope is a step."

I do that, and suddenly, my arms are by my chest again.

What? I'm in the air?

"Extend one arm at a time as high as you can reach."

I look up, grasping the rope over my head.

"Knees to your belly."

I raise them.

"Create a step with the rope."

I'm above his head, so he can't help me. I fight with the rope, then manage to trap it again. And I stand up.

I can do this!

I look down, searching for Gregor. He's moved farther away, lurking in the shadow of the castle.

Why has he done that?

"I wouldn't go much higher," Finley says.

I only do one more. Even though it's easier than dangling, my arms feel like rubber, and I see his point. I've done enough.

I'm well over everyone's heads. Valloria has arrived, and she looks mad enough to cut the rope with her teeth. She peers up at me, her hand shielding her eyes.

I realize I don't know how to get down.

I'm stuck.

My arms start to shake.

"If you're tired, create that step and use your legs to rest." There's a note of fear in Finley's voice.

I *am* way up here.

"I like the view from here!" I say. "Carry on!"

No one moves.

Great.

Should I slide down? Won't that burn my hands? Won't I fall?

My heart hammers.

Valloria calls out, "She said carry on!"

The guards spring back into action, including Gregor, who heads to the other side of the yard.

But Finley stays down below.

"You're all right," he says, more quietly now. "Just reverse the process. Use your step to brace you while you squat back down."

I try what he says, but my arms refuse to let go. "I'm stuck," I finally admit.

Valloria turns to Horitus. "Fetch a ladder. *Now.*"

Oh, God. This is too embarrassing. "No. I can do it."

"Of course you can," Finley says.

The commander arrives at my feet. "Return to your station, recruit."

"No," I say. "He's helping me."

The commander bows. "Of course, Your Grace."

"Close your eyes," Finley says. "Pretend your feet are on the ground, and you're about to sit down on a chair. Let your hands walk their way down the rope."

I close my eyes. It's definitely easier to shut off the visual of falling to my death. Or a broken arm, or whatever.

I move my hands as I try to sit down. The rope shifts alarmingly, then steadies. I open my eyes. Finley holds the bottom. "Keep coming."

Soon I'm scrunched up.

"Let go of the rope with your feet, straighten your body, and catch it again."

It's hard letting go of the stability of the rope-step. But I shake it off, praying my grip stays strong.

I lower my legs.

"I can help now. That's why I didn't want you too high." He wraps the rope around my foot. "Sit one more time."

I do it, and then Finley has me, his arms beneath my knees. I let go of the rope, and I'm in his arms. He quickly sets me down.

I don't want to let go of him, but the whole yard is watching, so I step away. "Thank you," I say.

Valloria rushes forward. "That's quite enough exercise for the day," she says. "Come back to your chambers."

Drat. At least I got to see them. I wave merrily at the guards. I wish I could spot Gregor.

Finley's grinning at me, though. Why was he the only one to step up?

"Your parents are going to hear about this," Valloria says. "You could have fallen. Hurt yourself." She opens the door to the palace, and we enter the side hall that leads through the staff wing.

I'm rarely here, so I slow down, taking in the simpler decor. The rooms are all closed up. Finley lives here somewhere.

Valloria tries to march us ahead, but I won't do it. There are only numbers on the doors, no names. There's no way to tell which one is his.

"Your Grace, are you listening?"

Something snaps. I turn to her. "Your job is to keep someone from stabbing me or stealing me or causing me harm. It is not to tell me where to go or how to act or when to leave somewhere. I'm done with this! I'm twenty-three! You treat me like I'm twelve! So, stop it or I'll marry the next man I see and leave the palace all together and never look at you again!"

She remains silent, following me at five paces as I stalk through the hallway. Maybe I was too mean, I don't know. But I'm done. Done with being a prisoner in my own palace. Done with being told who I can and can't talk to.

As of right now, I'm the biggest rebel this royal family has ever seen.

CHAPTER 16

Finley

I've just said good night to my mom and headed to my room when a frantic text comes through from Gregor.

Gregor: *The Princess asked me to meet her outside of the abbey. In town. I can't do that. What do I say to her?*

Me: *Holy hell. Did she sneak out?*

Octavia has lost her mind. She's a princess. It's one thing to go to the stables with guards. Or climb a rope. Another entirely to head into town.

Gregor: *She said to meet in fifteen minutes.*

So, she's gone.

Me: *You don't want to go?*

This relationship is unraveling faster than the ball of yarn in a cat lady's house.

Gregor: *No. Yes. I don't know. It's a lot.*

Damn. He's a grown man. He's acting like he's sixteen and sneaking out on curfew.

But I get it. This is the Princess. The poor guy is warring between his duty and this woman who has her sights set on him. I don't know if she understands what she's putting him through.

But, then I get a brainstorm.

Me: *Tell her you're with me.*

Gregor: *Ok.*

I wait. I can't intercept this myself. If I do, Octavia will know how involved I am. And honestly, I'm not doing it to protect Gregor. I'm protecting myself. She sees me as a friend. I don't want there to be distrust with her.

I sit on the end of my bed, waiting to hear. The minutes tick by.

Me: *So?*

Gregor: *She's already halfway there. She says you can come, too.*

Right. I totally need to be the third wheel on this date.

Me: *How is she getting out of the palace? The guards are everywhere.*

Gregor: *Beats me. She does what she wants lately.*

Me: *We have to go. We can't leave her out there alone.*

Gregor: *I know.*

At least he's on board finally. And now Octavia knows I'm coming.

So, I text her.

Me: *Big G says we're meeting outside the abbey. How'd you manage that?*

Octavia: *That's classified. If I told you, I'd have to kill you.*

Interesting.

Me: *I'm headed that direction.*

Octavia: *Excellent. You can stand watch.*

Great. She wants me to play lookout while they do their thing. This is getting to be way too much for me.

But this is Vi we're talking about.

Me: *Aye, aye, captain.*

I switch into my darkest pair of jeans and a black turtleneck covered by a black jacket. With my black guard boots, I figure I'm about as stealthy as an average Joe can get. I can't believe I got myself into this.

I pass through the bathroom and into the main room. Mom sits in her rocking chair, listening to an audiobook. Her eyes are closed.

I tap her arm. "I'm going out with some guys."

She glances at the clock. "This late? On a Monday? Don't you have training first thing in the morning?"

I shrug. "So do they. We'll be all right."

"You boys be careful."

I kiss her forehead and walk out her door.

I exit the staff wing, which lets out into the training yard where Vi climbed the rope this afternoon. There are a couple of the townies there, lifting weights late into the night. I admire their dedication to catch up with the others. They wave as I pass, and I give them a fist pump in the air.

A girl runs up to me. "Hey, Fin. Where you headed?"

I remember that voice, screaming my name behind one of the donkey sheds a couple of months ago. It's Janine, one of the gardeners. We were celebrating my acceptance into guard training.

As much as I'd like tonight's awkward wingman situation to become a normal group of four, I can't get entangled with her. "Meeting some guys."

"Can a girl come along?" Her voice drips with invitation.

"Not this time. Rain check?"

She runs her nail across my neck. "Any time." She watches me as I dart across the yard to the outer wall.

Nope, I'm not going to dally with her right now, even if I end up having to watch Gregor dally with — nope, not going to even let it enter my mind.

Gregor didn't say where to meet, so I text him. *Where near the abbey?*

No answer. If I don't hear shortly, I'll ask Octavia.

I pass under the watchtower, making sure my stride is correct and my hands are properly positioned. I approach the small pedestrian gate and click my heels. "Guard Trainee F. Bulgari requesting passage out of the palace gates."

The man leans over the ledge of the watchtower and peers down. "Oh, hey Finley. Venturing out late? All the shops are closed, even the bar."

"Heading to a friend's."

He nods. The gate pops open. That is a downside of living in the palace. My coming and going will be noted by this guard, by his log, and by the video cameras.

Unlike Gregor. Because he lives in the barracks outside the palace wall, he can walk off the grounds anytime he wants.

The abbey isn't terribly far from the castle, about ten blocks. I avoid Town Square, taking a backstreet among residential houses before cutting over to the avenue through the heart of Avalonia.

The abbey is closed up and dark. There'll only be two night guards there, both inside.

The church is tall and stone and intricately carved. The

spires disappear into the inky black of night, well above the reach of the street lamps.

A light in a window on the far side marks the guard office. I'm not sure where Octavia plans to meet us. Hopefully not inside somewhere. It's bound to be locked up in a way neither Gregor or I can penetrate without alerting the guards.

I step close to a stone pillar at the front corner of the cemetery next to the abbey. I tap out a quick message to Octavia.

I'm here. Where did you plan to meet us?

Octavia responds quickly. *I'm in the cemetery, near the middle. The tallest angel.*

Tallest angel. I like that. I tap on her contact information. I called her Rose Garden, same as what I typed into Gregor's phone when all this began. But I swiftly change her name to Tallest Angel.

I've wandered this cemetery many times. It was filled long ago, not with kings or queens or the royal family. They are primarily buried in monuments below the abbey itself.

Here are the royal ministers, chiefs of staff, and other notoriety. No washing women here. No guards either.

I weave my way through the tombstones, heading toward the center. This isn't a large space, maybe the equivalent of four sporting fields.

It isn't difficult to spy the tallest angel. She's huge, arms to the heavens, wings outstretched.

I hurry toward it. It takes a moment to spot Octavia. Like me, she's dressed all in black. The yoga pants from earlier today. Black tennis shoes. And a puffy black coat.

Her hair is in a high ponytail, gleaming black with its blue and pink strands.

"Hey," I whisper.

She turns my way. "Finley. You made it. Where's Gregor?"

Oh, boy. He better show.

"We had to use different exits. He should be here shortly."

She tilts her head, her ponytail swinging. "Why do you have to use different exits?"

"Because I'm palace, and he's barracks."

She frowns. "But he said you were together." She's not buying it. I don't like lying to her. So I confess.

"Look. We weren't *together* together. Just texting." That's the truth.

Her frown deepens. "Then why did he say you were the reason he couldn't come?"

She's figuring it out. "I think he's nervous about meeting you off the palace grounds."

She sighs. "I know. I'm so sick of being told what I can't do."

I lean against the tall granite crypt. "You really showed them on the ropes today."

"I would have humiliated myself if you hadn't stepped in."

"You just needed some coaching. We all did. Every guard standing in the yard had to be taught how to do that. Nobody expected you to climb like an expert."

Her shy smile breaks my heart wide open. "That's good to know. Thanks." She steps forward and punches my chest. "You are the most amazing friend I have."

I have to avoid her gaze. She might see right through me. I examine the crypt. It's oversized, eight feet long by four feet wide. The top edge is shoulder height for me. The angel looms above us, wings outstretched. "So whose grave are we hanging out with?" I ask.

She turns and runs her fingers across the carved letters. I can barely make out the words in the dim light of the lamp on the corner.

"Angelique Montgomery Matteson," she says, almost reverently. "Born 1794. Died 1817."

"She was twenty-three," I say.

"Just like us."

She continues to run her hand over the young woman's name.

"I wonder how she died," I say.

"No telling. She was important to the royal family if she's here."

I look up at the angel. "Really important, if she's the tallest angel."

We walk around the crypt. On the other side, her name is repeated, but this time there are other words.

Daughter. Wife. Mother to be.

"She died in pregnancy or childbirth," Octavia says, her voice low.

"Happened a lot back then."

"And we're the same age. She was married, pregnant, and died by now." Octavia leans her head against the granite. "And what have I done, even with all my privilege? Nothing. I haven't even kissed anyone."

Though I suspected this to be true, it's a punch in the

gut. She's been so sheltered. No wonder she's finally acting out.

She pushes away from the crypt. "Where is Gregor?"

Right. That's what we're here for.

I check my phone, but there is no response from him. "I'll find out." I tap out a quick message.

Dude. I'm here. Where the hell are you? We're waiting in the cemetery by the abbey.

He better answer. Until then, I have to distract Vi. I gesture toward another large crypt. "Who's the biggest honcho in the cemetery?"

I walk that way, and after a moment she falls in beside me. "Oh, that's the first Minister of Culture. He lived to be a hundred. He served two kings."

This crypt is taller than our heads and topped with a trio of young children, their mouths open in song.

"Do you come here often?" I ask her. "You seem to know the place well."

"Enough. But the main reason I know about that crypt is because of Rosenthal. It's well-known among the staff that he's trying to squeeze himself into this cemetery despite no one having been buried here for a century. We keep trying to tell him there's no room at the inn."

I run my hand along the smooth wall of granite. "I'm sure this is pretty roomy for one old man. We could probably toss Rosenthal in here after the fact."

Octavia breaks out with a melodious laugh. "He'd probably be down for it. All they have to do is add his name to the side."

We wander the cemetery. I keep waiting for my phone to buzz, but it doesn't. What is going on with Gregor?

Octavia's gaze falls to the ground, watching her feet as we move along the path. She draws in a breath as if she's about to say something, and I have a feeling it's going to be about how Gregor doesn't seem to be coming.

I quickly butt in. "I have a place I want to show you. Gregor can catch up if he ever gets his head out of his ass."

"Do you think he will?"

"Will what?"

"Get his head out of his...what you said."

"Sure. Let's have some fun." I pick up my pace and motion for her to catch up.

She rushes forward. "Where are we going?"

"You'll see."

I hold out my hand. She looks at it a moment, then places hers in it. I squeeze and take off in a run, pulling her with me. We dash through the cemetery and outside the gate.

I hope Gregor doesn't show. I'll get Vi all to myself. This is going to be an epic night.

CHAPTER 17

Octavia

I'm not sure how I end up running through the back streets of Avalonia holding Finley's hand, but happiness soars through me as if I'm a bird flying before the moon.

It's cold, but not freezing, and the air on my cheeks makes me feel alive.

"Look there," Finley says, pointing up.

The palace is magical from here, massive and strong, like a fort protecting the world. Lights shine on the Avalonian flags flapping from the two towers.

"It seems so far away," I say.

"Have you ever seen it from the road?"

"Not at night."

He grins and I have to grin back. We pause beneath the trees, looking for guards who might be on watch, then dash across the street to the other side.

We pass between the shuttered Italian restaurant and the bakery. Nothing is open this late on Monday night. Not this close to the palace. Long before my father was king, the curfew for Town Square was set early to avoid any trouble near the palace gates.

I have no idea where we can go. Anything within walking distance will be shut down.

We come to the alley behind the shops. It's dark back here so far from the streetlights. "Where are we going?"

"You'll see." His teeth flash white as he pulls me along.

We pass dumpsters, back doors, and piles of wood crates. Definitely a far cry from the palace halls. But it's all so fascinating. There's mud, broken asphalt, and chipped paint. The owners must have other priorities than making things look perfect. They're busy working, building families. Who cares about the alley side of a building?

The back side of the palace is as immaculate as the front.

"Up here." Finley grasps the bottom rail of a set of metal stairs climbing the side of a brick building.

"Is it safe?" I immediately want to retract the question. I didn't sneak through the tunnels to the abbey to be safe.

"As safe as climbing a rope." There's that grin again.

It instantly creates a matching one in me. "Let's go."

We rise into the sky, bricks to our left, the open air to our right, until we reach the lip of the roof. We're three stories high, as tall as any shop in the square, since Avalonian law states that no building in view of the abbey will be taller than its cupola, much less the spires.

Finley turns to help me up to the flat expanse of the pebbly roof. "Best view in Avalonia," he says, taking me to the front edge.

The height makes me clutch his arm. It's not like

looking from the inside of the tower, where I'm on a bench in front of an enclosed window.

Here the wind whips at my ponytail and the hush is broken by the rustle of tree branches and a car or two driving in the distance.

The palace is easier to see above the hedges and stone walls. My wing is dark and quiet off to the right. The main entrance blazes with light, even at this hour. Each stone column has a night guard before it. Looking at it from here, everything is peaceful and perfect, as if all is right in the land.

I look the other direction at the abbey and the quiet cemetery. I can see the tall angel in its center. It means more to me after reading the inscription with Finley. The two of us are the same age as Angelique.

What if my time was already complete? I had done almost nothing.

Finley looks off in the distance as well, his short hair a wild whip of dark brown. He looks different without the guard uniform and the mirrored sunglasses. More like the Dory I grew up with.

I have the most incredible urge to be kissed. It's over-whelming. The cold, the view, and…him.

"Hey," I say.

He turns, and my breath catches. The moon caresses his rugged, charming face. He's been with me every step of his new journey. I trust him completely.

"I need your help with something."

His gaze meets mine and something in my belly goes liquid.

"Of course."

"I—I'm nervous about something. Really nervous. And you're one of my best friends. And luckily, a boy." A nervous giggle tries to escape, but I clamp it down.

His eyebrows draw together the smallest amount, but he waits me out.

"I — I've never kissed anyone. I would like to try it. Would you do it? It wouldn't be like cheating on Gregor, I don't think. You're like a — a brother to me. Okay, that's weird. I would never kiss Leo. But you're a trusted friend. Someone who would tell me if I did it wrong. If I was bad. I mean, you'd *know*. You've kissed a thousand girls. You're an expert."

A muscle in his jaw ticks. "You should save your first kiss for Gregor."

"I don't think you would be my *real* first kiss. Any more than my mother kissing me goodnight or the French ambassador pecking my cheeks."

His Adam's apple bobs and his gaze cuts away. He's not going to do it. I've asked too much.

"I'm sorry. Nevermind. That was crazy. It'll be fine." I turn away from him to look out on the small park at the center of the square where the townspeople sing in the mornings.

"Kissing me wouldn't be like your brother, or your mother, or the French ambassador," he says. "Not at all."

Then he'll do it? I reach for his hand. "I know. I mean, sure. But we're friends. I only want the basics. Where do noses go? How do our mouths fit together? Then I won't be a complete mess when it happens for real."

It could happen tonight, if Gregor can find us.

"All right."

My heart leaps. He said yes!

I let out a squeal. "So, how do I stand? Do I lean in? Where do my hands go?" I hold them out, waiting for Finley to place them.

"None of that matters. You can do it a million ways." His eyes take in my face, and something uncurls deep within me when he looks at my lips. "All you need is proximity." He steps in close, and his breath feathers across my nose. "And touch."

He leans down. Somehow, my chin knows to tilt up, and his face knows to turn to the side. We don't collide, but our mouths meet.

I expect it to be bristled with unshaven whiskers and clammy, like a damp hand.

But it's not. His mouth is warm and soft and seeks my lips. His hand goes to my back to hold me steady, and my arms lift to wrap around his neck.

He tastes of peppermint and a bit of chocolate. Dessert maybe? I want to be closer, so I lean in more, and the warmth of his whole body envelops me.

Time stops. The wind whips around us as if we're at the center of a cyclone. My lips part, and our tongues meet. Electricity darts through me, as if Finley is the charge that lights my happiness.

His mouth moves, nibbling, tasting, loving my mouth. I love his back, following his lead, sensing that we're connecting in all new ways through this simple act.

He seems to be saying, *this is right, we are right, and it is only us in this whole wide world.* And I answer him back, *I am yours, this is perfect, and I never want this moment to end.*

But then he pulls away, staggering almost, and I reach

out a hand as if to steady him. "You're good," he says. "It's all good. You'll be fine. It's fine." And he strides quickly back to the ladder.

I follow him, my hand to my mouth. That was magical. Kissing is sorcery, a potion passed between two people.

It was so wonderful with Finley, a friend, someone who will kiss *any* girl.

I can't even imagine how much better it will be with Gregor, my one true love.

CHAPTER 18

Finley

I should not have agreed to that.

Never, never.

As I help Octavia onto the ladder and back down to the street, it's everything I can do to keep my hands off her.

If I thought I was in love with her before, now I'm wild with it. The feeling is physically painful, as if someone is repeatedly kicking me in the gut.

Her happiness is palpable, clearing the air around her. She spins in circles in the dark alley. "I can't wait to see Gregor again! I'm so ready!"

Every four-letter word I ever learned flashes in my head. This was a mistake. I shouldn't have kissed her. Shouldn't have let it go so long. I need to get her home.

"We should go back to the abbey," I say. "It's late."

"But we're waiting on Gregor!" She skips along the alley, whirling about as if it's a summer parade.

I trudge along behind her, trying to right myself. It was only a kiss. She was new to it, that's all. She responded with such openness. She came at me with no hesitation, no fear. It wasn't me. Just kissing. She's figuring out what a drug physical attraction can be. I should know. I wrote the book on it among the women of the palace staff.

We approach the back side of the bar, and she pauses. "Wait. I hear something."

She tiptoes along the building.

Right. The speakeasy. The bar has to shutter its front side at midnight, but those in the know are aware of the rear entrance. The owner serves drinks until the wee hours.

She leans her ear against the wall. "Yes! It's music! Glasses clinking!" She sizes up the building as if to figure out how to get in.

I relent. "The bar reopens in the back after it's forced to close."

Her eyes light up. "Can we go?"

"It's a bar. And you're the princess."

"Do you think they'll recognize me?"

"Your portrait hangs in the square."

She frowns. "But they've never seen this." She reaches for the elastic band in her hair and slides it out. She bends over, running her fingers against her scalp, making a mess of the sleek style.

Then she stands and tosses her hair back. It's chaos, flying around her face, landing on her shoulders and down her back. The colored strands weave in and out of the mess.

She knocks the breath out of me a second time. So, this is Octavia unchained.

"What do you think? Did I lose my princess vibe?" She shoves a couple sections behind her ears self-consciously.

"Yeah." Now she's a sexy, just-been-tousled-in-bed vixen.

I'm doomed.

Our gazes catch for a second, but I quickly dart mine away. I'm not here for romance. She belongs to someone else.

"So, can we go?" She's so excited, she's practically vibrating.

I can't tell her no.

"Sure. But be prepared to run for the abbey if you're recognized. I'll be right behind you."

I rap three times on the door, pause for a beat, and rap two more.

Her eyes light up. "There's a secret knock?"

I manage a grin, trying to keep my feelings light. "Not really. Basically, if you know there's a door here, you're good. But it's fun, right?"

She laughs. "Thanks for the truth."

The latch turns and the door pops open. It's Luka, one of the herders I used to know. He works here, which is how I know about the afterhours.

"Hey, Fin!" he booms. "Good to see you!" He pounds me on the back. "And you brought a town girl? Since when are you seen with town girls?"

It's working. He doesn't recognize her. "This is Vi."

He steps aside to make way for us. "Come on in. It's rather lively for Monday, a holdover from the festivities last weekend."

Octavia turns to me. "Does he mean the guard inspection?"

Luka laughs. "No, the gelding fest. The ceremonial

cutting of the nuts."

"Oh." Octavia's eyes meet mine. "He means the donkeys, right?"

"Yes." I hope this isn't too much for her.

But inside the bar, the crowd is mixed. Townies and herders, young and old, singles and couples. The lights are low, hiding the unfinished feel of the cedar walls, the low ceiling. Tables and chairs are scattered along the sides, but most are empty.

A space has been cleared for dancing, and everyone is on their feet, doing a bastardized version of the morning dance performed each day in Town Square.

Luka moves back behind the big oak bar.

Octavia leans close. "What are they doing to the Avalonian anthem?" The couples grind against each other, and her eyes bug out. "Oh! I want to do that."

First kissing, and now grinding on the dance floor. She's testing my limits.

"Let's knock back a drink first. What do you like?"

"Champagne? Sherry?"

Oh, boy. I nod and head to the bar, leaving her to watch the dancers. She's practicing, moving her feet and rocking her pelvis.

Luka gives me a wink. "She's a tall drink of water. Where'd you meet her?"

"Her family came to the guard inspection." That's not a lie, at least.

"She likes a man in uniform."

"Something like that. She's a lightweight. What you got? Champagne?"

Luka laughs. "You're a lark. Champagne in a joint like

this. I have cider, though, a sweet one."

"That will work. I'll have a lager."

Luka pours them up. "Looks like she's ready to get in the thick of the dance." He slides the glasses across the bar. "Somebody's in for a fun night."

Right.

I slap cash on the bar and take the drinks. Octavia tucks her phone in her coat pocket as I pass her a glass.

She lifts the drink to the meager light for examination. "What is it?"

"Cider. Luka thought you'd like it."

She takes a sip. "I do!" She gulps half of it down.

"Go easy if you don't drink a lot."

Her eyes narrow, and as if I'd dared her, she drains the rest of the glass.

Okay, then.

"Bottoms up, Dory. I'm out for the night, and I want to dance." She lifts my glass to my lips.

So that's the way it's going to go. I drain my beer. When I slam it on a nearby table, a cheer goes up.

"Come on, Finley," someone calls, and I spot a couple other herders on the dance floor. "Bring your girl!"

The Avalonian morning dance comes to an end with a great shout.

"Oh, no!" Octavia cries. "I missed it!"

"Again!" someone shouts.

The old man in the corner strikes up again on his fiddle, and everyone arranges in the traditional circles like in the Town Square ritual, women on the inside ring, men on the outside. Octavia joins her group, and I jump into mine.

At first, nothing is different. The two rings go in opposite directions.

But when the two circles come together, pairs linking elbows to make a pattern, the traditional dance veers off course. The music changes tone. The round robin of elbow links end, and couples form with whoever's closest.

As the men spin the nearest women, Octavia looks at me expectantly. "So." The other couples have begun the grind.

I take too long. My hesitation means some other man snatches her. He sweeps her up against his body, grasping the back of her knee to drive their bodies in sync.

Her eyes go wide. "Whoa!"

"Like it?" the man asks. I've never seen him before. He's probably a townie. With his collar popped and his designer label jeans, he probably goes to university.

"It's something!" Octavia concentrates on the moves as the man leans her back so far that her hair dusts the floor. She's still wearing her puffy black coat, so there isn't too much contact.

I clench my fists. I'm ready to snatch her back.

The man picks her up and twirls her in a circle. The music becomes a quick staccato beat, and men stamp. That's the cue, so the women jump, wrapping their legs around the waists of their partners.

"Oh!" Octavia says, but she gives it a try. Now she's straddling the guy, and he's into it.

I've had enough. I'm about to jump in, but then I see we have a bigger problem.

Gregor storms into the room and heads straight for them with a murderous look on his face.

CHAPTER 19

Octavia

He's here!

I texted Gregor, letting him know we weren't at the abbey anymore, but at the bar. I felt so worldly telling him about the back entrance!

Maybe he already knew, but at least now he knows I do, too!

I pull away from the random guy and our awkward dance. But before I can even greet Gregor properly, he's grabbed my arm and started dragging me toward the door.

"I wanted to dance with you!" I cry. "Let's stay!"

"This is no place for someone like you," he growls, low enough that the others can't hear him. I'm grateful he's not blowing my cover.

I'm torn between digging in my heels and going with him. At least we can be alone. And we have no deadline, not until morning. As long as I'm back before Valloria comes to relieve Tyson, it will be fine.

I glance back at Finley. He's striding toward us, but

when he catches up with us at the door, Gregor lets go of my arm and punches him in the face!

"Oh, my gosh!" I reach out for Finley as he staggers back, surprised by the punch.

"You brought her here, didn't you? You can't be trusted!" Gregor turns to me. "Come. Now."

My loyalties become divided. Gregor had no reason to punch Finley! I can't just leave him.

"I wanted to come," I say to Gregor. "So, stop it."

Finley has recovered and stands menacingly, his arms dangling like he's ready for a fight.

I stand between them. "Are you okay, Finley?"

He's not bleeding or anything. Maybe guards know how to strike in a way that doesn't leave a mark.

"I'm fine." But his eyebrows are one fierce line of anger.

I try to keep my voice from shaking. This night has gone all wrong. "I'm going to let Gregor take me back, okay?"

Finley shifts his gaze to me for only a second, then he's back on Gregor with a quick nod. "Understood."

I realize the music and dancing have stopped. We're the center of everyone's attention. I know I should probably hate this. I mean, Gregor hit Finley after he's been so amazing!

But it is a *little* thrilling. I'm really living now!

I'm sure I can clear up the misunderstanding. Gregor thought he was saving me. And he's probably right. I shouldn't be here, if for no other reason than if I'm caught, I'll never sneak out again.

But everything is all right. I'm getting time with Gregor. I don't need a crowd.

I wave at the gawking room and move toward Gregor. "Let's go."

Gregor yanks the door open and waits for me to pass through. The cool air is a relief. As we walk along the alley, Gregor's pace is hard to keep up with. It's definitely not the love-struck moment I was hoping for. He plows ahead, taking us back in the direction of the abbey.

Soon, I'm unzipping my coat, even though we're outdoors. I'm almost running to keep up.

Then, I stop. This isn't right.

He goes an entire block before he realizes I'm not with him.

"You have to come," he says. "It's not safe."

"I'm not running to keep up with you." A tendril of despair curls through me, cutting through my elation over how the night has gone up until now.

"Your Grace—"

"Don't call me that! I'm Octavia! You're acting like the guards!" The cold invades my lungs and steals my breath. All the joy is pushed away.

Gregor glances around as if he's afraid someone will see us. He's wearing sweatpants and his hair is sticking up, like he got out of bed. He didn't bother to put on regular clothes to meet me?

I'm ready to cry. What is happening here?

His tone softens. "Your Gr—Octavia, it's almost one in the morning. I'm sworn to protect you. And I can't protect you on the night streets out in the open. Please, let's get back to the abbey. Is someone there prepared to get you back into the palace?"

"I have a way back that is safe."

"All right. Then let's go. We should stick close to the buildings and only cross the main thoroughfare when we are near the church."

"Will you at least hold my hand?" It's hard to ask, but I want my perfect night. And I hope he's going to kiss me, although maybe it's not right to kiss two different people in the same evening.

No, it doesn't matter. Finley was only my practice for Gregor. I want to see how much bigger the fireworks are with him.

Gregor stares at my outstretched arm like it's a tentacle. Then he relents and takes it.

Happiness shoots through me. Yes! It's working!

He slows down, and we walk along the alley together. I could sing. I'm free at night in Avalonia with Gregor! It's finally happening.

I feel daring. Bold. I danced with a stranger. Climbed on a roof. I pull on Gregor's hand and drag it behind my back so that his arm is around me.

Now we're close. Gregor concentrates on the road ahead, but he keeps his arm in place. This is heaven. Our steps match, and the crunch of the gravel beneath our feet is the soundtrack of our first real time alone.

I want to sigh.

"Isn't it a beautiful night?" I ask.

Gregor grunts.

"You don't love walking in the moonlight?"

He sighs. "I don't like an unprotected member of the royal family in an alley."

"I'm not unprotected. I'm with you."

We turn the corner. Across the street, the abbey looms against the sky.

Gregor removes his arm from my waist, rushing ahead to peer around the building as if we're on a secret mission. Then he turns. "It's safe to cross."

"Of course it is."

He shushes me, and another dart of unhappiness cuts me. Why can't he enjoy our moment? I guess we'll have to meet on the palace grounds after all, if he's going to be like this in town. Maybe we can try the kitchens or even the Great Hall. There have to be suitable spots that aren't guarded. Maybe I can sneak him into the billiards room. There are good hiding spots there.

He motions me forward and runs across the asphalt like we're common criminals. At first, I refuse to go, arms crossed over my chest like a petulant child. Then I stalk across the road.

"Where now?" he asks. "How do you get back?"

"I have ways." I can already see what's happening. There will be no kiss. No romance. He's too worried about me.

So I tell him to go home and disappear into the hedge that hides the short granite hall that goes to a secret door to the abbey that eventually leads to the hidden door to the tunnels.

Before I'm totally underground, I text him, *On my way back. I'm safe. Don't worry.*

But he will.

Like Valloria.

Like my father.

Like everybody.

I'm not a person.

I'm a princess.

Nobody sees me as anything else. Not even him.

CHAPTER 20

Finley

I wake up wired after a restless night. Neither Gregor nor Octavia answered my texts last night after they took off, so I can only assume they got home all right.

Despite the late hour, I'm early to training. I want to be there the moment Gregor arrives, so I can find out what the hell happened.

Those efforts are in vain. Gregor jogs up at the very last moment, right as Sergeant calls us into our lines for warm-up. Gregor chooses the opposite corner from me, so there is no way to get even a minor question to him as we go into our stations.

He avoids me through the morning routine, but he can't prevent me from approaching him at lunch. I catch up to him before we enter the Great Hall. Octavia might be in there, and I don't want her reading anything into our body language or tone.

Especially if I punch him like he did me last night. It could happen.

He spots me aiming for him and heads away from the palace doors.

"Dude! You can't skip lunch. It's not like you to walk away from a conversation like a skulking punk."

This gets him. He halts and waits for me to catch up. Everyone else has already passed through the rear entrance of the palace. We can't delay too long, or Octavia will notice we're not there.

I stop only a couple of feet from him. I want him to feel my anger. "What the hell happened, man? Why did you punch me? What happened with Octavia after you left?"

"I don't answer to you. We're not friends. Anyone who would take a member of the royal family to a sleazy, illegally operating hole in the wall, where people are dancing like it's a strip club, is no friend of mine."

Oh. I see. This is his judgment. Holding me to his standards.

"She was having a great time. She was perfectly safe."

"She was half drunk and letting a stranger grind his junk on her." He shakes his head. "I'd call the whole thing off, but it's clear my relationship with the Princess must remain in place if I'm to protect her from the likes of a rogue like you."

A rogue like me.

I like it.

"So, I take it you walked her back to the abbey?"

"I did. Then she disappeared. Obviously, there's some sort of secret passageway."

I nod. "As long as she's safe. I didn't hear from her last night. You either. I care, despite what you think."

"I have no idea when she got in. She wouldn't respond to me either."

That's interesting. She was ecstatic when she left with him. "Is she mad at you?"

"We're done here." He slashes the air with the flat edge of his hand. "This friendship is over."

What a drama queen. "You're breaking up with me, Big G?" I smack him on the back. "It's fine. Do what you have to do."

I sound a lot more laid-back than I am. Last night was a revelation. The Princess, literally letting her hair down. The dancing. The drinks.

That damn kiss.

It appears Gregor might be out of the romantic picture. At least on his end.

I wonder if she knows that yet. And how she'll feel when she figures it out.

Gregor stands firm on the path outside of the palace, his arms crossed, a glower on his face. I guess he's waiting for me to go in. He doesn't want to be seen together.

Fine by me.

I rush toward the building and into the Great Hall. I immediately direct my gaze to the serving table.

She's there. Trussed up again with her glorious hair disguised in an elegant updo, wearing a pale green dress with a pristine white apron that sets her apart from the rest of the servers.

We've dallied so long that the line has dwindled. I hurry to the end and wait for a tray.

I receive my servings in silence until I reach the end.

Octavia stands there with her tongs, in charge of the bread again.

"Good afternoon, sir," she says. "Have a roll."

Her guard is much closer today, standing only a couple feet from the end of the table where she can watch both Octavia and the room. Smart maneuver. That's what I would've done.

"Thank you." I give her a wink.

Her lips press together tightly, and I know she's trying to hold back a smile. There's a sparkle in those golden brown eyes that wasn't there before.

That tells me all I need to know. She's not mad at me.

Just as I'm about to walk away, her whole body stiffens, and the muscles of her face freeze in place.

I pretend not to notice and move on, casually turning to see where she's looking.

It's Gregor. He's completely changed her demeanor.

Whatever he did or said to the Princess, most likely to admonish her for her behavior, she's not having it.

I don't blame her.

I sit down at a table with some townies, hoping for a random conversation that doesn't require my attention. But I watch as Gregor goes down the line. If a person could turn to stone, that is what Octavia looks like as he gets nearer and nearer.

He's not much better.

I need to know more. I have to talk to her. Maybe she'll respond to my text today. I watch Gregor leave the table and find a spot across the room from me. They didn't even exchange pleasantries.

He keeps his back to the serving line, although it

doesn't matter. They all pick up their bins and head to the kitchen.

I eat quickly and head to the rose garden. She met me here before. I wonder if she can again. It's worth a shot.

I wind my way through the hedges. The roses have come a long way since I first saw Octavia here a week ago. More buds are peeking out from the spindly stems.

I tug out my phone to text a quick message. *I'm in the rose garden. Would love to talk about last night. Gregor seems upset. Are you okay?*

It might take her a moment to respond since she's in the kitchen.

Or she might not at all. I sit on the bench to wait. I have a good fifteen minutes before Sergeant will call us back. I'm happy to hang out in the gardens.

I see Vi everywhere. Young, running down the path in her little dresses with shiny black shoes, her nanny and guard close behind.

A memory surfaces, probably not too long before we were parted. She wears a riding habit, funny khaki pants with flared hips. Her white shirt is tucked in, and her hair is covered with a billed cap.

She's getting her first riding lessons, and she hopes that I can come with her. I'm used to going everywhere the Princess goes, running about the castle, playing billiards, watching movies in the theater.

But this time is different. We're sitting on the ground inside the rows of roses in full bloom, playing jacks. Her legs are crossed with her riding boots, sleek and black. Red petals drift to the ground and land around us.

Her nanny says it's time for her to go, and Octavia says, "Come along, Dory."

But the nanny shakes her head, and the guard holds me back.

This is the first activity I can't join her in.

Soon after that, I lose her completely.

Melancholy washes over me. If what's happening now goes wrong, I'll lose her again.

I can't let that happen.

I hold my phone out, willing it to buzz.

Then it does.

It's Vi.

Can't leave the kitchens. Guard is waiting in the hall. Go through the herb gardens to the back kitchen door.

Works for me. I tap a quick *yes* and hurry through the rows. It takes me a moment to find the tiny gate that leads to the herb garden. I haven't looked for it since I was a kid.

The low wooden growing boxes are mostly empty, but the signs of spring are already hitting them too in the tiny sprigs of life. By the time I reach the kitchen door, it has swung open, and there she is, my Octavia, still in her apron.

She steps down, holding the door open. "I only have a moment."

I want to touch her, hold her hand. "Are you okay? Did Gregor walk you back?"

"The royal family has their ways to move about," she says. "I ditched Gregor and came back." She hesitates. "I would have rather gone back to dancing."

Hope rises within me, even as I press on with my questions. "Was he harsh with you? I swear I didn't intend to get between you two."

She shakes her head. "I don't know. He's not exactly good for adventuring if he won't even let me dance."

"I'm sorry."

We stand there, the sun streaking through the vines overhead. My heart hammers. "Now what?" I ask.

She shrugs. "I've had a taste of freedom. I loved it."

I'm absolutely going to seize this opportunity. "I'm happy to take you again. There's so much more to see."

Her eyes lift to mine, and I swear my body could power the entire town of Avalonia. I feel so bright.

"We should do that. Text me." She disappears inside the kitchen.

As I head back through the herb garden, there might as well not have been any ground below me. My feet don't touch the earth at all.

CHAPTER 21

Octavia

When I return to my chambers and pull off the annoying scratchy dress, I throw on some jeans and sit on my bed.

What's happening with Finley? Are we flirting? Did we agree to a date?

His kiss was fantastic, but I have nothing to measure it against. If movies are to be believed, all kisses are that good, unless they're unwanted or your braces get caught together.

I need more data. Am I going to have to kiss a stranger now that things aren't good with Gregor?

I'm totally mad at him. He was so wrong last night. So wrong.

But he sent me those amazing songs. And he was so romantic and kind until he saw me dancing with another man.

Wait.

That's what happened!

He saw me dancing with someone else, and he was so overcome with anger and jealousy that he acted out of line.

This is the plot of so many romance movies. Didn't Hugh Grant get a pummeling in *Bridget Jones 2?* And that guy in *Wedding Crashers?* Oh, and that classic, *Pretty in Pink.*

It's practically a requirement that the hero slug someone to defend his lady's honor.

Maybe this can be repaired. He's so kind to the other guards. I know he's a good man. The best. It makes sense that he didn't like seeing me in a bar in the middle of the night. He was probably really angry at the man I was dancing with and didn't calm himself in time.

Gregor didn't understand that I wanted to be there with *him.* Who else would I risk all this for?

I can fix this.

I sail across the hallway to my sister's room. She's lying on her bed in her usual position, on her back, fingers flying over her phone. Her jeans are way more ripped than mine. I wonder if I should take scissors to my pair. Or hers. I've taken to wearing some of Lili's smuggled clothes when we won't be seeing our parents.

I sit on the end of the mattress and wait her out. She hates to be interrupted when she's in the zone.

Without even looking up, she asks, "Should I be on TikTok?"

"You want to do funny dances?"

"No, no. TikTok is very broad now. It's taking over. I should be there."

"But I thought you chose Instagram to make everything beautiful and perfect. It's all about your princess feed."

"I was thinking to not be myself."

"Then you can't show your face."

"Oh, there are apps for that. I can do entire videos with a completely different face and hair."

I scoot next to her. "Really?"

"Watch." She opens an app and turns on the camera. When she begins talking, I don't recognize her at all. I can see her on the bed saying the words, but the view of her on the screen is of a completely different person. Red hair, long fringed eyelashes, dramatic dainty chin.

"Lili, that's freaky."

"I know. I can be anyone."

She shuts off the recording and drops the phone to her bed. "So, was he at lunch?"

"Of course. We didn't really talk. Valloria was three steps away."

"Did he at least try to apologize?"

I run my fingers across the rips in my jeans. "I think he may have overreacted to seeing me grinding against another guy, even if everyone was doing it. I talked to Finley."

"What did he say?"

"He's happy to keep taking me out if I want to do more things."

"I bet he is."

"What do you mean by that?"

"I know you guys used to be childhood friends, but I don't think he feels that way anymore. Be nice to him." She waves her hand at me. "You're a lot. A princess. Perfection."

"I am not. I'm too tall, too hippy, and my nose is too big."

"Whatever. You glow now. Absolutely glow." She leans in. "Did you do something dirty?"

I didn't tell her about the kiss. That's private.

"Of course not. I mean, other than the dance. That was pretty dirty, I guess."

"So, what's your next move?"

"I'm going to apologize."

Lili pops up on her knees. "What for?"

"I feel like I cheated on him. I danced very provocatively with someone else."

"So what?"

"I'm serious, Lili. I was, like, *straddling* that guy. I'm sure it looked really, really bad. I was supposed to be meeting *him*."

"He's the one who punched Finley in the face! Why not that other guy, if he's so freaked out?"

"He was overwrought. Finley's a guard. Gregor thinks he should be protecting me, not taking me to bars."

"Girl, this is called a red flag. Clocking some guy because they don't like what their girl is doing? Hell to the no."

"But I've been watching him for months. He's such a good guy in training. The best."

Lili's face goes bright red. She's mad. "Around other men! Now you see what he's capable of around women."

I fall back on the bed, my hair flying out around me. I'm not sure that Lili's right. It feels thrilling. His behavior makes a weird sort of sense.

"I want that kiss, Lil. I need to move forward with my experience, even if it's with the wrong guy."

She sighs. "Okay, okay. A kiss doesn't take very long.

Can you meet him somewhere in the palace, get your smooch on, and then be done with this craziness?"

I sit back up. "Yes. I can. I was able to see Finley for a few seconds. I can do the same with Gregor."

"I think you're better off making out with someone else." She picks up her phone again.

She might be right. But it's hard to be alone with someone. It takes time and effort and sneaking around. I'm already invested in Gregor. I have his number. I can get to him. Despite last night, he's an obvious choice for my second kiss.

Finley gave me a taste of the magic.

I want more.

CHAPTER 22

Finley

Gregor avoids me again all afternoon. I'm feeling done with him by the time I get to my shower and dinner with Mom.

Hopefully Octavia is the same. Done with Gregor.

Mom slides a plate of fried sandwiches in front of me. "Did you have a good time last night?"

It all flashes by. The tall angel. Octavia on the roof. Kisses. Drinking. Dancing. The punch in the face.

"It was all right."

She peers at my cheek and lifts my chin. "What happened here?"

"Got roughed up during training."

She nods. "That'll get you tough."

My phone buzzes. I want to ignore it, but Tallest Angel flashes on my screen. Mom's sharp eyes catch it.

"Tallest Angel, huh? That doesn't sound like one of the guys."

Damn it.

"Yeah. Someone from last night."

That perks her up. "Someone interesting?"

"She's probably not for me."

She points at the phone, which buzzes a second time. "She doesn't think so."

I need to leave my phone in my room during dinner.

After the third buzz, Mom says, "It's not very gentlemanly to keep her waiting."

I take a bite of fried ham and cheese and unlock the phone to see what Octavia is saying.

Tallest Angel: *Gregor is ghosting me!*

Tallest Angel: *Did he say anything to you?*

Tallest Angel: *It's because I was all cold at lunch, isn't it?*

Mom glances away when I snatch up the phone so the messages can't be read. The lunch part would tell her it's someone in the palace.

Me: *He's struggling. He wants to protect you.*

Tallest Angel: *I knew it! So why won't he write me back?*

Me: *What have you been saying?*

Tallest Angel: *I want to meet him for a moment, like I did with you! Surely he can do that?*

Me: *Maybe. He's not in the palace.*

Tallest Angel: *Right. In the barracks. Can you get me to the barracks? I can sneak out once my night guard comes.*

Oh, boy.

Me: *The barracks aren't safe for keeping secrets. They're all guards. Plus, they'll recognize you for sure.*

Tallest Angel: *Well, poo.*

I read the line while picturing Octavia as a six-year-old. I almost laugh, and Mom smiles to herself while averting her eyes. She's definitely getting the wrong impression.

Tallest Angel: *Can we go back to the bar?*

Me: *Is that a good idea?*

Tallest Angel: *I want to go somewhere! Meet me at the tall angel in three hours!*

I want to say no. That it's too risky. That Gregor won't come again.

But I also want to see her.

Me: *Okay.*

Tallest Angel: *Yay!*

I set down the phone, ready to focus on the meal with my mother.

"So, that was quite an exchange." She lifts her water glass and watches me over the rim.

"Yeah."

"You going to see her?"

"Looks like it."

"Tonight?"

"Yes, in a bit."

"Don't stay out too late."

"I'll be careful."

Great. Now I have a hopeful mom as well as an over-exuberant princess. This is a real mess.

I leave early to take the walk through town to the abbey. I cut back and forth along the streets, looking back, wondering if I'll catch Octavia and see how she's escaping the palace.

Once again, it's late enough that the restaurants and shops are closed. The streets are mostly empty. I slip inside the gate to the cemetery and head to the center. What should we do this time?

I imagine the blazing kiss again, but have to set that aside. Octavia already got her practice.

I'm basically a travel guide.

I'm tempted to text Gregor to knock some sense into him. He needs to at least be polite to the Princess. But most likely he'll ignore me, too. Once I've gotten a read on Octavia's mood in person, I'll force him to listen to me at training tomorrow.

The chill is more intense tonight than before, and the winter grass crunches with frost as I pause in front of the tallest angel. I stare up at her long body stretched toward the night sky.

"Hey."

I turn to Octavia's voice. She's not in all black this time, but ripped jeans and a red coat.

"Hey." I want to be cool and nonchalant. She just told me how upset she was that Gregor was ghosting her.

But she's here.

With me.

I can't help but feel a rush of exhilaration.

"So what should we do tonight?" she asks. "I assume Gregor's not going to show."

"I don't think so. We can go farther afield."

"Out of Avalonia?"

That might get me thrown in the brig. "Away from Town Square. Here, the curfew is early. Get away from the palace, and things get more normal."

She holds out her elbow. "Lead the way."

I tuck her arm under mine and use my free hand to call a car to drive us away from prying eyes.

The herders often piled into cars to escape the palace, far enough that our shenanigans wouldn't get back to the guards.

Funny how things have gone full circle. Now I'm the guard trying to avoid being seen.

Octavia peers at my phone. "What's that?"

"An app where you call a car to take you somewhere."

"Really? Like at the palace?"

I chuckle. "Sort of. Except you have to pay for it."

"With cash?"

"No, you set up the app with your bank information or a credit card."

She frowns. "I don't have access to those."

"Will you ever get it?"

"Leo got it when he turned eighteen, but he was going on trips with Father as the Crown Prince. The princesses are apparently palace decorations with no need for money."

"I hate that, Vi. Can you ask?"

"We've tried. They simply arrange to get what we want, if it's approved. We never get actual money."

We reach the front gate near the street where the car should pick us up. I lean against the pillar to wait.

"So…" she says.

And her tone makes my heart speed up.

"Yeah?"

"Since we're here in the dark, can we practice the kiss again? I liked it. A lot."

"Don't you want to wait for Gregor?"

"No."

She's tempting me so hard. I don't think I should do it, but she's so close, leaning against me, her hands on my chest. She closes her eyes, and the moonlight caresses her skin.

There's no way I'm going to deny myself this.

I press my lips to hers, gently, like last time. I take it easy, telling myself to watch it, not to fall into it.

I nibble along her lips, capturing her mouth. But when her lips part, I pull away.

"Good?" I ask.

"So good." She bites her lip. "But last time we opened our mouths, just for a second."

She's killing me. "We did."

"Let's do that part." She leans in again.

When I don't move in right away, she opens her eyes. "Are you going to give me a movie screen kiss or not?"

Hell yes, I am.

If caution is a yellow flag, I fling it out of sight. I clasp the back of her head, threading my fingers through her hair. I pull her to me roughly until our bodies are flush together fully along their length.

I bend down and don't wait for her to come to me. I pull her face to mine, delving instantly into her mouth. She opens in surprise as my tongue licks against hers. She's warm honey and peppermint, yielding and soft.

After a moment, her body molds into mine. Her tongue comes for me, and her pulse flutters beneath my thumb at her throat. She lets out a sound and presses her pelvis against me.

With only a few inches between our heights, she lands where her body instinctively knows where to aim. I respond instantly, stiffening between us.

She pulls her face from mine, her eyes big as she looks up at me. "Is that…"

I want to grab her hips and grind into her. I'm fiercely in need. But I control myself. "It is."

"What do I do with it?"

Oh, I could tell her.

She goes on. "Should I pretend it isn't happening? It didn't when I danced with that random guy. How often does it happen?"

I draw in a ragged breath. Her innocence is shocking, delectable. I want to break it wide open, right here, against a brick wall, pounding her until we both disintegrate into nothing.

Down, boy.

"You don't have to talk about it. A guy knows it's happening. It's natural. Part of the process."

"Already? Just from kissing? I thought we had to be naked. And ready to do that thing!"

"It can happen anytime."

Her eyes go even wider. "Like at dinner? Or while driving a car?" She draws in a sharp breath. "Around your grandma?"

Okay, with that thought, I no longer have a problem. I let out a breath. "Probably not around a grandma. It's a stage in the process. It's not as obvious in women as men."

"Is it happening to me?" She glances down at her jeans as if she might produce an erection or some other obvious sign. "Wait. Is that what they call a lady boner?"

I can't stop myself from laughing. "Sort of. But not literally. You don't have an outward sign."

"What is my sign?"

Jesus. "A dampness. It's called getting wet."

"I've heard that phrase. They mean down there!"

"Yes."

"It's not pee, is it?"

"Oh, God, no. Didn't your parents have someone teach you about this stuff?"

"Hell, no. And don't bring up the internet. We have nanny software that blocks anything interesting."

"Right."

She bites her lip in thought, and it's so inadvertently sexy that my jeans get tight again. She lets out a rush of air. "So, it was okay when we were kissing, and I sort of happened to be against it."

"Sure."

"Let's do that again."

God. "Vi, I—"

But she's on me, her mouth on mine, her body against me. She grabs me around the waist so we're tightly together.

I know I should get control of this situation. We're way out of line. But she feels so good. She breaks the kiss, only a breath away from my mouth. "What is my next step if a guy gets like this? Is it right to touch it?"

Fuck. *Be the good guy, Fin.*

"You can go with what moves you. It can be different for every couple."

"But what does me touching it *say*?"

"That you're ready for more."

"More being…"

"Well, if he hasn't touched you yet, he would definitely do that if you touched him."

"And if he's already touched me…"

"That you're ready to consummate the thing." God, she

does know about sex, doesn't she? Surely. "You know what that entails?"

"Right. Sex. The deed. He puts that into me. I got it. I know the mechanics, just not the steps. That bit gets rushed or hidden in movies. And romance novels — well, they're sort of the idealized version, you know?"

I don't know, but I nod.

"Not good at all for telling me what will happen in real life. What expectations are. How it goes for regular people."

"Thankfully, this isn't a romance novel."

"Oh no, of course not. If it was, well, I guess we'd be going about this the entirely wrong way. You'd be the hero. I'd be in love with you."

My mind feels jumbled. I don't even know what we're doing.

We breathe together for a moment, her heart skittering against my chest. I try to rein in my control.

She shifts against my body again. "Are they always that big?"

I choke on my own spit and start coughing. We break apart, and she bangs me on the back.

"Dory! Are you all right?"

Tears smart my eyes as I try to get my breath back. When I'm finally quiet, she's looking up at the palace, thoughtful. "So, we can verify that I'm super awkward and say all the wrong things."

"Vi, you're all right. You've been sheltered. You didn't get to learn from peers, or listen to gossip, or sneak porn."

"Porn! That's it! Would that help me learn? My phone blocks it, but yours wouldn't!"

Watching porn with the Princess. That would most definitely get me thrown in the brig.

"Not recommended. It's not realistic. Not at all."

"So, you've watched it?"

"I mean, sure. It's a thing teen boys do. And others. Can we not talk about this?"

"Okay." She walks in circles, occasionally stealing a glance at my crotch. She's all worked up.

But this is the end. I'm not doing one thing more with her until we clear up this business with Gregor. I've crossed a major line, even if she asked me to. I'm the one who knows better. I have to be the one who stops.

Thankfully, the car shows up. Hopefully, the kissing lessons are done for the night.

Because I'm the guy who never has brakes, who goes in for the kill, devil-may-care with anything in a skirt.

But Vi is different.

And I can't take much more.

CHAPTER 23

Octavia

The pulsing of the music vibrates the ground as we walk up to the open door of a flat-topped building painted all black. I want to squeal with excitement. This looks fun with a capital *F*.

A bald man in a black vest sits on a stool by the door. "IDs," he barks as we approach.

Oh, no. I don't have a driver's license. Any identification I do have is locked in the palace vault, and I wouldn't dare use it. Either I'd immediately be outed due to the "Her Grace, Princess Octavia of Avalonia" emblazoned across it, or they'd assume it was fake.

But Finley is unfazed. He steps closer and claps the man on the back.

The man's expression lights up. "Donkey Puck!"

I glance between them. "Donkey Puck?"

Finley shakes his head, but he's smiling. "Barato here called me that back in our herding days. He used to make me shovel the dried manure from the donkeys that walked the palace grounds."

"You did that? Shoveled poop?"

Barato laughs, his mouth red beneath a long mustache twisted at the ends. "And so much more. So Donkey Puck finally found himself a girl."

"I'm Vi," I say, since that's how Finley introduced me before.

Barato leans in. "You robbing the cradle?" he asks Finley.

"I'm two months older than him," I say. "And I'm never letting him live it down."

Barato laughs and waves us in. "Have a good time. Tell Dresden at the bar I'll spot you a round."

"Thanks." The two men shake hands, and Finley turns to me. "Let's go."

So, that's why Finley brought us here. He's been able to sidestep the problems of me being a princess by going places where he knows people.

And they all seem to like him.

Inside, light dances from every direction. Beams of it spin and slice across the big open room. Rotating discs of color cross over the walls and briefly illuminate tables and chairs.

A blue rectangle lights up part of the floor, a dozen dancers moving about on top of it. Their shoes are bright, but they become silhouettes by the time you get to their faces.

It's hypnotic, and the music drowns out any other sound.

Two girls wander by, both in skirts so short that I wonder how they sit down.

"Hey Finley," one says with a red-lipped smile. "Haven't seen you since you started guard training."

She's got her eyes on him, for sure. My chest goes tight. Does he want to dance with them? Or do more? Do people hook up in the dark corners?

This is his thing. My face flushes when I remember the rumor about him and some girl on the back stairs. And here I was asking to touch him!

"Who's this?" the other one asks, looking me up and down.

Next to her, I look plain. Her hair flows in soft waves. If her cleavage was any higher, it would bump her chin.

"It's Vi. We're getting a drink. Catch you later." He steers me past them and leans in close. "Drink, dance, or watch?"

I'm relieved we've moved on. I scan the room and spot an empty round booth.

"There." I grab his hand to go toward it. I need to get my bearings. How many of Finley's women will I have to meet tonight?

I scoot around to the center. Finley closes in.

"I can't pay for anything," I tell him.

"It's all right. I've got it."

"Can I have one of those cider things again?"

"Absolutely."

A waitress comes around, and Finley orders for us. The music thumps, vibrating my body. I gradually start to relax. No one else approaches, and the last thing I want to do is waste my time here feeling insecure.

All around me are people dressed so differently. Tiny skirts. Big loose sweatshirts. Jeans and camouflage. Boots and high heels. The colors wash over everything and strobe lights make it hard to focus on any particular thing.

One song blends into the next, and more dancers hit the floor. They are all over each other, moving together, making out, laughing. It's stirring, watching them be so free with each other. A buzz starts in my body.

I turn to Finley. "Kiss me again! I want to be kissed in a wild place like this. I want to feel like everybody else!"

I can see his hesitation. And I get it. I'm a childhood friend. But is this so hard? Don't people do this all the time? Lili told me about Tinder. You can swipe right and get yourself a one-night stand!

That's it! "Make me your one-night stand!"

His eyebrows shoot up. "What?"

I grab his hand. "I could be your one-night stand! Just do it one time. Then we never speak of it again!"

He looks like he's choking on something. I smack his back. "What do you think?"

Our drinks arrive. He passes me mine. His never makes it to the table. He takes it and down it goes, like at the tavern last night.

Maybe this is normal. So I pick mine up, and chug-a-lug.

We both slam our glasses on the table.

He stares at his. He hasn't answered my question.

Damn it. He doesn't want to do those things with me. I'll have to convince him. I read an e-book once called *Losing Her V-Card*. I think it snuck past the censorship on our phones because they thought it was about Valentine's Day.

It was all about this girl going to college and wanting

her best friend to be the one to take her virginity.

Just like Finley!

This is perfect. I mean, his body was clearly up for the task in the cemetery. He's used to being with girls only one time!

He needs a push.

I look around, trying to spot a behavior that might convince Finley that I'm serious. In a booth on the other side of the dance floor, a girl is sitting facing a boy, straddling his lap. It looks very much like they could be doing something right there!

I have to try it.

Their table must be farther away, because as I turn toward Finley, my hip bumps the edge. I try lifting my leg to throw over his lap, but I get stuck, trapped between the table and his thighs.

He scoots back. "What are you doing?"

I get it. He was too far forward. I shove him into the cushion and manage to get my leg over.

There. Now I'm facing him.

Except, his face is too low. The other girl must be a lot smaller than her man.

Doesn't matter. I'm here.

I lean down for the kiss. Finley pulls his face back. "Vi? What is this?"

Nope. No talking. I silence him with my mouth. Ha! Just the opposite of the romance books. I don't care. I'm doing this.

I scoot my knees forward until they press into the cushion of the bench.

He's surprised at first, and I don't think he'll kiss me

back. But then he says, "Oh, Vi," against my lips and it's back on.

Our mouths move over each other. It's so much wilder here than the last two times. The music invades our bodies, the *thump, thump, thump* of the low notes becoming a beat that makes us feel like one person.

His arms go around me, drawing me close. I feel weightless, lost. It's so different sitting down than standing up. I feel a shift between my legs. It's him, changing, filling that space. This time he's right where he would go if we were naked, and I instinctively push down to get that pressure where I want it.

He groans. "Vi."

I won't let him stop. I have to convince him to do this thing with me. It's the perfect idea. He's interested. His body can't lie. And we've known each other forever. This is so much better than a random hookup. Or Gregor, who's proven to be unreliable.

Forget kissing that other guard. I want to go all the way with Finley.

I'm frustrated by the bulkiness of his coat and mine. Besides, I'm getting hot. I unbutton mine and fling it onto the bench beside me. Then I work on his, tugging down the zipper.

When it opens, I can get so much closer to him. The heat of his chest seeps through his shirt.

Our mouths have figured each other out, continuing their soft exploration. Our tongues meet, fall back, and meet again of their own accord.

I want to touch his skin. I pull on his shirt, moving it aside.

"Vi." Another note of warning. His voice is husky.

I like the sound of it a lot.

Touching his belly is nothing like holding hands or even caressing a cheek.

It's a part of him I've never felt before, warm and muscled and firm. Something private.

His abs have definition, and I run my thumb along the grooves.

My heart is so loud that even the tremendous thump of the music gets drowned out. In fact, it's almost as if the world has gone dim and quiet, fading out of existence.

My focus is sharp. Skin, muscle, how he moves with short, tight breaths.

I'm terrified and exhilarated, the buzzing in my body reaching a fever pitch. This must be what it feels like to get an electric shock.

My hands keep sliding up inside his shirt. My fingers find the larger muscles of his chest, and one delicate tip crosses a nipple.

His hands tighten on my waist, and the bulge beneath me somehow gets even bigger.

How big is it?

Romance novels never mention inches. Or girth.

There are jokes about cucumbers. And pickles.

That's pretty big.

Finley's eyes are closed, his breath coming fast. "Vi, we have to stop. We can't do this. It's not right."

He's saying no.

My Finley is turning me down.

I slide my hand out of his shirt, my hope deflating. "I'm sorry," I say. "I shouldn't do that. If you were the one feeling me up in a bar, it would be something terrible. An invasion."

His jaw is tight. "Yes. Let's hit the brakes."

I slide off his lap and sit beside him. I'm crushing my red coat, but I don't care. I don't even know what to say.

"I'm really sorry," I say again. "I'm no good at this."

His hand closes around mine. "It's all good, Vi. It's fine."

"Can I have another drink? I think it will help."

He nods and flags down the waitress to order another round.

But, even as I steal glances at Finley, trying to figure out all the turns my emotions have taken in the last five minutes, beneath it all is that is the new thread of emotion. It's a tingle, a funny urge. I want to press my hand to myself, but, of course, I can't. I'm in public.

But this is the sort of itch you know that, very soon, you will need to scratch.

CHAPTER 24

Finley

When I finally get home from the club after ensuring that Octavia was safely returned to whatever secret path she takes into the palace, it's hard to sleep.

The wicked visions of her in my lap at the club keep me wide awake.

I don't need to sleep to dream about her. I've felt her in my arms, pressing against me, her mouth, her body, her timid hands wanting to touch my skin.

It's too much. I have to put a stop to this.

I've known all along to tread carefully with her. Not just because she's a princess, and I'm a guard.

But because she is so new to these feelings. All the normal avenues a typical kid has to learn about relationships and sex were taken from her. There's no normal progression. Kissing behind a school building. Having some friend shout that you like someone across a crowded lunchroom.

First dates. Those awkward kisses when you're young and don't expect to keep going.

Now she's a full-blown woman and figuring out that this is fun. Really fun. And she's experimenting on me.

I don't know why the King and Queen thought hiding her away was a good idea. They have sheltered her but not protected her. She found a way out into the world, and she has very little experience in dealing with what's out there. She's beautiful and self-possessed. We went to one local bar and men were grinding on her instantly.

I should have seen that coming.

And I shouldn't have kissed her and started this whole thing rolling, even if she was the one who insisted. Even if it started so innocently.

Now look where we are.

I've been committed to helping her, especially as she navigated this first crush on a fellow guard. I couldn't let him hurt her.

But I'm in over my head.

Way, way over.

I'm the very thing her parents sought to protect her from.

What *I* tried to protect her from.

Morning finally arrives, and I throw the covers aside. As a herder, I might have been able to sit among the donkeys and think this through. But I'm a guard. I have to train.

Two late nights in a row take their toll. I'm sluggish on the obstacle course, and, while racing up the vertical wall, I slip and crash back to the ground.

"Bulgari!" Sergeant roars. "What the hell is wrong with you today?"

For a split second, Gregor snaps his head toward me with a scowl.

I wonder what he knows. Did Octavia ask him to go out again last night? Is he guessing that I went in his stead?

He can't know what went on. Surely Octavia wouldn't have told him. If she had, my ass would be canned.

But, even without proof of my transgressions, his expression tells me I've made an enemy out of the squad leader.

I jump up and brush myself off. "Sorry. I need to focus."

"You sure as hell do," Sergeant barks. "Now start over."

I jog back to the beginning of the course, determined to nail it this time.

My feet dig into the cold ground as I race toward the course. I fly through the rows of tires, knees high. Then I sprint even faster, leaping for the first set of hanging rings.

My legs propel me as I hurtle hand-over-hand along the metal circles, then fling my legs forward to sail over the mud patch at the end.

I return to the climbing wall. *Pound, pound, pound.* I pump hard, then leap in the air, getting halfway up the wall with my first hold. I step my way up, then my shoulder clears the top. I grasp the rope on the other side and swing out beyond another mud pit and land on the earth on the other side.

Sergeant gives me a brisk nod. "That's more like it." He turns his attention to others.

This is where I need to put my attention. This is where my future is.

I will respect the Princess, and probably always love

her from a distance. But last night, things definitely went too far. Even though I let her lead the way, it was still too much for a fatherless, penniless, laundry worker's son. She can never belong to me.

It's time to back away.

CHAPTER 25

Octavia

I don't text anyone for three days after the club.

I feel exhausted. Wrung out. Confused.

I hole up in my room, watching murder mysteries and avoiding anything with romance. I'm already plagued with an unyielding pulse in my body.

Fin. Fin. Fin.

And it's not only the new stuff I'm obsessing over, like kissing him. Drinking. Straddling him at a club.

It's the old days, too. Running through the rose gardens. Sitting with donkeys. I don't know what to make of it. It's too complicated. There are too many storylines rolled into one.

Friends to lovers. Forbidden romance. Secret affair. Every virgin story. Such a cliché. I'm not bold at all. Not brave.

This Saturday morning, I'm hiding in the tower. Lili's probably sleeping. The only days the trainees are off are Sundays, so they're down there on the field, working out as always. I haven't laid eyes on any of them since the last time I served lunch on Tuesday.

Gregor is the leader, as usual, encouraging the other guards. He's bent at the knees, hands braced on his thighs, yelling at a much more slender man to lift a giant barbell over his chest.

I feel nothing when I look at him. I can scarcely remember why I obsessed over him for so long.

I shift to Finley. I catch him glancing up at the window from time to time. I assume he thinks I might be here. I stay to one side so that my shadow isn't visible.

He looks good today. Strong. The cold snap earlier in the week has lifted. He wears the dull green short-sleeved shirt that goes under the uniforms. I marvel at how his biceps stretch the ends of the sleeves. Looking at his chest, I'm reminded of touching it. When he lies back on the bench for his turn at the weights, I see the shirt settle into the ridges of those muscles I explored.

That tingling returns. I've told no one about what happened between us. When Lili asked how my night out had gone, I told her we'd used a special app to drive out to another club. I described the music, the lights, the drinks.

But not what I had done. Kissing him. Feeling him hard against me — twice. How I'd gone a little crazy in the booth.

No, that's too much to explain to anyone.

Instead, I stay up in my tower, looking down. The guards work out, then spar. They strip off their shirts to run out into the fields, and I can barely catch my breath seeing all of Finley, that skin that was mine so recently.

Then they're gone, only specs in the distance.

Valloria raps on the door and steps inside. "Time for lunch. Will you be dining with your parents, or should I send for someone to bring up a tray?"

Her eyes dart to the window, then back to me. She knows what I'm doing. Of course, the men are gone, so she's fine to look.

"Up here, I think. It's nice watching the hills slowly turn green." I gesture to the window, feeling confident since the yard is empty.

She peers out. "It's a warm day. Would you like to walk in the gardens?"

"No. Maybe. I don't know. But I'll lunch up here, I think."

The men will come back, eventually.

Valloria nods and pulls her cell phone out to do my bidding.

Most of the people here do that. She can't push back at me. She won't tell me I'm doing something wrong. Only Lili would do that. And Leo.

I sure miss my brother.

While I wait for my lunch, I send him a quick text.

Me: *Hey. How is Sunny feeling?*

It takes a few minutes, but he replies.

Leo: *Good. First trimester is over, and she's not throwing up quite so much.*

Me: *I'm glad. I miss you being here.*

Leo: *Sunny's enjoying being around her own family during these early days of the pregnancy. We'll be home plenty once the baby comes.*

Me: *I can't wait.*

He knows nothing about the guards, or that I've seen Finley again, and, suddenly, it's too much to tell him. I set my phone down. Am I wasting my life here? What's next for me? Don't my parents want me to marry, eventually? They sure pushed Leo into it.

I lay my head on my arms. I don't worry about hiding from the window now that the men are gone. As soon as my eyes are closed, though, there's Finley again. His chest, his skin. I can connect the vision with the touch.

I've got to scratch this itch.

Not having money is a total pain in the butt.

I managed to load the Uber app on my phone, but it's no use to me. Just like Finley warned me, I need payment to be able to call a car.

I fling myself onto Lili's bed in frustration.

My sister looks up from where she is sitting sideways in an armchair by the window. "What's getting you this time?"

"I want to go back to the club. I want to find a decent-looking guy, and I want to have a one-night stand like any other twenty-three-year-old."

She sits up straight. "Octavia! You wouldn't!"

"Why not? This is ridiculous. I should be dating."

I'm sick of being naïve and dumb. If I can get to the club, I'm sure some guy will buy me drinks. One thing will lead to another, and goodbye V-card.

Lili rushes over to the bed. "Oh, no. No, no. Girls like you get roofied in clubs. They slip a knockout drug in your drink and next thing you know, you're abandoned in some alley."

"That won't happen."

"It could! And what about sex trafficking? Do you know the danger signs? It's wild out there! Girls have to travel in packs to protect each other."

"I don't have a pack! Mother and Father made sure we never had a pack. We only have each other!"

She frowns. "We do have each other."

"At least you know about roofies. And sex traffic. But how do you know about that stuff?"

"I'm better at getting around the censorship software than you are."

"Then come with me." I frown. "Actually, you're no help. To call an Uber, we need a credit card."

She bites her lip. "Actually, I can solve that problem."

"Really? How?"

She glances through the open door to the antechamber and the hall, where our guards wait. We're in her room, and Botania is not quite as invasive as Valloria is with me. Still, she waves me to her closet.

We enter the room, and she tosses aside several shoe-boxes to find the one she's looking for.

When she opens the lid, I gape at the contents. "Where did you get all these gift cards?"

"I told you. I have fans. Sponsorships. Influencer perks."

I grab a handful. Restaurants. Clothing stores. And

then I see what she's talking about. Uber. Lyft. Another car ride company called Speed Ride.

"You ever use these?"

She shakes her head. "I'm saving them for a rainy day."

I snatch up one of the Uber cards. "Can I have it?"

She nods. "But you can't go by yourself. I won't let you do that."

She sorts through the box until she finds a rubber-banded group of gift cards with the word Visa on the bottom.

"What are those?"

"You can use these anywhere. They have a pre-set amount of money on them."

The back of the cards have numbers written with black marker. 50. 25. 100. I quickly add them up. "There's nearly a thousand here. Mostly in American dollars."

She nods. "America is where it's at for influencers. I have some in Euros, of course. For here in Avalonia or wherever."

She pulls one marked "50" out of the stack, then another. "We should have these just in case."

"We?"

"I can't let you go alone,"

I give her a huge hug. "Tonight is going to be epic."

"It doesn't change the fact that we don't have IDs. I'm not even twenty-one. In some countries, you only need to be eighteen to go to clubs. But not in Avalonia."

"I can handle that part. I know the guy at the door. I met him." I snap my fingers. "What was his name? Barato. I'm almost positive I can get us in with him there."

Lili stuffs the other gift cards back in the box, setting aside the ones she's pulled. "I'm okay with going to a club, Octavia. But I'm still not sure about the one-night stand. What are you going to do? Stay in a hotel? Go to his apartment?"

"Of course not. I mean, maybe I can just meet the guy. Maybe I can do the actual hook-up later. I don't know. Maybe we can do it in a car?"

"For your first time? You really want that?"

I crumple into a ball on the floor. "There's no telling when this house arrest is going to end, Lili. When we're twenty-five? Thirty? What are they doing? Why do we have no say?"

She shakes her head. "I'm hoping that when the baby comes, Leo will be here for good. Then maybe things will change. Like the guards."

"I wrote to him earlier. He says they'll come when it's closer to the baby's due date. Palace life stresses Sunny out."

"I don't blame her," Lili says. "It *bums* me out. But we have bigger things to think about."

"What's that?"

"What to *wear*." She scans her closet.

"Last time there was everything. Sweats. Sparkly dresses. Jeans."

"That was the middle of the week," Lili says. "You probably saw the hard-core clubbers and the outliers. Tonight, people will go all out for Saturday. If you want to catch a guy, you should do it up."

She pushes aside swaths of dresses, scrunching them

tightly against each other. "I have some things that I would never wear around the palace. Never, ever."

When she's exposed a section of the wall, I see a hidden hanging suit bag. She pulls it out. "This is the stuff we need for tonight."

She lowers the zipper, and it practically explodes with brightly colored dresses. Hot pink lamé. Sapphire blue with rhinestones. Black with bold white stripes. There's a couple dozen of them.

I pull out a siren-red number with cutouts across the chest and waist. "Holy smokes."

"That's what you call a fuck-me dress," Lili says. "Try it on."

We go through numerous outfits before settling on our club wear. Lili takes it easy, choosing a simple black dress. She softens the low cut with a white denim jacket. She isn't interested in drawing too much attention.

I wind up too tall for the red dress with cutouts. If I bend over even the slightest bit, my panties pop out beneath the super-short hem.

We go with all-white instead. The dress is strapless and fits tight like a bustier. The skirt is short, but long enough to cover me, and has slits on either side. When I walk, I show an outrageous amount of thigh.

"Prepare for pain with your shoes," she says. "You want hooker heels for a night like this."

I definitely have nothing appropriate. Lili finds a pair of clear stilettos with slender silver heels that were too small for her. They're close enough.

Lili pushes my hair behind my shoulders. "We can't do your makeup until after the night shift begins. Valloria will be all up in your business if she sees you looking like a tart after dinner."

I agree. We fold our outfits together and hide them under a stack of sweaters. Now we have to wait until it's time to make our escape.

CHAPTER 26

Finley

By Saturday night, I can barely take the silence anymore. Normally, I would head out to the bar with a few of the guards or maybe some of the old herding crowd.

But something tells me to stay close to home tonight.

I haven't heard from Octavia since the night of the club. I don't think Gregor has either. I know he's super pissed, but if he gets into a problem with the Princess, I'm pretty sure he will come to me.

I respect her space, but the tingling sense that something might be wrong sticks with me. She hasn't served the guards lunch since the falling out. But I know she's grappling with feelings she's never had before.

And I've given her the tools to get out into the world.

Around eleven, I finally text her. *Miss talking to you. How are you hanging in there?*

I sit back in the recliner. Mom has fallen asleep watching a classic movie in black and white.

She hasn't asked about Tallest Angel. She's good like

that. She might bring it up in the moment, but she doesn't pry.

The movie is an old Hitchcock film. A man in a suit climbs wooden steps in a church, looking distraught. It must be *Vertigo*.

I get caught up in the scene, then realize fifteen minutes have passed with no response.

Is she asleep?

Staff members aren't allowed to wander the main palace at night. There are guards at the end of our wing, as well as more guards at the entrance to any of the royal family's wings. I'd never make it to her room.

I watch the show a while longer. My anxiety rises. Maybe I should've gone out somewhere to blow off some steam.

I must've dozed off, because the buzzing of my phone snaps me awake.

An hour has passed. It's almost midnight.

And it's Octavia.

Tallest Angel: *Finley? Is this you? Octavia only put the name Dory in here. We need your help. Are you there?*

I knew it.

Me: *Yes. I can come right away. Where are you? What's happening?*

A call comes through. I jump out of my chair and dash to my room to avoid waking my mother.

"Octavia?"

"It's Lili. Octavia's sister."

"What's happening?" But I can already guess. I hear thumping music in the background.

"Octavia wanted to go back to the club you took her to.

Your friend let us in. She was insistent on having a normal night out. Meet some guys."

Octavia's words blast through my brain.

One-night stand.

"Did she go off with somebody?"

"Of course not. I wouldn't have let her. But she's gotten trapped. I think she wants to get away. But they've got her in a booth and won't let her out. They're laughing and think it's funny. I don't."

I shove my feet into shoes. "Did you get Barato?"

"I tried, but some other guy is out there, and there's a line to get in. I can't risk him kicking me out."

Right. She's underage. "I'll get there as fast as I can. Don't let her out of your sight."

"Should I stay on the phone?"

"Hell yes. Talk me through what you're seeing."

"I need to get closer again. I didn't think I could hear you in the main part of the club. It's so loud."

I race out my door and sprint down the corridor out of the palace. "Do you have earbuds? That will help you."

"No. I didn't think to bring them."

"How do you have her phone?"

"She didn't have any pockets. I was holding on to it while she danced."

I race up to the guard station. "F Bulgari, requesting exit."

I don't know this guy, but he buzzes me out. I'm sure it's been busy. It's a weekend. A big chunk of the staff doesn't work tomorrow.

The moment I'm outside of the palace walls, I open the

app and call a ride. Thankfully, there's one already coming down the street, and they pick up my request.

It's torture, waiting at the intersection for the car to arrive. "Come on," I mutter as the dot inches its way toward me.

When I can see the headlights, I tell Lili, "I'm about to get in a car. I'll be there fast. Watch your sister. If they try to take her anywhere, grab a server, a patron, anybody."

"She's sitting with them. They keep trying to make her drink something."

"She can't do that!" My stress reaches a peak as I run toward the car.

"She knows not to! I told her what a roofie was."

Thank God. "Maybe we're assuming the worst."

"They've had her trapped for an hour!"

She's right. If they're willing to do that, no telling what else they might do. "Are you safe?"

"Yes. They're not paying attention to me. One of them asked her to dance, she gave me her phone, and then the others showed up on the dance floor. Then they took her to the booth and put her in the middle."

The gray SUV arrives, and I wave it down. When I'm in the back, I say, "Go as fast as you can. I'll cover any ticket."

The gray-haired lady in the front turns to stare at me. "Are you out of your mind? I could lose the gig!" She takes her time putting the car back into drive.

Great.

As if to make me crazy, she goes exactly the speed limit down the main thoroughfare of Avalonia to the highway. It's only two exits, and driving faster probably wouldn't get us there much quicker, but I feel like I'm going to crawl out of my skin with frustration.

The moment she pulls into the parking lot, I slam my finger on the button for payment and leap out of the car.

Barato is walking back to his post and thumbs the other guy to head back inside. He spots me. "Saw your woman," he says. "About time you caught up with her. She looks pretty smoking."

I ignore him, his comment not landing like he might expect. I want to punch him for saying it.

The room feels pitch black, even though it was dark outside. It's outrageously crowded. How in the world am I going to find the younger princess in this?

"Where are you?" I say into the phone.

"I'm coming toward the door. I'm in a black dress with a white denim jacket."

I spot her coming toward me, the white jacket floating like an apparition. I don't know Lili at all. She was a toddler when I was friends with Octavia, and she hasn't exactly been part of our expeditions.

I wave her down, and she runs up to me. "Thanks for coming."

She's wearing a lot of makeup and a pair of white cat-eye glasses. Her hair is pulled into two round buns on either side of her head. She's done a good job of looking nothing like her portrait on the square.

"Where is she?"

I realize I maybe should've brought Barato with me as we approach the table. There are four men with Octavia, two on either side. One of them, the man on her right, bumps her shoulder with a sneering laugh. I want to bash his face in. They're all in their thirties, easy, and ought to know better than to trap a young woman.

If they realized who they were messing with, they'd be scared shitless. The King would lock them up.

I don't take the time to go back for Barato. When I see Octavia's helpless expression as she stares down at the table, my rage flashes hot.

My best strategy is for them to not know what hit them.

I race up and immediately grab the jacket lapels of the man on the outside edge and throw him to the ground. That ends my element of surprise.

The sneering man whips his head around. "What the hell?"

He's harder to reach, deeper inside the booth. But I grab him by the arm and drag him sideways onto the floor.

He tries to stumble to his feet, but I shove him hard, sending him flying backwards.

I turn and hold a hand to Octavia. Her mouth is gaping. "Finley?"

"Come out, now."

But the other two men have figured out my game and slide out from the booth.

Even so, I help Octavia to her feet, using every ounce of my guard training to watch my peripheral vision for anyone moving forward to attack.

Sneer-face makes the first move. "What do you think you're doing? That's my girl."

"I don't think so. This lady looks like she's done with you."

He comes at me, but he's slow and clumsy, and untrained.

All I have to do is bend at the waist, drawing my shoulder into his gut as he arrives.

And I stand up. He flips over me easily and lands on his back with a bone-jarring crash.

Octavia runs to her sister. "Go to Barato at the door," I tell her.

"No!" Octavia says. "I'm not leaving you with these jerks."

As if to prove her ability to handle herself, she lifts her foot and stomps her toe on the sneering man's shin. The stiletto part would've done more damage, but I don't correct her.

The other three men watch from the side. They probably spotted my training and want no part of it.

It doesn't matter. Barato's the bouncer, and he's already heard the ruckus. He rushes up, assesses the man on the floor, and me standing, my legs shoulder width apart in a fight stance.

"What the hell's going on?" he roars.

"These gentlemen trapped my lady in a booth. Your staff didn't help her."

Barato's eyebrows draw in as he frowns. "Who did they talk to?"

Lili points them out.

"I'll deal with them in the second." Barato kicks his boot against the sneering man's arm. He's still on the floor. "Out of the bar. All of you. Out."

"We're regulars," one says.

"Not anymore. Get out of here before I have you arrested."

One of the sneering man's friends gestures for the door. "Come on. There's always another 'ho for a bro.'"

"They were trying to make her drink that drink," Lili says. "You need to check it for drugs."

Sneering man gets to his feet, smacking the side of his head a few times as if he needs to bump something back into place. "There's no drugs in them, you little bitch."

For that, Octavia stomps him again, this time using the stiletto.

It pierces his pricey tennis shoes, and he yelps in pain.

Octavia's face is bright red. "Don't call my sister a bitch, you — you bitch!"

Barato has to force himself not to smile. My lips twitch as well.

"Come on," Barato says. "Out!" The men stumble toward the door.

Most of the bar hasn't even noticed the commotion. The dancers remain on the colored floor. The booths are full. The lighting makes it hard to see, and the music drowns out all other noise.

I turn to Octavia. "Are you sure you're okay?"

"I think I hurt my foot by stomping him."

Her face is pulled into a frown. Then suddenly, I'm done. So done.

"Are you finished here? Or did you have some other guy you wanted to try out? Maybe one who's less trouble?" The adrenaline is draining out of me, and I feel exhausted.

"You don't have to be an ass about it."

"Octavia!" Lili shouts. "He just saved you. Don't be mean."

I can see Octavia doesn't want to back down. Her pride is at stake. She's upset.

"Vi, let me get you out of here. We don't have to go home. There are some all-night diners. It's still time away from home."

The lights flash over her. She crosses her arms over her chest. Now that the moment is over, I see Barato is right. She's smoking hot.

Her hair falls in soft waves over her shoulders. The white dress is form-fitted to her body in a way that makes you crazed with the need to run your hands along that waist. And it's strapless, showing off her shoulders and arms. There's no bra. Not possible. Her cleavage is pushed high and round.

I have to tear my gaze away. I can't take it.

"I could go for some greasy food all right," Octavia says. "Please take me somewhere with booze, though. I need a drink."

"All right." I can see I've been a delightful influence. I should never have gone anywhere near the Princess.

I call another car and take the three of us to an all-night diner that serves mimosas. I don't feel like eating a thing, but Octavia scarfs hash browns and pancakes like she hasn't eaten in three days.

Finally she says, "Thank you. That situation sucked."

"Men suck," I say.

"You don't," she whispers.

Except I feel like I do. These men trapped her at a table in a bar, but they didn't play with her innocence. They didn't kiss her in cemeteries or awaken feelings she could do nothing with.

I'm as big an asshole. Worse, since she trusts me.

I sit back in the booth, sipping on a cup of coffee, completely unsure how to deal with this.

I catch Lili's eyes across the table, and she gives a shrug.

In the wee hours of the morning, I take them back to the abbey, where they disappear into the hedges. I walk the quiet streets of Avalonia to the palace and wonder how to get out of this terrible situation that's causing both of us so much misery.

I want to be the one to save her, to be the one who's there while she goes to these difficult growing pains.

But remaining only a friend is impossible now.

CHAPTER 27

Octavia

I don't even know what to do with myself for the next few days. I dress like I'm supposed to. I take all my meals with my family.

Mother seems pleased. She remarks one day at lunch that, "I am turning into a proper young lady, at last."

What does that mean? I was a wild child? How? There was no opportunity!

Lili and I glance at each other across the table. Is it possible that she knows everything we've done and hasn't confronted us about it?

It doesn't matter. Her compliments don't exactly come with privileges.

Does everyone have parents as distant as ours? Even when seeing them two to three times a day at meals, there is little conversation. Father's work is always completely uninteresting. Land disputes. Zoning. Who wants to hear about zoning?

Mother has her philanthropy. Perhaps if she focused on

children, or even hospital work, I would be interested in helping with those.

But no. She doesn't go out in the community and do things. She reviews grant applications. In her office.

Things should get slightly better as the weather warms. There will be ribbon cuttings. Festivals and photo ops. I like them well enough, because at least I get out of the palace.

But we never get to mingle with the crowd or have a spontaneous conversation with another human. We're guarded and set apart. Put on podiums or stages. Escorted in and escorted out.

I'm grateful for Lili. She feels the limitations more acutely than I do since her social media presence is so high. Her online friends attend trade expos, fashion shows, conventions, and meet-and-greets. I often find her lying on the floor of her room, staring at the ceiling.

Two birds in a cage. That's what we are.

We're sitting in the billiards room on a Friday, the doors wide open, our guards standing outside, when the trainees pass by on their way to the Great Hall for lunch.

I'm tempted to stand up and close the doors, not wanting to hear Gregor or Finley talking. I don't know if they've written to me. I let the burner phone lose its charge.

If I learned anything from our expedition to the club, it's that Finley is right. I'm naïve. I know nothing. And even though my sister has more knowledge, her experience didn't help us with that tricky situation either.

Understanding that problems exist and knowing what to do when they happen are two totally different things.

We get that now. I also know that my lack of street smarts is evident in my face, my posture, and the way I respond to people. Those who want to trick me or trap me see it from a mile away.

I'm an easy target, and I don't know how to fix that.

Right now, it seems best to avoid everyone.

Lili leans on the pool table, idly rolling the cue ball back and forth. "They're coming."

I pull a soda from the fridge. "Doesn't matter."

But then I hear Gregor's familiar rumble.

"No. Not today. I'm taking a walk after lunch."

I don't recognize the next voice. "But you're our ringer in three-on-three."

"Tomorrow."

A third voice. "Did I hear Gregor's not playing today?"

The second voice. "He's off to smell the roses again."

The third one. "What's so great about the roses?"

Gregor says, "I need to think."

Does he, now?

I nonchalantly pass the door. The guards have all entered the Great Hall. I can't see inside the room from this angle.

I could go to the garden. Confront Gregor about why he quit writing to me.

It's more interesting than sitting here, and I'm not in any danger with him.

And who knows? Maybe there's a way to work this out.

Maybe he can be the one to scratch this itch. At least we have history.

I check the time. The trainees just entered lunch, so they'll probably exit again in fifteen to twenty minutes.

They all eat fast so they can play basketball before afternoon training.

I can be in the rose gardens when Gregor comes.

I glance at Valloria. It's been a long time since she's experienced an incident with us. Not since I climbed the ropes. She's relaxed a little.

"Are we going to finish this game, or are we quitting?" Lili asks. The cue ball bounces off the felt edge of the table.

"Let's finish." It will help pass the fifteen minutes I have to wait. And, this time, I don't think I'll let Lili in on what I'm doing. For one, she'll try to talk me out of it.

And two, if I go alone, that cuts the guard presence down to one.

Valloria maintains her five-step distance as I walk through the rose gardens. It's much warmer today, and almost all the rose bushes are showing green growth. Occasionally, I spot a tightly closed bud.

I don't need a jacket, although once I'm beneath the arch and out of the sun, a chill creeps in.

But nothing could deter me today. I'm back on track. Maybe this can be a complete do-over. I'll meet Gregor in the gardens. We'll have the conversation we should've had weeks ago. There will be no mistaken identity leading to Finley as intermediary.

Just me. Just him. We will figure things out.

I sit on the bench with a notebook I dug out of a cabinet in the billiards room. It's for keeping score, but I'm using it as a sketchpad.

Valloria is likely not fooled. I've never pretended to be an artist in my life. But she won't say anything, not as long as I don't make trouble.

Even if my pencil sketches are terrible, it's nice sitting here among the early rosebuds, keeping my mind clear.

The twenty-minute mark clicks by. It has to be getting close to when Gregor will enter the gardens.

I look up at Valloria. "I'm going to walk to the back of the kitchen and see if someone will make me a sandwich. I'm hungry, but I don't want to leave." I gesture to the path. "I'm feeling good here. Happy."

I walk toward the back gate to the herb garden. Valloria follows. When we pass through the small gate separating the gardens, Valloria says, "Tell me what sandwich you want. I'll go to the back door and request it."

Perfect. She's falling for my scheme. Now to protest. "You don't need to do that. I'm happy to handle it myself." I continue on between the rows of wooden boxes holding newly budded plants.

She speaks up again. "It's not appropriate for Your Grace to ask for food at the back door. Stay near the gate between the herb garden and the rose garden, and I will do that for you."

I stop. "All right then. A simple ham and cheese sandwich will do. Spring water. Some grapes, if they have them."

I circle back to the fence between the gardens. "I'll sit here and draw the flowers near the gate."

Valloria nods. I pass through the low gate and sit nearby. I situate myself so she can see my shoulders in a bright yellow sweater. I want the color to be highly visible.

Valloria raps on the back door of the kitchen, quickly turning to make sure I'm where I said I would be. I wave and focus back on my drawing.

And I listen. So carefully. Unless guards are being stealthy, they walk with intention, the metal base of their heels ringing with each step. It's how they're trained.

There is almost no breeze. No rustling of leaves. I'm close enough to the kitchens that I can hear an indistinct murmur of the workers.

The first guards must exit the building, as there's a burst of laughter from a distance. My heart hammers. In the corner of my eye, I spot Valloria turning to make sure I'm still there. This time I don't acknowledge her, pretending to be focused on my work. I'm heavily obscured by rose bushes, and should mainly appear to her to be a swath of yellow.

Then I hear it. A ringing sound, separate from the others. The footsteps grow louder. A guard has entered the gardens.

I most definitely will not make the same mistake as before. I won't assume I know who I'm speaking to. I'll check before I talk.

I slowly slide my bright yellow scarf from my neck and tie it to the branches of the nearest rosebush, spreading it for maximum color.

Hopefully, this will be enough to convince Valloria I'm still sitting there while she fetches the sandwich.

She's speaking with a staff member. This is my chance.

The ringing footsteps get closer. I duck my head and run, zigzagging along the path to get to the arching trellis. Mother and Father are home, and so are the full complement of directors and staff members in their offices on the floors above. I can't take the chance that anyone is looking down to see me in the gardens alone.

When I'm safely covered from above, I slow down, listening as I walk. The other steps and I are heading toward the same destination. The bench in the deepest part of the garden.

He's whistling, and I recognize the tune.

Wake Up Alone. It has to be Gregor. He's whistling the song he sent to me.

My heart races. This is it. Finally, we will talk, naturally, like we did the very first time at the stables. There will be no bar, no punching someone. No lunch line with onlookers.

Just us. This time I'll get the real him, the one who sent me sweet songs, who told me he was transfixed and entranced.

Hope rises in my chest.

He's slightly ahead of me, and his footsteps go silent. He'll be visible at the next opening. I race forward, ecstatic to finally fall into his arms.

I clear the last rose bushes.

And stop dead. It's Gregor all right. I'd know him anywhere. His height. His broad shoulders. His strong back.

But he's not alone.

He's with a girl from housekeeping. I recognize the pale sea-foam apron over her blue uniform.

And they're kissing.

And not gently. It's a full on make-out session, hands in each other's hair, mouths wide open.

I back away slowly. When did this happen? Had he always had this other girl but didn't know what to do with the Princess asking for him?

I swallow my sob. Nothing is ever as it seems.

I run back to the herb garden, feeling like I might throw up. Valloria's on her way back, but I plop onto the ground, snatching my scarf from the branches, furiously dragging my pencil over the page.

Valloria calls my name, a strident note in her voice, then sees me on the path. "Oh, there you are."

She sets the pretty tray of food on the bench. "I hope this will do."

I choke out a quiet, "Thank you," and continue drawing. Vine. Stem. Leaves. My focus is sharp. I can't think about what just happened or I will fall apart in front of my guard. I have to make it through the next few minutes, calm myself, and get to my rooms.

I draw, draw, draw. Stem. Leaf. Rosebud.

Like me, the flowers on this page will never bloom.

CHAPTER 28

Finley

I leave the back of the palace after lunch, not feeling up for playing ball today. The rose garden looms ahead and to my right, but I have no intention of going in there. I've been avoiding it in the days since rescuing Octavia from the club. She hasn't returned a text from me since.

The beauty of the flowers and the memories of all my times there bring me down, and I have to keep my energy up to focus on training. We're approaching the final weeks until our assessment. Soon, this walk out the palace doors will no longer be part of my routine.

My graduation has clearly been assumed, because Sergeant has already forwarded paperwork asking me to make my top choices for assignment.

I don't want the abbey, where I might spot the Princess sneaking out. Nor anywhere in the palace. It's too much. I need distance. Hopefully, I will be assigned to the city center, or maybe the royal airstrip.

Those might be far enough.

As I approach the entrance to the rose garden, a young

woman from housekeeping exits the gap in the tall hedge. I'm guessing from the flush on her cheeks and the pinkness to her mouth that the garden path has been her trysting place.

I slow down, waiting to see if someone follows her out. The ringing stride of a guard breaks the silence. Huh. Her affair is with one of us. Curiosity makes me wait and see.

I take a step back when I realize the man is Gregor. Our eyes meet for only a second, and his brow furrows as he barks, "What are you here for?"

"I'm just walking."

He turns away from me sharply and heads toward the training yard.

I'm about to walk past the entrance, when something literally grabs me by the gut and tells me to go in. I walk swiftly into the rows of rose bushes, scarcely noticing the advent of spring on the vines.

I've arrived under the shadow of the trellis overhead when someone careens from a corner and smashes into me from one side.

Fists pummel my shoulder.

I turn to grab them. It's Octavia!

"Finley! Why are you here?" She's full-on sobbing.

"What's wrong?" I ask her.

"Why didn't you tell me that Gregor had a girlfriend all along? I'm so embarrassed. It's horrifying. It's awful. The worst."

She's barely standing, tears streaming down her face.

"Where's your guard?"

"I lost her in the maze when I heard footsteps coming

back in. I thought you might be Gregor. She'll be here any second."

I pull her to me and press her head to my shoulder. "I didn't know. In fact, it was the first thing I asked him when you told me to give him your number."

Of course, his answer flashes through me. *Nope. Not really.*

I understand. He was dallying with this other girl, but willing to set her aside for the Princess. And he's gone back.

"It's humiliating. He sent all those messages to me, and now he's with her." She hiccup-sobs.

"Princess, you're a lot. He wasn't up to the task."

Her fists pummel me again. "Take it back! I'm not a lot!"

I grasp her wrists. "I love that you're a lot. I love that you sneak out. I love that you want more than palace life. But it's a lot to take on." I'm on the cusp of saying even more when an angry voice penetrates the hedge to our left.

"Octavia. This isn't funny. Return to me immediately."

"I think that's your guard."

"I don't care." She lifts her chin to me and in any other circumstance, I would kiss away all that fear. All that self-doubt.

But, I can't. Not now. She's so mad.

"Save your ability to escape later by playing it straight."

"Why? So more men can trap me in a booth? I'm useless in the world, and even the men I meet at the palace would prefer to kiss someone else!" Tears pour out of her again.

I want to hold her. To reassure her, but it's too late. Her guard is about to find us.

"Come see me, Vi," I say. "Come to me. Tell me where you want to go, and I'll take you. And I'll teach you anything you want to know."

This gets her. She stares up at me. "Anything?"

"Anything."

"All right. Get out of here. Don't get caught." She pushes me away.

I step around the hedge so I won't be seen. I wait there as her guard approaches.

The woman is red-faced and angry. "That's enough for today. You're going inside."

"I'm not a child," Octavia says.

I wait until the two of them have exited the gardens. I don't blame her for not wanting to live this way, for reaching for something she wants and finding a way to get it. She is absolutely treated like a child.

I wish there was some way I could save her.

But, I'm only a guard. Only a laundry worker's son. I have no power.

We haven't even been called back to the training yard when she buzzes my phone.

I'm taking you up on your offer. Meet me in the trees in the hills later tonight. I want to know everything I've been missing.

I tap out a quick *yes*.

I hope I know what I'm doing.

CHAPTER 29

Octavia

The tunnels feel spookier than usual tonight.

I'm used to walking through them alone. Night. Day. It's all the same down here, pitch black, until each lamp illuminates briefly to light my way.

I shouldn't be afraid of where I'm going or what I'm about to do. This is Dory we're talking about. I know him better than most anyone, other than maybe my sister.

But things are going to happen tonight. He promised I could ask for anything. I'm obviously no longer saving myself for Gregor.

And Finley's the perfect choice. Hell, he's probably been with most every woman in the palace.

I have condoms to protect myself from all the things. Lili had a stash. They're promotional, printed with the name of a dating app.

I pat the pocket of my skirt. They're still there.

I thought very carefully about how I wanted to dress tonight.

The skirt is because there's too much possibility of

someone finding us. It will hide what we're doing, whether it's him touching, like we talked about. Or his face, like he did on the stairs to some other girl.

A nervous thrill darts through me.

Or, if we do the whole thing.

Will we do the whole thing?

Dory will do the best he can to make it go easy for me. I trust him.

But giving up a V-card is well covered in books. I don't believe the romance novels for a moment, what with their three orgasms the first time she has sex. I'm not that dumb.

The young adult and coming-of-age books are better. They talk about the pinch. The pain. The importance of relaxing into it and not being all tense. That it might not be so great, but at least it will be over.

I know about as much as I think I can.

I wore cute panties. Not that it matters. I don't have to seduce Finley. And it's not like he needs to be in love with me. I'm quite certain he hasn't been in love with every girl he's tangled with in the hayloft. Or the hills. Or the back stairs.

In fact, unless I was going to hire a professional, as if that could even happen, Finley's probably the best choice. We've been friends all our lives. He's very experienced.

He's the one to get this done.

I hold my flashlight tightly. Valloria may have fixed all the lamps inside the palace tunnels, but I doubt she walked all the way out to the hills. This is the emergency escape route for the royal family, the one used with Leo.

This is a longer stretch, farther than even the abbey. I have a lot of time to think about what I'm about to do.

Something scurries across my path, and I yelp, pressing myself against the cold stone wall.

Right. I'm well beyond the palace. And it's spring. There will be critters. I press my hand to my chest and slow my breathing. It's fine. I will be fine.

I force myself to keep going until I recognize a marker on the wall. It's not far from the exit into the ruins on the hillside. I hope I can open them. Leo did it last time.

I didn't tell Finley about the tunnels, although he must have guessed that we have a secret passage into town and out into the fields.

The family has always been warned never to trust anyone with this information other than our personal guards. Leo, in particular, was read the riot act by our father. "Don't try to impress girls with them. You will compromise not only our safety, but the safety of every generation to come after us."

I haven't forgotten.

The smell of the tunnels gets earthier as the path angles up. I'm rising to the ground level. One wall lamp goes out as I pass, but the next one doesn't illuminate.

I click my flashlight and hold the beam ahead. There are three quick steps to the door. The last exit. I'm in the hills.

I press my hand to my chest. I'm wearing several layers. A soft blue T-shirt. A lightweight cardigan. Then a long down coat, in case it's cold or if we need something to lie on in the woods.

I'm doing this.

I check my phone. It's close enough to the surface that I have bars again. I can text Finley to rescue me if I have to. I don't have to mention the tunnels, and I don't think he'll ask.

But, hopefully, I can manage the exit myself.

Something glints at the base of the door, and I'm relieved to see that it's the crowbar Leo brought the last time we came this way.

I pull on the door handle, but it doesn't budge. I had a feeling it wouldn't. It's been months since it was opened last.

I shine my light on the door, noting the marks where the crowbar was used before. I pick it up and slip the thinner edge into the crack.

I lean into it, feeling the seal pop as I put pressure on the gap.

The door eases open. Thank goodness.

I return the crowbar to its place and slip outside. The fallen stone pillars cross the exit, hiding it from casual discovery. The moonlight filters through the ruins.

I pick my way through the rubble until I'm out on the hillside. The moon shines clear overhead. The newly green grass is gray in the low light. The outcropping of trees is ahead.

I cross it carefully, watching for stray rocks or holes. When I get about halfway to the line of trees, a figure separates itself from the shadows and walks my way.

For a split second, my heart speeds up like I've been discovered, then I recognize the lanky walk.

Finley.

It's almost a cliché, the two of us coming toward each other in the fields. The moonlight shines on his hair.

Everything engages. A fluttering in my belly. The quickening of my pulse. And something sweeter. A quiet, simple joy. I'm happy to see him. I'm *happy*.

The feeling surprises me after the anguished ups and downs of the last two weeks. This isn't hard at all. It's easy. Simple. It feels right.

We stop a couple of feet from each other. "Hey," he says.

"Hey yourself."

The silence ought to be awkward. I'm going to ask him for this big thing. And he surely knows I will. Understanding was in his expression when he told me he would do anything I asked.

But, there is no discomfort here. Just the two of us. Kids who played together. Now, we've come back together as adults for one last forbidden act.

He holds out his hand. "Let's walk for a bit."

I nod. We take a roundabout path back toward the trees. I assume that's our destination. There's nothing else out here. It's too risky to go back to the stables. And I know better than to meet in the palace. Besides, if the rumors are true, pairings out here are a regular event. It wouldn't be so common if it didn't work.

"I think spring is officially here," he says.

Weather. He's talking about the weather. I want to laugh.

"Seems the right time of year for having sex in nature."

It takes a moment, as if he's shocked that I said such a thing, but then the laugh arrives, deep and throaty.

"I'm sure you're right. It will be us and the rabbits and the birds."

"I'm trying to picture birds getting it on. It's not working."

He laughs again. "I'm sure there are YouTube videos."

"I bet even those are blocked to avoid sullying an innocent princess."

He sobers. I've reminded him of who I am and the magnitude of his role in what we're about to do. Deflowering the Princess of Avalonia. I sound like a romance novel. Maybe I should write it.

After tonight, maybe I can.

He squeezes my hand. "I brought some things."

"What things?" Sex toys? Porn? My heart clambers in my chest.

"A blanket. Some food."

Oh. That's easy. "Is anyone else out here tonight?"

"There was. But they've all gone home. It's late for the working folk."

I glance at my phone. After midnight. Technically, it's a new day.

He leads me into the tree line and pops on a flashlight, shining it over the stones and roots in our path.

The trees get even thicker for a moment, then there's a small clearing. The light crosses over a red plaid blanket, a small green cooler, and a wrapped bundle of white roses with a single pink one in the center.

I kneel on the blanket and pick up the bouquet. "That's not symbolic or anything."

He laughs. "I thought you'd find it amusing. Also, you know, the rose garden."

I like that he's been thinking about this. Planning. And that he's telling me, without having to say it, or me having to ask outright, what he knows I came here to do.

I lift the flowers to my nose. "Thank you."

"You sure about all this?"

I hold the flowers. "Yes. I'm living in the now. It's all I have. This very moment."

"You've thought about this a lot."

"It's all I think about. I don't have a future until I take charge of it."

He sits beside me and opens the cooler. "I brought ciders, the kind you like, in case you need to take the edge off."

"I think I might."

He extracts one and pops it open. I take it, reveling in the cold biting my skin.

He takes one. "Bottoms up, like the first time?"

I grin. "Okay."

We both down our drinks. He tosses the empties into the cooler. "Come over here."

His voice is different. He's always spoken to me in this gentle, friendly tone. But here's a version I've never heard before. It's darker, lower, and hits me right between the legs.

I lean toward him, drawn like a compass seeking true north. That's enough for him, and he grasps my hips and drags me across the blanket. I fall into him, catching myself on his chest. His lips meet mine, and we're back in familiar territory.

I tense for a moment, realizing that this is no experiment this time. We will continue, keep going. We're alone, no guards, no one rushing in. We have all the time in the world.

Finley keeps it easy, nibbling along my lips until I open for him. Then we dive into each other, tongues tangling, my body resting against his.

He unzips the front of my coat and slides his hands beneath it. The next two layers are thin, and I can feel the strength of his hands and fingers as they slip around my waist and grip my back.

He pulls me even closer, and I shift, my legs falling on either side of his outstretched legs so that I straddle him.

The skirt bunches up between us, and I jolt at the sudden contact of my panties with his jeans.

He pulls me even closer, and the bulge of him presses against me. One of his hands moves to the small of my back, forcing me to arch toward him. The other finds its way back around the front, clasping a breast in his hand.

My heart beats so hard, I can feel it in my throat.

This is happening.

CHAPTER 30

Finley

I'm never nervous with a woman.

Not the first time I did it. Not the most recent. Not any in between.

But I am today.

Our mouths know each other. She tastes of cider, both the apple and the berry. Her hair cascades down her shoulders, pieces of it tickling my neck.

Her breast is heavy in my hand, the tip of her nipple so tight that I can feel it through her shirt and bra.

I want everything to be perfect for her.

In my head, I think of us as a couple. I can't rush like I do with those rapid-fire hook-ups I'm known for. I'm not Finley, and she's not the Princess. We're Dory and Vi, best friends since we were small, moving into the newest phase of our long lives ahead.

I have to tell myself these things, or I could never do this. Not with Vi.

Her hands grip the back of my head, fingers clutching my hair. The pressure of her body on my cock is making me crazed. I reach behind her for the bra clasp and release it. Her back is warm and smooth. I move my hands to the base of it and slide them up her naked skin.

She sighs against my mouth.

My thumbs reach around, slipping beneath the curve of her breasts, caressing that deep hollow. The bra lifts away, and I cup both at once.

She gasps, sucking in a breath, her hands gripping my shoulders.

Her eyes open and stare into mine. I pause, waiting to see if it's too much, if she will back away.

But she comes at me, mouth on mine again, a low groan escaping. I squeeze her, thumbing both nipples, and she gasps again. Her body grinds down on mine like it did at the club. Everything ignites. I can't get enough of her mouth, her skin.

I lean forward to press her down on the red blanket. I lift her shirt up out of my way and push aside the bra. My mouth slips down, kissing her cheek, her jaw, then skipping over the fabric.

When my lips take in a nipple, she arches up with a cry. "Dory!"

I clasp the breast, allowing myself to take more of it into my mouth. She says it again, "Dory! Yes!"

I can't help but smile against her soft skin. I knew she had so much passion in her. I felt it from the first kiss on the roof. It's what turned me inside out.

I move to the other side, tucking her coat around her to make sure she doesn't get cold. She holds my head, her hips moving against me. She's rolling with all the sensations, knowing instinctively where they lead.

There are no brakes tonight. She won't want to stop. Already she seeks more pressure, lifting up to get closer contact. She can't control the grind of our bodies while lying on her back, and she wants more.

I'll give her more.

Her skirt is in disarray, slipping up her thigh. I keep my mouth on her while a hand reaches for her leg. I bump against something crinkly in her skirts. A square wrapper caught in her pocket. I smile again. Yes, she's ready for tonight.

I take my time working my palm up over her knee, her thigh, allowing my thumb to slip along the lace edge of her panties. She jolts up, away from the ground, another gasp.

I pause, but she says, "Please don't stop. I want you there. Right there."

I ease beneath the silky fabric, running my thumb over the hot, swollen skin beneath the cap of curls. She stills, her breath coming in short, quick bursts, one hand holding my shoulder.

I take my time, learning every curve and valley of this part of her, keeping it easy. Then I move my finger ever so slightly inside her body.

She lurches again, crying out. "Yes, please. More. More."

I pinch the lace of the panties and drag them down, tossing them on the blanket. She'll get more.

I slip a finger fully into her. Her hips rise. She's so wet, deliciously so. I can't resist a taste.

I move down her body so she isn't surprised, leaving a damp trail on her belly. Then my tongue replaces my fingers.

"Oh my God," she says, her hands moving to my hair. "Holy shit!"

My Vi can cuss. I chuckle against her skin. My thumb opens her wider, and now I can get inside. As her breathing increases, so does my pace. Her chest heaves, and I look up her body, moonlight touching the tips of her breasts, her shirt bunched up at her neck beneath the open coat.

Her multi-colored hair is spread on the blanket, chin high. She's beautiful, glorious, mine.

I slip a finger back inside her, then another, maintaining the pressure of my tongue on that tiny bud that's appeared now that it's swollen.

Her body almost vibrates, and I know where we're headed. Does Vi love on herself? Does she know this feeling?

Her hands grasp the blanket, tight fists crinkling the surface. "Finley!"

I curl my fingers back and fit my mouth over her clit, sucking hard.

"Oh my God!" She writhes beneath me as she pulses against my mouth. Then she's perfectly still, letting it hit her, wave after wave. I take my free hand and cover one of hers. She lets go of the blanket and holds my fingers instead.

Her hips have lifted from the ground, but they gradually fall until she's settled again. I slow down my movements, kissing these intimate parts of her until she's released the blanket with her other hand, her arm crossing over her forehead.

I pull away, lowering her legs to the blanket. She's lost her shoes, and her skirt is all bunched around her waist.

I run a finger along her thigh and trace the contours of her knee. "You okay, Vi?"

She stares up at the canopy of trees. "I am. I guess I've read about this, but it's something else entirely to feel it."

"It is."

She lets go of me and sits up on her elbows. "Is it this good when people do it, you know, alone? By themselves?"

"I would think so."

"You mean I could have felt this all along?"

I guess that answers that question.

"Sure. There is something to the connection, though. You always know what you're going to do to yourself. With someone else, there can be surprises."

"You sure surprised me! How could you do that? How did you know what would work?" She sits up and shoves off the coat.

I start to pull her skirt down to cover her, but she stops me. "Tell me. How did you know?"

"I paid attention. When you liked something, I expanded on that theme. If you didn't respond, I tried something else."

"Can I do that to you?"

"Sure."

She pulls at my jacket. "Take this off. Will you? Is it too cold? I don't feel cold."

My cock jumps to attention. "Okay." I strip off my jacket, then my shirt. "What do you want to do?"

"Everything," she says, her hands already on my chest. "I want to do everything."

CHAPTER 31

Octavia

Finley shirtless in the moonlight is the most breathtaking thing I've ever seen. He's like that statue in Italy, plus every Abercrombie and Fitch ad, plus he's *here*. I can touch him. All of him. I'm allowed.

"Let's be naked," I said. "I won't be shy. You're not shy, right? No, of course you're not shy. You've banged every chick in a ten-mile radius." I pull off my cardigan and drop it on top of my coat.

Finley reaches out. "Hey. Vi. I'm sorry about that. I'm sorry you know about it."

"It's in the past! And look! I'm benefitting from your experience."

Hell, yes, I am. Nothing, and I mean nothing I ever read or saw anywhere prepared me for what just happened. My whole body became something else. Vibrating, pulsing, electrically charged. I became one with the universe.

I want to do more.

I reach for the bottom of my T-shirt, but Finley stops me. "Let me do that."

He pulls it over my head, taking the bra with it.

"Stand up," he says.

I do. He tugs on the skirt, letting it fall at my feet.

Now I really am naked. But I won't back down. It's too wild. Too exhilarating. I want this too much.

It's chilly, but not freezing. My nipples tighten with the cold.

He stands beside me and starts to unsnap his jeans.

"Nope. My job." I move his hands away.

It's hard to see what I'm doing in the dark, plus, I'm tall, blocking what little light there is. So I kneel in front of him to work the snap and the zipper.

When I glance up, his eyes are all over me. I can imagine what this looks like. All my skin, me with my mouth right there.

Okay, why not?

I peel the front of his jeans away. He wears gray boxers beneath them. I pull on the elastic and bring them down.

"Vi…" he says.

"Shhh. I'm concentrating."

His laugh puts me at ease.

I can see the top of him, but it's tucked down inside. Is there a sexy way to do this? Something classy? I don't know. I reach in and pull.

He sucks in a breath, and for a second I think I've hurt him. But everything here seems all right. He springs up in front of me.

I should have watched porn. Should have, should have, should have.

But it's clear what should be done. I wrap my hand

around the girth of him. He's warm and thick, and there's a pulse there, the slightest throb.

I move my thumb along the length, and it jumps in my hands.

"Oh!" I cry, surprised. Then I laugh. I look up at Finley. He swallows hard.

He's so damn handsome. I can see the boy he once was, and the man he is now. His jaw is unshaven. I can still feel those bristles on my thighs. A rush of heat goes between my legs. Getting wet. That's exactly how it all works.

I look back at this new body part. I grip him with both hands. It's beautiful. I'm not afraid.

I lean forward, touching my tongue to the tip. There's a small indentation at the end. I take more into my mouth, hoping this is what's expected, and Finley groans. His hands move to my hair.

It must be the right thing.

It goes in my mouth, more and more, and then I relax my tongue and find even more space. Finley's breathing is like mine was, fast and hard. This is what he means. Pay attention, expand on what you've learned.

Sex is like anything. Figure it out.

I move faster, taking him in and out. A breeze wraps around us, and I shiver, but I'm not cold. I feel wildly alive, this half-naked man at my mercy. I'm a completely different person than I was an hour ago. All this is so wild, so untamed. I'm so free. I can do what I want. Feel what I like.

I want to burn.

I grip him more tightly, my mouth flying over him. I

feel a twitch in his skin, as if all his energy has moved to his part of his body.

"Vi, Vi."

I love hearing my name come from his mouth. I want him to lose control like I did. I want him to vibrate, to sense the universe breaking wide.

He grabs my head. "I want to come inside you. In the condom, of course. But in your body."

I pull away. "Yes. Yes. I want that."

I want to do everything.

He kicks off his boots and I help him drag his jeans and boxers down.

I lie back on the blanket, then move the down coat beneath me.

"You might bleed on it," he says.

I shake my head. "My hymen broke when I was nine. Riding horses. They thought I was getting my first period already. But, no. It happened already. It had to be documented. Royal stuff."

He brushes my hair off my face. "Was that traumatizing?"

"Sure. I survived. But if I bleed more, if I wreck the coat, it's fine."

He nods. "My condom or yours?"

"Whichever you think is better." Nerves hit me again, my belly bursting with flutters. This is happening.

He reaches for his jeans and extracts a condom. I watch in fascination as he rolls it over his length. I sit back up to examine this. "How do you know they will fit?"

"They generally do." His grin is mischievous, and my

stomach calms. "I'm going to start in a basic position in case it hurts. That way, I can control how it goes."

"I trust you."

I think he will go straight to it, but he doesn't, his mouth covering mine. We don't taste like cider anymore, but it's nice. Like people. Like sex.

His hand reaches down, and his fingers are inside me again. I would have sworn I was done with the good stuff for the night, but now that my body has gotten a taste, it definitely wants more.

My hips rise to meet his touch. His mouth takes my nipple in again, and our skin connects in a thousand places.

It's almost overload. His hard chest, the brush of his arms, his lips drawing my breast in, and his fingers inside my body. I stop thinking about it and just feel the weightless sensation taking over again.

The trees rustle in the breeze and I'm wrapped in nature, the outdoors, and our connection. The heat pools where he works me, and I suck in a breath as it suddenly increases in need. "Yes, Finley."

He aligns himself over me, spreading my knees wide. His skin is bronze from the training. I reach out to touch him again, refusing to be afraid. It's just another step. We've already taken so many.

"Here we go," he says, and I feel the pressure of him against me.

I prepare myself for the pinch, the pain.

But he slides in, and I expand for him. I feel full, like we're part of each other.

It doesn't hurt.

"You okay?"

I look up into his eyes, full of concern as he pushes my hair back. "It's fine. It's nothing. I'm good."

He pulls back, and I think he'll go all the way out, but when he reaches the end, he slides in again.

And this time, something else happens. A friction, a tightening, something harmonious and right. I clutch his shoulders. "Finley!"

He moves slowly, taking his time, his jaw clenched in concentration. I clutch his shoulders, moving with him.

His pace picks up, and there is no time between each pulse of pleasure. They get closer and closer together. We breathe at the same time, connected in a way I never knew was possible.

I wrap my legs around his waist, drawing him deeper, sensing there is more we can do, farther we can go.

He understands, and his careful movements become faster and harder.

Soon, I can't catch my breath. The energy builds, different from how it was with his mouth. It's farther in, like there's an infinite well inside me, creating something new.

Finley wraps his arms around my body, drawing me up until I straddle him like in the club, like all the times I felt his body reaching for mine.

He plunders me, both of us working, finding our rhythm together. I can barely stand the pressure between us. It's so intense and full and reaching a breaking point.

Then it does.

It's a star exploding, a blast of particles, energy releasing.

I'm lost in the intensity of it all. Finley holds me, and I realize his body is pulsing inside of mine. There's no change there, the condom holding it in, but our muscles talk, working around the presence of the other.

He holds me tightly and I clutch him back. I bury my face against his neck, feeling, in this moment, that we're no longer two separate people.

We're connected, two pieces of a puzzle fitting into another to create a whole. He's the boy I loved when I was small, the light in my long days surrounded with grownups. He's the man I took for granted while I chased after someone else.

He was always here.

It's clear to me. I love him. He has seen me through this crazy transition.

We belong together.

The glow fades, and soon it's only us in the trees, gripping each other.

"Vi," he says, and it's almost like a prayer, as if my name is sacred.

I want to stay here forever. Him inside my body, our naked skin together.

But the wind suddenly whips and I shiver.

"You're cold." He reaches for my white coat and wraps it around my shoulders.

"I don't want to leave here." Tears prick my eyes. How can I go back to my guards and my palace wing? How can I not be with him all the time? Doing this all the time?

"Me either."

My heart soars that he's said it. Maybe I'm not simply

another woman he seduces. Maybe our childhood means something to him too.

Maybe —

We both hear the noise at the same time. His arms tighten around me.

It's not small. Not a creature living in the woods.

It's big. With heavy footsteps.

Guard footsteps.

Finley snatches at my skirt. "Get this on. Be prepared to race back."

I nod, pulling away, thrusting my legs in the skirt and shoving my feet in the shoes. They're coming fast. I'll have to leave my other things behind.

Finley jerks on his jeans. "Leave all this," he says, shoving his feet in his boots.

He takes my hand, and we race away from the blanket. I realize too late I've left my flashlight and my phone. But I'll make it. Only a small part of the tunnels doesn't have working lamps. I will be brave.

We race through the trees, and I button my coat to cover my nakedness.

But when we reach the treeline, it's clear we're way too late.

Lights blaze.

There are cars.

Guards. I make out Tyson.

Then Gregor.

And then...

My father.

CHAPTER 32

Finley

Gregor was right. There is a brig.

It's old school, a dungeon beneath the heart of the palace. The walls are all stone. Rusting metal bars separate the cell from the corridor. Picture *Beauty and the Beast*, Belle and her father. I sit on a metal bench I'm assuming serves as a bed. I'm shirtless, with bare feet since I was in too much of a hurry for socks and my guard boots have been confiscated.

I didn't know the guards who brought me here. The King's Regiment doesn't hang out with the trainees. Any attempt to chat them up was met with a roaring, "Silence!"

On brand for where they put me, for sure.

I know Gregor's father was involved. He's the head guard and made the order to bring me back to the palace. I spotted Gregor skulking off, as well as the girl from the gardens.

Gregor must have called him after seeing us. It appears he was in the woods with his lady, too.

We didn't stand a chance after that.

I picture Octavia and her screams of anger. Her tears. Naturally, she wasn't manhandled and thrown in the back of a car like me, but her trauma might be bigger than mine.

It's not every night you lose your virginity, get caught by your dad, and watch your lover get taken away by guards.

I can't do anything to help her. I have nothing but my jeans and my attitude.

If I thought the first time Octavia and I were separated sixteen years ago was going to ruin me, I had no idea what was coming.

Every time I close my eyes, I see the blazing lights, feel the branches of the trees brushing against our bodies as we run.

I don't care what happens to me. But Octavia is bound to be in utter distress. I try to refocus, remembering the hour before the bad one. Vi in my arms, finally. Our bodies moving together. That quiet stillness that broke open into joy when she became mine.

A door squeals down the corridor, and several sets of footsteps ring on the stone floor.

I'm trained to gauge the size, the weight, and the stride of people approaching. I can assess a threat. Prepare myself.

There are four men. Three are guards. The fourth one wears rubber-soled boots, not the guard-issued ones.

Is that the King? No. The step is wrong. It's not someone heavy like him. Someone who is trying to sound heavy. Trying to intimidate.

They can't kill me. Even a monarchy has rules. Hearings. A trial. But those would come only if they thought I forced myself on her.

And they might. That might become the official story. I should've prepared myself for that.

I wasn't thinking.

Well, I was. But not with my head.

Gregor was right. Consorting with the Princess is dangerous.

As the four men appear on the other side of the bars, I'm about to find out how much.

The three guards form a triangle in front. When they part, they reveal the fourth man, who steps up to the bars.

He's inhumanly tall, trim, but not muscled. He wears all black, which makes the skin of his face and hands, the only parts visible, exceedingly pale.

His eyes are tiny blue marbles, fixed on me with a steely glare.

I'm not afraid of him exactly. I could take him one-on-one unless he has some unexpected ninja training. But he's unnerving. I'll give him that. He looks like he'd be thrilled to peel back your fingernails to make you talk.

"Finlandorio Bulgari." He's not asking. It's a statement.

I stand. "Yes."

"You have been summoned here to explain your role in the removal of Her Grace, Princess Octavia from the security of her wing. She was discovered with you, far from her guards. Explain yourself."

I have no idea what Octavia has said or what she would want me to say. I stick to the simplest facts. "I met her in the fields."

"Are you aware of how she got there?"

"I assume she walked."

"Do not get clever with me." He clasps his hands tightly in front of his black belt. "What happened after the two of you found each other?"

"Is there going to be a trial? Can I save my story for the jury?"

"You tell me." His eyes are half-lidded, as if he's casting a spell on me. Maybe he's Merlin, still alive after all these centuries. He just needs a black cat and a tall, pointy hat.

"Is the Princess all right? She was quite upset when you dragged her off."

"Her Grace's status is no concern of yours."

I figured. "Will I get my phone back?"

"Unlikely."

I nod. That's a week's pay to replace. Not that I have a job anymore. I'm quite certain getting caught with the Royal Princess in the woods means you're not cut out to be a guard.

The man watches me, the tip of the diamond formed by the four men. I assume he's the Director of Justice. He fits the description I've heard.

But I'm a guard, almost fully trained. I know very well the rule of negotiations where *he who speaks first loses*. I clasp my hands in a mirror of his gesture. I'm the one behind bars. I have nowhere else to be. I can wait all night.

Seconds tick by. The man's knuckles grow white as he grips his hands.

I'm tempted to sit back down, maybe take a nap.

But then he says, "Did you or did you not sully the innocence of Her Grace?"

Jesus. Asking that in front of three guards. Nobody needs to know her business.

"A gentleman doesn't kiss and tell."

"You will tell. The Princess is being examined by the Royal Physician."

Ouch. That sucks. But if what she told me was true about her riding debacle years ago, there will be no proof of what happened between us. She will have no change inside her. And she didn't bleed, not as far as I could tell.

I wasn't able to discard the condom properly due to the rush, but if they want to comb through all the tossed condoms in the woods, they can spend a year testing them all. There are no doubt hundreds.

But she won't have my semen in her.

Jesus. I never thought I'd be thinking about that.

I don't think Octavia will tell them anything. And I bet she'll deny any evidence they think they find.

It doesn't matter. They can come for me on that account if they want. No one is underage. But they will not hear it from me.

The stalemate of silence continues. I finally decide, screw it, and go sit down on my bench.

The Director turns on his heels. One guard follows him, but the other two remain. I'm not sure what he wanted from me, but I don't think he got it.

I guess I'm stuck here for the night. I assume Mom is sleeping. I'm not sure what she'll think when she wakes to find me gone.

It might be all right. I've left early for training before. Hopefully, she'll assume that's what happened.

But, even more, I worry for Octavia. Tonight's events will have consequences for her, even if it's not a stone cell. I'm not sure which of our fates is worse.

CHAPTER 33

Octavia

The moment I refuse to unbutton my coat, the Royal Physician is summoned.

I refuse to tell them anything.

But they're assuming. It's probably obvious. Finley wasn't wearing a shirt, and if they searched for our things, they found plenty of clothes strewn around. I still have condoms in my pocket. I have to resist patting my skirt to check on them. And if anybody forcibly removes my coat? They'll get an eyeful.

Mother has been trying to convince me to move to the bedchamber so I can be examined. I have refused, sitting in the antechamber on a high-backed chair. If anyone gets within two feet of me, I scream.

It worked when I was two years old. Still does.

Based on the way they are treating me, it seems like the appropriate tactic.

The physician arrives and instantly gets too close, so I let out another bloodcurdling wail.

"Octavia!" Mother admonishes. "That's enough!"

"Then leave my room. You can see that I'm fine."

I've no doubt that whatever Finley is going through, it's worse than this. Is he being beaten? Is he down in the dungeon? I learned about the old stone cells accidentally, when I took off running from my nanny at eight years old. We were down in the vault to choose suitable jewelry for my first banquet, and I spotted a corridor that looked like something from Harry Potter.

I ran straight for it, down a few sets of stairs, through an iron door, and there they were. A whole row of tiny rooms with metal beds and iron bars. They must've been unused for years. Cobwebs and dust had accumulated in the corners.

This was old. Centuries old.

I froze in terror, imagining I could be put here if I was naughty enough.

The guards caught me and brought me back to the nanny. After that, trays of jewels were brought to my bedchamber to choose from.

I didn't return to the vault until my eighteenth birthday, when the royal crowns were deemed too risky to bring up for me to choose from for my coming-of-age ball.

There was a shiny steel door where I remembered the old one, the kind shown in movies to secure a bank. I wasn't sure what that meant. Was it more likely someone would be held there now? Or were they trying to keep me out?

Crimes in the palace are handled in the way of most civilized countries, even though Avalonia is a monarchy. The regular police arrive, arrest them, and take them to the city jail to await the judge. We've had petty thieves, and, more than once, a fight has broken out between staff members.

But my situation is a deeply private matter of the royal family. I'm not convinced Father will want to risk Finley blabbing to cellmates in town.

I know Finley would never say a word. But Father won't take that chance.

Regardless, I refuse to give them the opportunity to even pretend to examine me and draw any conclusions.

I realize everyone is still standing around, staring at me. I am so over this. It's the middle of the night, coming up on morning.

"You will not get anything else from me. I'm not letting you examine me. And I'm not talking to anyone about what happened tonight. It's my business. My life. I wandered into the fields. Everything that happened was on me. Now everybody leave, or I will start screaming, and I won't stop this time."

Father shakes his head. Mother steps close, within the two-feet zone, and I open my mouth to let loose.

She holds up her hand. "Octavia. Stop. No one is going to forcibly examine you. We're trying to make sure you're not hurt. We need to understand the situation." She glances around. "I would like everyone to leave me alone with my daughter."

Uh oh. I don't like the sound of this. Being alone with Mother is worse.

She turns to my guard. "Tyson, your duties tonight will be performed by the hall guards. Please instruct them to stand outside Octavia's door. I will personally see to her safety during the night by remaining inside with her. Thank you."

Great. A sleepover with the Queen.

Everyone files out. The guards exchange places, and the door shuts, leaving them in the hall.

It's just me and Mom.

"Would you like to change clothes?" Mother asks.

"I would."

"You have sticks in your hair."

I reach up a hand. She's right. "I guess I should shower, too." That will get me some time alone. I need to think.

She nods. I'm about to walk by when she holds out her hand. I swear, the world stops with that movement.

"Can you assure me you will not be pregnant from whatever transpired tonight?"

"One hundred percent."

"All right. That is the one secret you can never keep from me. One thing you understand quickly as a grown woman of a royal family is that your children do not belong only to you." She gestures to the walls. "They belong to your country. They are the future ruling family."

That's a hell of a thing to think about. No wonder Leo had it so hard getting married. I'm seriously glad to be second in line and not first. When the baby is born, I'll drop to third.

Fine by me.

"Where is Finley?"

"The boy you were with?"

"His name is Finley."

"I don't know."

"Find out." I've never in my life spoken to my mother this way, but tonight I no longer feel like a girl.

She considers me for a moment. "I'll inquire about him while you shower."

She positions a chair in front of the tapestry that hides the tunnel and sits in it. I understand. There will be no more escaping tonight.

I move into my dressing closet and pull out a pair of pajamas. Now that I've been sitting awhile, parts of me feel swollen.

This makes me smile. One, I'm glad I didn't allow a snoopy examination. And two, it's proof that what happened was real.

I head to the shower. I almost don't want to wash. I lock the door and pull the condoms from my pocket. I carefully unwrap a bar of soap, tuck them inside the packaging, and wrap it closed again. This soap I shove in the back of the basket to be smuggled out of the room when no one is around.

The shower hits me from three angles. It's heaven. For the first time since this entire ordeal began, I let myself think of what occurred in the cluster of trees.

Magic. It can be described as nothing less. The way our bodies worked together. That sense of the infinite. I'm getting the picture. It isn't always this way. The very idea of doing any of these things with Gregor, especially now that I know he was a part of our betrayal, absolutely repulses me.

I saw him. He tried to sneak away. My anger burns so hot that I swear the steam rising is from my body.

Everyone thinks Finley is the one who should be punished. That he did something terrible.

But it's Gregor, the very man I thought I was in love with.

Which means, I guess, that my feelings can't be trusted.

Exhaustion sets in. I wash my hair quickly and turn off the spray.

I dry myself, looking in the mirror. This is the face of the woman who knows everything. All the secrets that have been kept from me are now mine.

At this point, it's only a matter of how much I will have to pay for them.

When I return to my bedroom, Mother isn't alone. Two members of the housekeeping staff have spread suitcases on my bed.

My pulse quickens. "Am I going somewhere?"

Mother stands. "You are. It seems you need a little getaway. The pressure of the palace has been too much."

I'm too old for boarding school. Where can she be sending me? Is there some island for bad princesses?

She pats my hand. "Don't fret. I'm sending you to New York to visit your brother and Sunny."

This I can scarcely believe. "Really? I get to go? And hang out with them?"

She smiles. "I thought you might be pleased."

"Can Lili come?"

"Of course. It's good for the two of you to be together. I will send Valloria and Botania with you, however."

That sucks. But I'll be with Leo. He'll send them away. And they have to listen. He'll be the boss.

The women walk back and forth from my closet to load the bags.

"When am I leaving?"

"We've already summoned the plane. I want to let your sister sleep, but as soon as she is packed, you will head out. Hopefully, by eight o'clock."

I won't get to say goodbye to Finley.

This is clearly also part of her plan.

The phone with our messages is lost to me. I've memorized his number. Gregor's too, for all the good that is. But I'm back to square one on the phone. I have no way to write to him safely.

But maybe, when I'm in America, I can find a way. Leo will help. If not, Sunny surely will.

I'll find a way to talk to him. I have to.

But then a dark thought crosses my mind. Are they sending me away so I never know what they do to him?

"Mother, what is going to happen to Finley?"

She frowns. "I conferred with the Director of Justice. He will be stripped of his guard status and no longer allowed to live at the palace. In fact, he is being asked to leave Avalonia."

"What?"

Mother holds up her hand. "I'm aware of your friendship and that you've been seeing the guard who reported you. No good can come of such a rivalry. It's best that you escape it altogether."

"So, is Gregor banished, too?"

"Do not let it concern you."

"No. Tell me. Because Gregor is the traitor. He's the bad guy here."

Her face becomes a familiar mask of serenity. "Octavia, Gregor did exactly as he was trained to do. His father is the head of our guards. Because of his involvement in this matter, he will never be assigned to the palace grounds nor given a leadership position. Most likely he will be sent to watch over our ambassadors somewhere else entirely. But it is well within his right to remain a part of our security. Your father is grateful for him."

"But, Mother!"

"No more of this. You and I will spend the night in one of the guest wings. When we return after a few hours of sleep, your bags will all be packed, and your sister will be ready. And you will go on your next adventure."

She opens the door. Her personal guard waits for us and follows at a distance as we head into the empty guest wing.

A room has been prepared, one with two beds. I scan the walls. There is definitely no tunnel entrance here. Not that I would try it.

Suddenly, I'm exhausted.

When I get to my brother Leo, I will deal with how to get hold of Finley. Make sure he's okay.

But for now, I'm stuck.

CHAPTER 34

Finley

In the end, I don't see the King. No more Director of Justice, either.

It's Sergeant who comes for me, opening the iron door. "Come on, then." He tosses me a plain white T-shirt. I'm still barefoot.

He keeps his gaze on the stone floor. He's mad about this. Mad at me, maybe. Or how it all went down.

I pull on the shirt, and we walk along the corridor to a vault door.

"What's happening next?" I expect transport to a regular jail. Or a lawyer visit.

"You pack," he says. "Your citizenship to Avalonia has been revoked. Per our agreement with the EU, you can apply to become a citizen of Belgium or Luxembourg or a few other choices. This will be outlined in your paperwork."

Paperwork.

"What about my mother?"

"She's free to stay. It's clear she knew nothing about this. She has been a long-standing employee of the palace."

A guard opens the vault.

The air is different on the other side. I didn't realize how musty and dank it had been until I take a fresh, cool breath.

"Naturally, you're no longer a part of the guard training. It's too bad. You were a star recruit."

"Is Gregor still head trainee?" I have to ask.

"You are no longer authorized to receive information about the training program. We ask that you no longer comport yourself in the manner of a guard." He glances at the curl of my hands.

I flex them out of the guard pose. "I understand."

We climb an endless number of steps until we finally reach the back staircase. The bustle of the kitchen in the next room means it must be a meal. I have no idea which one. Time meant nothing in the dungeon.

A server passes with a large bin of rolls. I recognize her from the guard lunches. So it's that time. She meets my gaze for only a moment, then scurries away.

The staff wing is quiet. Two guards stand at the end. "Take him to his rooms to pack," Sergeant says to one. He turns to me. "In about an hour, a man will arrive to drive you to Brussels. What you do once you cross the Avalonian border is up to you, but to cross back over without permission of the crown will result in your immediate arrest."

"I understand."

He gives me a nod and heads toward the Great Hall. He's spent part of his lunch dealing with me.

But where is Octavia?

When I arrive at my door, it's wide open. Mom has dragged our suitcases into the living room. When she sees me, the big bag drops, and she rushes over. "Finlandorio! What happened? You're moving out? They gave me the day off to help you." She presses her hands to my cheeks.

I wrap my arms around her. She's faced so much hardship in her life, and I've given her more.

The guard waits by the door. I walk Mom to the bathroom. I understand what Octavia went through, unable to escape being watched.

"Did they say anything else?" I ask her, already trying to spin this in a way that doesn't upset her.

"That you left the guard program. Why would you do that?" Her watery eyes about kill me.

"I'm going to see what life is like outside of Avalonia," I tell her. "You know. Travel the world."

"I don't understand." She closes the lid to the toilet and sinks down on it. "You were so close to getting your stripes."

I can't lie to her. I kneel in front of her. "Mom, it's about Octavia."

"The Princess?"

"Yes. She's the Tallest Angel."

Her eyes go wide. "On your phone?"

"Yes. I fell in love with her. They found out."

"So, you have to leave."

I nod.

She stands up abruptly. "Then I'm leaving, too." She opens the cabinet and starts yanking things off the shelves and piling them in the sink.

"Mom. No. You have friends here. A job. You've always lived in the palace."

"I can't be here if you're not here."

"Can you let me get settled first? Find us a place? I have to apply for citizenship somewhere else."

Boxes of Kleenex fall from her arms to land on the floor. "They revoked your citizenship?" She presses a hand to her chest.

I should have been more careful.

She pushes past me for the bathroom door. "I'm going straight to the King. I know where they have lunch."

I reach for her and hold her by the arm. "Mom. You'll never get past the guards. Don't get yourself fired."

"This isn't right. None of it is right. She trapped you. She wrote you, but you are the one who has to go? Is she the one you kept sneaking out to see?"

I close the bathroom door. If the guard thinks it's weird we're in here together, he can shove it.

"Mom, there's nothing we can do about it now. They won't let us be together."

Her gaze meets mine. "So that's why they fetched linens for the royal plane. I had to pack them early this morning."

My jaw tightens. "What does that mean?"

"When the royal plane is taking an international flight, they need fresh bed linens for the bedroom on board."

The timing is too convenient. "They flew her out of here."

Mom sits on the toilet again. "Did something bad happen? You didn't come home last night." She glances down at my bare feet. "That isn't your shirt. It's too big. Where were you?"

I can't tell her I was in jail.

"I was with the Princess. We were reported."

Her hands fly to her mouth. "Did you...did you..." She can't say it. "I knew you kept company with many of the palace girls. But the Princess?"

Of all the things that have happened since last night, this is the worst.

I slide down to the floor. "It's Vi, Mom. We have history. She's been trapped here. I..." Actually, I don't know what to say anymore. There is no excuse for me. "Nothing was her fault."

The dark descends. I haven't faced it in so long, I'd almost forgotten it existed. There is a hole I can fall into. Inside it are the kids who made fun of me for not having a father. Getting the worst jobs in the stables. Losing Vi as a kid. Watching Mom be so lonely. Hearing her cry.

For years, I thought the blackness would swallow me up. Sometimes I'd hide in the upper levels of the stables, not moving, unable to make myself do anything.

As I became an older teen, I found ways to cope. Women, mostly. But being the wildest of the wild got me points with the other boys. I couldn't be the butt of the joke if I was the one on top. I got all the prettiest girls. I was never lonely. If I didn't belong, at least I had company.

But the dark is back. The color washes out of my vision. A dull thud hammers behind my eyes. There's rage. Then despair. Then nothing. I have to silence that part of me completely.

I've been so focused, I forget Mom is in the room until she slides to the floor next to me. "When you were born, it was the only light I'd known for a long time."

She's never said things like this. That I'm her light, sure. But not that it had followed the dark.

"There was a time when I thought I couldn't make it through. Your father..." She falters, and I squeeze her hand. It's a word we never use. "Your father left Avalonia when he found out about you."

"Bastard."

"He took his wife and son and left."

I'm shocked silent. I never knew this.

"Don't think too ill of him. I knew he was married. I knew all along. I'm not the saint you may have painted me to be. I'm just a person, someone who thought she was in love and that love would win in the end."

She rests her head on my shoulder. "So, I may understand things better than you think."

I wrap my arms around her. The bathroom is quiet, the bustle of the palace far away. We could be anywhere. A hotel. A house in the country. A city apartment.

Soon, I suppose we will be.

I clear my throat, uncertain words will come out. But they do. "I love her. I always knew we wouldn't work, but I wanted whatever we could get."

"Exactly." Mom holds my hand tight. "So what do two fools like us do now?"

"I'm about to be escorted out of here," I tell her. "But you're allowed to stay. Work a little more. Let me find us a place. Then you can decide if you want to come or not."

"My life is where you are," she says. "I can fold laundry anywhere."

"Okay." I kiss her head. "I'll let you know when I have a place for us."

We work quietly together, choosing items for me to take now, and what will go later.

The man arrives to drive me out of the country of my birth. I hug my mother and promise to get a phone so I can call her as soon as I'm on the other side.

And then I'm loaded into a sleek black car.

The palace is merely an object in the rearview mirror.

CHAPTER 35

Octavia

I sleep the whole way to New York. When I wake, Lili braids my hair, making the most of the color.

"You okay? You've been out the entire flight."

"It was a long night."

"You want to tell me about it?"

And I do. The whole thing. Miracle sex with Finley. Gregor calling the guards. Mom. Dad. Finley's punishment. The words spill quietly in the bedroom portion of the plane. Lili plays music to cover our words since the plane isn't soundproof.

"I have the extra phones," she whispers. "They're in my makeup case. You can call him once we land."

"If he has his phone." I doubt it. And no one has told me when — or even if — I'd get mine back. It wasn't official, so they may not even know it's mine if they find it. I've lost all our messages. We've never taken a picture together.

The only proof he existed is in my memory.

"We'll find him." She glances at the open sliding door to

the main compartment, where six guards and two members of the staff sit in the short rows. "Leo will help."

I'm not feeling confident. Finley was ousted from the country. He could be anywhere. Even if I do figure out where he is, I can't get to him.

Valloria approaches the door. "We have ten minutes until we descend. We'll take a car to the hotel where the Crown Prince is currently residing."

At least I will be with my brother. If I had to stay in that wretched palace with my disapproving parents after all this, I would have been forced to run away.

But they knew that. This was the best solution they could come up with. They gave an inch, but only after I stole a mile.

Every time my thoughts turn to Finley, tears squeeze from my eyes. Lili tugs my braids like she did when she was small. "Don't do that. We're going to fix this. And Octavia's Life 2.0 will be way better than the first version."

I don't see how that can happen, but I nod.

I've never been to New York. The ride from the airport into Manhattan is brilliant and bold. The bridge is enormous. Then the buildings! They stretch into the sky like nothing I've ever seen.

Lili seems unfazed by the view, tapping on her phone. A new one lies in a box beside me, clean and empty, an unfamiliar phone number written across the top.

I can't try to write to him yet and when I do, it will have to be from one of the burner phones. I can't use my name, but hopefully, if he does still have his old number, I can say something only he will know is me.

Blue frosting? Hiccups of doom? Our Webkinz. There

are so many possibilities. I feel confident about that part, but not about reaching him in the first place.

Valloria and Botania sit across from us in the back of the limo. I avoid their gazes, propping my arms on the window ledge. There's so much to see here. So many ways to get lost. I can see how Leo sometimes evaded his guards. Can I do it, too? Will he teach me? He went to other countries. Could I? If I find Finley, can I go where he is?

Or would that make things worse?

They always catch us in the end.

We turn into a parking structure, driving slowly up the levels. The car stops next to a small red awning. A man in a uniform stands there, as well as two more palace guards in blue. Part of Father's King's Regiment, it seems. They're older, and I'm sure the type of guards that convinced Leo he needed to hire new, younger ones.

I ruined two of them. One is gone and the other can no longer do palace work. I wonder if Leo knows. If he's mad. They were the best ones.

The driver opens the door and Valloria exits first. Lili shoves her phone into her bag and hops out. I pick up the box and my purse and follow her. Botania takes the rear.

The King's Regiment turns to the side as we pass. Two more wait inside the doors.

And then there's Leo!

I race forward and fling myself into his arms.

"Baby O," he says, holding on to me. "Baby O."

He only calls me that when I'm in distress, so he must have been briefed on what happened. At least their side of the story. That's good. He'll tell me everything, and we can compare stories and figure out where to go from here.

I'm more safe with him than our parents. He understands. I won't be judged or punished or confined. We'll come up with solutions and ways to cope.

Sunny comes up and wraps her arms around the both of us. The faint scent of lemon and violets envelops our trio. "We've got you," she says. "We know how it is."

I want to stay in this embrace forever. When was the last time our parents had hugged any of us? I couldn't remember. They were so proper. Hugs came from nannies or kindly staff when we were little. But once we were teens, nothing.

"Let's go up," Leo says. "We can talk."

He releases me. The two of them are dressed in jeans and sweaters. I try to spot a baby bump on Sunny, but it's not obvious yet.

We pass a security station and enter a small hall with an elevator. This is one thing I'm used to from the traveling I've done with our parents. Private entrances. Back elevators. Keep us away from the ordinary people, like we're so much more important.

I want to take off. Race down the ramps of the parking garage and out into the open air. No guards. Nobody I know. Just walk and look and be free.

I understand my brother so much better. I regret any ugly thought about how his actions might have caused our parents to lock us down more tightly.

He did what he had to do.

And so did I.

And I will again.

When we get in the elevator, Lili says, "So I guess I'm chopped liver?"

Leo wraps his arm around her neck and rubs his knuckles in her hair. "Noogies for the baby!"

She ducks out of his grip. "Leo!"

"How's my social media mogul? Did you take over Instagram yet?"

She grins up at him. "I joined TikTok. Be nice to me or I'll make your snoring go viral."

"Lilibug, I made myself go viral with way worse than that."

Sunny takes his hand. "In a rooster Speedo no less."

"That was epic," Lili says. "I'll never reach that level of visibility."

It's nice, watching happy family talk. I wish we'd been able to do this a long time ago.

The doors open. Two guards step out first, then we follow.

"We have the entire floor," Leo says. "Feel free to run up and down the halls screaming."

I might do exactly that.

"Let's do some shopping later today," Sunny says. "Get out and see New York."

"Yes!" Lili says. "I have a list of places!"

Sunny laughs. "Anywhere you want to go."

We stop in front of a door. "This is your set of rooms," Leo says. He turns to Valloria. "Guards stay in the hall."

Valloria frowns. "But Your Royal Highness, we must keep — "

Leo stops her. "When separated from the King, the Crown

Prince makes the rules concerning comportment and security for the good of the royal family. Guards in the halls. You will be relieved of your duty for time off and rest." He gestures to a guard in blue. "Augustus will create a schedule that allows for your own enjoyment of the city. Please go with him."

Lili and I glance at each other with barely contained smiles as one of the King's Regiment leads our personal guards to the end of the hall.

"I feel so free!" I say, turning in a circle. "They've refused to let us so much as close the door to our chambers!"

"That's ridiculous," Leo says. "We'll use common sense in the city, but when you're here in the hotel, there is no need for constant lock and key."

I give him another hug as the other guard in blue opens our room.

"We'll come get you in an hour," Sunny says. "Shopping and dinner, if you're not too tired."

"No way," I say. "I slept the whole way here."

We step inside and close the door.

And we're alone.

"I'll get the phones," Lili says. "If we can't get any of the US sim cards to work, we'll buy one on the street. There's a guy on a corner about eight blocks from here who sells them." She rapidly texts on her phone.

"Who are you talking to?"

"I'm meeting up with some influencers." She bites her lip. "I need to get to a salon before tomorrow."

"Leo has his stylist Aisha here. She could do it."

"A wig might be better." She unzips her bag. Before I

can ask her why she needs a wig, she says, "Let's get your phone working."

We spend most of our hour trying out cards in the various phones until we finally hit one that works. With the Visa card, we're able to sign up for a US plan and soon, my test phone call to Lili has worked, as well as a text message.

"Time to try," Lili says. "Prepare yourself to not reach him, though."

I nod.

I create a new contact for Dory and type in his number. My thumbs hover over the letters. What to say? He has to know it's me without anyone else knowing it's me.

Missed you at training. You around? I wanted your advice on how to get in touch with that girl we talked about. The freak-ishly tall one who likes to hang out in cemeteries to look at the angels. Write me back.

Lili looks over my shoulder. "That's good. Sounds like one of the other guards. It's natural they'll write him to find out where he's gone."

I press send.

Now to wait.

CHAPTER 36

Finley

The apartment is definitely a downgrade from the palace.

And a downgrade from the cottage behind the stables behind the palace.

It took a couple of days, but at least I found something.

I open the box with my new phone. It's imperative that I at least try to get back in contact with Octavia.

I'm grateful I memorized her number from the first day, and I tap out the digits, my stomach already clenching with the knowledge that nothing will come of it.

I know I can't tell her it's me. Even if this phone gets through to her, they'll be watching.

Always watching.

It takes me a moment to get the message right. But I think she'll know it's me without anyone else being the wiser.

This message is to inform you that your Webkinz Fuzzball is due to expire in 30 days. To ensure you do not lose the data for your important friendship with Webkinz Blockhead, please contact customer service at this number.

That should work.

I send it and stare at the phone for five straight minutes, willing a quick response to come.

It doesn't.

She could be off somewhere without her phone. Ball gowns don't come with pockets.

Or she may have hidden it and only checks occasionally.

Anything, really. This isn't the end.

I sit on the scruffy sofa that came with the place, edging away from the stain I'll have to clean later. I text Mom.

Me: *Got my new phone. Got an apartment. I'm fine.*

Her response is immediate.

Mom: *Send me pictures. And the address. I'm going to give notice.*

Do I want her to do that? I don't feel sure about anything.

Me. *Can you hold off a few days? I'd like to find a job first. And I'm trying to see if I can get in touch with the Princess.*

Mom: *She's not here. Kitchen staff has confirmed it. Both of the princesses left on a plane that same morning, just like we suspected.*

Vi could be anywhere in the world. And if she's in some other country, her phone might not even work. I have no idea if my message will reach her.

Me: *Thanks for that. I'd still hold off until I find work.*

Mom: *I can do that.*

I wander the space. It is definitely the smallest home I've ever had, beating out even the tiny cottage where I had to sleep on a mattress behind the sofa.

Here, I will have to sleep *on* the sofa. At least when Mom gets here.

I pause in the kitchen. Scuffed-up appliances look like a mismatched set from the salvage yard. I turn on the burners. Three out of four's not bad.

I open the fridge. The light doesn't work, but cold air brushes against me. Good.

The faucets have water.

Things could be worse.

Or could they?

I can't seem to grasp any of my old swagger. What used to make me feel like I could do anything? Seduce any woman? I can't find my bearings. Nothing makes sense.

I used to shovel donkey dung for a living. Nothing about where I am now is any worse than where I've been. And yet, nothing feels right.

I know it's Octavia. In all those years I worked in the stables, there was always that chance I could run into her. She wasn't far away. And even if I didn't see her, I knew where she was.

Now, I don't.

I move to the bedroom and sit on the bare mattress. I spend a solid hour scrolling through social media looking for any reference to the Princess. Lili has an official Instagram account, but it's been silent for days. Her absence has been noticeable enough that a few people have asked where she is.

I scour her feed, looking for pictures of her sister.

It's mostly gowns and shoes and gems. Selfies of Lili putting on makeup, adjusting her hair.

But I find one. She and Octavia wear near matching

sparkly gowns, two slightly different shades of rose gold. Six months ago, before I saw her again. Before guard training.

Farther down, I find another one of Octavia, trying on a ruby tiara, white gloves sheathing her hands.

It's hard to keep going after a while. The darkness tries to take over, and I don't have anyone to help me out of it this time.

There's no point sitting here any longer. I should be looking for a job.

I grab the piece of paper with my address and shove my new phone in my back pocket. Hopefully, my old ID will work for applications, or I could be stuck even longer. I don't have a clue about applying for citizenship, and I'm assuming I can work in Belgium without it. I've never had to wrangle red tape. I was born into a place, a job, a life.

Time to figure out this new one.

The apartment's on the ground floor, so I exit my door, cross the parking lot, and hit the sidewalk. I need to scope out public transportation in case I get an interview out of walking distance. Until I'm working, calling Uber is a luxury I can't afford.

I pass a grocery store with a "We're hiring" sign and head in. A woman at the customer service desk tells me to visit the website and fill out the application. She doesn't know if they can hire Avalonians. Someone will contact me if they can.

I grab a few basic supplies there and take the long way back around, scoping out the shops in the neighborhood.

There's a bar on a backstreet, and despite having two

plastic bags of groceries, I decide to pop in for a quick drink. Why the hell not?

The place is mostly empty, with tall tables and chairs scattered throughout the dark wood-paneled space. It's modeled after a British pub. I sit on a stool and drop the bags onto the floor between my feet.

A potbellied bartender holds up a finger to tell me he'll be there in a second, jabbing ice with a silver scoop to break it up.

The rear wall behind the bottles is mirrored, so I can watch the place without having to turn around.

I like it. This feels like a place where I could become a regular, like the one on Town Square with the rear entrance after hours.

The thought of it conjures the image of Octavia pressing her ear to the wall and proclaiming it open.

And the dance.

And getting my jaw clocked.

Gregor tarnishes all the memories.

The bartender adjusts his apron as he walks over. His black hair is thick and graying at the temples. He's rather dapper for the place. "What can I get you?"

"You have a good dubbel?"

He nods and tosses a pint glass in the air, neatly catching it and sliding it under the tap. He pulls the wood handle. "Day drinking. Long face. Avalonian accent. You a tourist?"

"Just moved here. Got an apartment two blocks over. Been hitting the pavement looking for a job."

He nods. "There's a fair number of those about, what with summer and the travel season approaching. A young buck like you will have no trouble. What did you do before?"

He slides the beer down the well-oiled bar.

I catch it. "Security. I'm trained." I say nothing more. Anything about the palace would invite questions I don't want to answer.

He leans on the bar and eyeballs me. "You ever been a bouncer?"

"No. But I reckon I could toss somebody out on their arse if they needed it."

He laughs. "You're definitely built for it. I've been going without one for a month. My last one's wife had a baby. Didn't want him to go on manhandling drunks. You interested?"

"I might be."

"We could do a trial. Have you here for a week, and at the end, we'll both decide if you should stay?"

I nod. "I can do that."

"Pay's the Belgian minimum, plus a house bonus based on the crowd."

"All right."

He nods at the beer. "On the house. Two per shift as well. Come by later tonight. Seven or there'bouts. It's a Saturday, so we'll be packed."

I lift the glass to him. "I can handle that."

"Good. I'm Roger. I own this place."

"Finley. I'm glad I stopped in."

"Me too. I hope it works."

I sip the beer, turning on the stool to assess the place. Bathrooms on one side, offices on the other. The long bar fills the back wall other than a door to a kitchen or storeroom. For the customers, though, one way in, one way out. Easy enough.

My phone buzzes and I practically fall off the stool, yanking it out of my pocket.

But it's a message from the new phone provider. *Welcome to our service.*

I jab it away with a sigh.

I finish my beer and tell Roger I'll see him tonight.

I guess the first day of the rest of my crappy life starts right here.

CHAPTER 37

Octavia

After hitting four of the shops Lili insisted on, including a beauty store where she selected a shoulder-length red wig, Sunny suggests we head to the flagship Manhattan Pickle deli for dinner and to hang out with her family.

The restaurant is huge and packed. There's a line out the door. Sunny ushers us past the throng of patrons and winds us through the busy tables until we reach a door marked *staff only*.

"We have space back here for family," she says. "Max and Jason aren't here, of course, but Anthony is in from Boulder. He's using the test kitchen to try out some new recipes. It's always fun."

We enter a quiet space, a big room with bright green sofas and a long white table in the center, surrounded by chairs.

"This is where we have meetings or family dinners if the restaurant is open," Sunny says. She glances at me and Lili. "If you're tired, you can chill here for a bit. I'm going to see what Anthony is up to in the back. Uncle Sherman might pop in. He's hands-on during the rush, but he'll come back here to take breaks."

I haven't seen any of these people, other than Sunny, since the royal wedding. I glance at my brother to see what he's going to do.

Lili speaks first. "Can I do background shots for my Instagram feed?"

"Sure," Sunny says. "Uncle Sherman believes all publicity is good publicity." She elbows Leo. "Unless maybe you're wearing a rooster Speedo."

My brother will never live down being the King of Cock.

"I'm starving," Leo says. "I'm down to eat anything."

"Are you now?" Sunny asks, and the invitation in her voice pangs my belly. I can see myself saying something like that to Finley. But I may never see him again to get that chance.

Even if he was trying to reach me, and I don't know that he is, isn't he all about the one-night stand? I'm not going to assume I was like any other girl to him. We have a history. But when it's clear I'm no longer an option, someone like him moves on. There's always another *ho for a bro*. I shake off the memory of the club where Finley came to rescue me from those men.

"I'll go with you," I say. Everyone is looking at me expectantly, since I'm the one they're all worried about. No one wants to leave me alone in a room.

Sunny pushes through a pair of swinging doors, and soon we're in the bustle of an industrial kitchen. The rush is on, and workers in green aprons hurry about. Some of them carry vats of vegetables. Others have baskets of bread.

It's not unlike the kitchens of the palace, although we have fewer to feed.

There's a sense of purpose in the room. Everyone has their job and does it. I envy them. I never have anything to do. Never have any purpose.

In the back corner, I recognize Anthony. He's directing a young man to chop a pile of slender, green vegetables I've never seen before.

Lili is also intrigued and hurries forward to snap photos.

"Sunny!" he calls. "I see you brought visitors!"

Some of the workers pause to watch our guards. They definitely stand out in their blue and gray uniforms. Valloria is with us, as well as one member of the King's Regiment.

Leo would prefer they wear regular clothes. But there are some directives even he doesn't have the power to rescind.

Lili leans on the counter. "What are you making?"

Anthony grins at her. "A new kind of pickle."

She's interested. "Even hotter than the one that went viral on TikTok?" She's been paying attention.

"Unlikely. After the cooking show fiasco, I prefer a little sweet with my heat."

"Oh, that's good. Is that what it's called?" Lili's fingers fly over her phone screen. "Sweet with my heat?"

"Maybe so. You going to post it to your princess feed?"

She glances up and quickly sends her phone screen to black. "I don't know."

What's she up to? I know when her voice is going evasive. First the red wig. Now this. Interesting.

Anthony pushes the jar toward Sunny. "See what they think of this one. Is there going to be a family dinner tonight?"

Sunny unscrews the top. "There can be. Should I call one together?"

"Totally. Let's get the gang all here."

Sunny grabs a knife and pokes at a pickle until she can withdraw it from the jar. She rests it on an empty cutting board. "Is this 'sweet with my heat' generation one?"

"Sixteen, actually. I'm struggling to get it right."

"What are those green things you're chopping?" Lili asks.

"This one's a jalapeño." Anthony pushes a narrow pointy vegetable toward us. Then he picks up a fat orange one. "These are habaneros."

"No ghost peppers,?" Lili's got her phone open again. She can't help herself.

Anthony shakes his head. "My ghost pepper days are over."

There was some reference to this in the days following Leo's wedding. A TV show that went wrong. Anthony getting in trouble. I think that's how he ended up with his fiancé. There are so many Pickles, I struggle to keep track of them all.

Sunny slices the pickle and spreads out the pieces. "Buckle up, buttercups. Give it a try."

I like this expression. Americans have such colorful language. *Buckle up, buttercup.* I want to say it to Finley.

Leo snatches up a pale green disc and pops it in his

mouth. He chews thoughtfully at first, then his eyes go wide. "Water!"

Sunny laughs. "Milk is better. My poor, poor, wimpy-mouthed husband."

She picks up a piece and tries it herself. "There isn't enough heat, cousin. Could you maybe use the ghost pepper for the first six hours of the soak and pull it out?"

"That's an idea." He picks up a piece of the pickle himself. After swallowing, he says, "You're right. Not hot enough."

Leo fans his mouth. "Um, still dying here. Can someone help?"

"Come on," Sunny says. "Let's get some milk."

As they wander off, Anthony turns to us. "I'm guessing after that I don't have any more takers."

Lili reaches out. "It is commonly known that Leo is a spice wimp. I'll do it."

She takes a still photo of her hand holding a piece of the pickle. Then she switches it to selfie mode, shifting so Anthony can't see the screen.

I can, though. And she's using that filter she showed me a few days ago. Her hair turns fiery red and her lashes get long. She records herself this way, popping the pickle in her mouth. "First tasting of the secret new pickle." Her eyes go wide. "Oh, no! Gosh!"

She stops the recording.

Anthony looks alarmed. "You, too? Sunny went to the fridge. She can grab you some milk."

Lili shakes her head. "No. I think it's perfect." She grabs another piece and chomps down on it.

Anthony nods. "Anything for the feed."

"You get me."

I start to understand what she's up to. The red wig. She's started that new account she was talking about, using the filter. And she's planning to meet someone and not be Princess Lilianne of Avalonia. I'll have to ask her about this new persona when we're alone.

The whole situation is a pleasant distraction. Sunny and Leo return, arm in arm. The pang in my chest hits me again. I check my phone. No word from Finley. I quickly calculate the time difference. It's late there. He's probably already in bed.

Which means either he didn't get the message, or he's been threatened not to talk to me anymore.

Either way, it seems like we're done.

The Pickles decide to hold the dinner in the private deli space, going for a combination of their own food and dishes ordered from another restaurant.

Tall, broad Uncle Sherman shows up, along with two members of the Pickle clan I've never met. One is Rory Sheffield, a business lawyer who was only discovered to be one of Sherman's children nearly forty years after the fact. She brings her fiancé, Mack, a sports agent who spends every Christmas season working as a volunteer Santa.

The couples interest me the most. Of course, I've seen Leo and Sunny a million times, but I watch this new pair, Mack and Rory, with fascination.

I discover they've been engaged for six months, but haven't made plans for their wedding yet.

When Lili asks about it, Mack says, "I'm trying to knock her up first."

Rory rolls her eyes. But he draws her close against him, and her dreamy expression makes me wonder if they've already succeeded and not told anyone.

These are the things I've been missing all my life. Seeing ordinary couples in their natural habitat. At state dinners, ambassadors and their wives, and certainly the other royal couples, all behave with stiffness and formality. I have no idea what anyone looks like behind the scenes. Even my own parents act that way during ordinary family dinners.

I watch how their gazes lock, how Mack occasionally drops a kiss in her hair. Jealousy slices through me. Am I ever going to have that? Am I destined to have a formal relationship, even with my own children? It's all I know.

But then Leo scoops up a bite of pasta — way too large of a bite — and shoves it toward Sunny's face.

He's caught her mid-laugh, and it all goes in. She clamps down on the spoon, sputtering. She manages to swallow it and cry, "Leopold the First!" Then she stops. "Oh, that's good. I want more of that."

He smiles knowingly. "I knew you would."

She takes his plate and starts eating off of it. I could never in a million years imagine this exchange between my parents.

So maybe there's hope.

When we've all finished eating, Sunny moves down to sit by me. "How can I help?"

Am I that obvious? I shrug. "I don't think anyone can."

Sunny's grandmother, Alma, comes up behind us,

placing her hands on Sunny's shoulders. "We Pickles are a wily bunch. If there's something to be done, we will find a way to do it."

The conversation hushes and all the attention is on Alma.

Rory glances around. "I know this quiet. This is the silence I remember before you guys put me on a plane to Alabama on Christmas Eve."

I don't know the story. Lili and I glance at each other. She doesn't either.

"Go on," Mack says. "Tell her the whole thing."

As Rory relates the account of feeling sure that Mack was no longer interested in her, but then getting the text that led the Pickles to call their friend Dell Brant to fly her across the country to see him on Christmas, the pain slices too deep.

She got her happy ending. But she was free to do it. She could just go to Mack. He wasn't banished from her country.

Before she's finished with their tale of finding Mack's father and getting him to the holiday festivities as well, I'm bawling.

And not some beautiful silent tears flowing down my cheeks. Full on *boo-hoo*.

Grammy Alma's arms go around me. "Please, child. What's going on?"

It's Leo who speaks up. "My sister fell in love with a palace guard. They've been friends since they were kids. Dad found out and banished the dude from our country. Now they can't be together."

There's a collective, "What!"

Sherman stands. "What are you going to do? Where is this guy?"

Lili speaks up. "Our Dad is freaking *king*. We can't exactly defy him."

"This isn't Avalonia," Sherman says. "He's not the King of Manhattan."

I push my phone out to the center of the table. The burner, not the official one. "I can't get hold of him."

Leo sighs. "They almost certainly took his phone." He picks up the burner. "This isn't one of ours. Where did you get it?"

I cut my eyes over the Lili, but I would never rat her out. "That's classified."

"Good. Don't tell me anything else about it." Leo passes it back. "Who would know where he would be? Who are his friends?"

Certainly not Gregor. "His mom works at the palace."

Alma comes around to sit beside me. "What time is it in Avalonia?"

"Close to midnight," Lili says. "No one's awake."

Alma folds her hands together. She looks devious, like she's going to solve the whole problem herself. "When will his mother be up?"

"She does the washing," I say. "That's probably an early shift. Maybe in seven hours?"

"Would he leave Europe?" Sherman asks. "Is it likely he's still on the continent?"

I shrug. "Probably. They don't have a lot of money. He was herding donkeys before he started training as a guard."

"He probably went to Belgium then," Leo says. "That's where revoked citizens are usually dropped off. It's close."

"Does this happen a lot in your country?" Sherman asks.

"We're small," Leo says. "Our kings tend to make problems go away."

"Leo won't be like that," Sunny says quickly. "We're changing everything."

"Not fast enough for poor Octavia," my sister says.

Alma squeezes my shoulders again. "We have seven hours until we can ask his mom where he is. What should we do to help sweet Octavia pass the time?"

"I say we get her back to Europe," Sherman says. "Can we get her there without anyone knowing?"

"Not on the royal plane," Leo says. "Trust me. I've tried it."

"We could commission a private one," Sherman says. "Or is Dell around? We're always borrowing his plane."

"Donovan and Havannah have the plane right now," Anthony says. "She's on a trip to choose things for the castle they're building outside of Boulder."

Lili perks up. "They're building a castle in America?"

"We have a few," Alma says. "Hers will be a grand estate for weddings."

"So, we're short a plane," Sherman says. "And the royal plane is off limits."

"Call me crazy," Lili says, "But why don't we put her on a commercial flight? There's bound to be something tonight, right? If price is no object?" She looks pointedly at our brother.

Leo snort-laughs. "Princess Octavia of Avalonia flying knee-to-knee with strangers?"

I sit up. "I can do it. I don't mind." Could this work?

"You'll have to slip your guards," Leo says. "And I'm not sure you should go alone. We have to keep you safe."

"Then you go," Alma says. "Take your sister back."

Sunny squeezes his arm. "Yes, Leo, you know all the tricks. Take your sister back and help her find her great love." She turns to me. "He is your great love, right? He's worth it?"

I can barely squeeze out the words. "He's totally worth it."

Alma pops out of her chair. "Then why are you all sitting around? Get this girl to the airport!"

CHAPTER 38

Finley

Compared to the craziness of Saturday night, this Monday crowd is nothing.

I sit on a stool inside the door of Roger's Pub, eyeballing the group of guys heading up the sidewalk. Not a one of them looks old enough to be out of secondary school, but then, the legal drinking age in Brussels is sixteen. They don't have to graduate to walk in a bar.

Unlike in Avalonia, and certainly strict places like America, Brussels doesn't ask for identification for proof of legal age. I'm the bouncer, and I call the shots. Someone could be forty, and if I don't like the looks of them, I can give them the boot.

But, it's hard watching these young bucks coming in to order a pint. As they approach the door, I say, "Don't you have school tomorrow?"

They know not to piss me off. I can kick them out, and the nearest pub from here is a fair distance to walk.

"Holiday tomorrow," one says. "Getting our beer on."

"All right, then."

271

Roger will watch them. He won't serve them any more than they can handle.

We've already established a good communication of glances, glares, and gestures to signal if we think trouble's coming, or if one or the other should intervene. I like Roger. He's friendly, easygoing, and has a wife and two kids.

I wonder if I could do something like he does. Save up and own a business. Now that I'm out of the palace, my future isn't set. I can do anything I want.

Other than find my princess.

The darkness threatens to take over, but I focus on the job. The street is clear for the moment, and the inside seems in order. The young fellows settle at a long table. There's an older couple at another one, and a few men bellied up to the bar.

Otherwise, a quiet night.

The cold air coming in the open door feels good. An occasional car passes, its headlights piercing the dark. The streetlamp on the corner is out. The damp streets and the shuttered businesses on the other side aren't exactly cheerful.

Brussels isn't home. Maybe it will feel more like it when Mom comes. I sent her the address now that I have a job. She gave notice this morning. Roger knows several of the business owners through a civic group and thinks he can get her work pretty easily. Everyone likes former palace employees.

I haven't told him I went through the guard program. He's very much someone who lives in the now. It comes with working in a bar. The past is something patrons are here to forget.

I wish I could.

Another couple comes up the sidewalk, arms tightly around each other. Their heads are pressed together, and every few steps, they stop to kiss.

I have to look away. I never envied couples before. In fact, I distinctly remember thinking they were poor saps stuck to one relationship for eternity.

But I get it. I met the right one when I was small. And she was an impossible dream.

The couple enters the bar, and I give them a quick nod. They won't be causing any trouble. Unless, of course, they get too frisky in a booth. My memory flashes to Octavia in my lap, the light and colors pulsing around her.

I push it aside. This couple takes a seat at a table, scooting their chairs close together.

This might be a long night.

My phone buzzes. It can be one of only two people. Mom or Roger. Since Roger is pulling beers, that leaves Mom. I tug out my phone.

Mom: *Are you working tonight?*

Me: *Yes. Until midnight. You okay?*

Mom: *Perfect. Slowly packing. Text me if anything interesting happens.*

That's an odd thing to say. But this is the longest we've gone without seeing each other. Living on the palace grounds like we did made us take that closeness for granted.

I shove my phone into my back pocket.

The street is empty again. Behind me, the young men

start playing pool, laughing loudly. They already sound tipsy. It's been ten minutes. They need to pace themselves.

A funny old Volkswagen Bug pulls up to the curb. It's bright yellow with flowers painted all over it. The back door opens, and what looks to be a member of the Avalonian King's Regiment steps out, his distinct blue uniform visible in the light from the pub's awning.

I sit up straight. What now? Have I done something wrong already?

But next out is the Crown Prince. Good God! I jump from my seat, ready to bow, but then I remember I'm no longer a citizen.

But this is Octavia's brother.

My heart hammers as I stand by the stool. No one inside has noticed anything.

The Prince approaches, his head tilting as he watches me. He looks like anyone else in jeans and a New York Mets jacket. But I know him. His photo has been everywhere. And I met him a few times before I was ejected from the palace as a kid. He was a young teen then, and constantly in trouble.

I always wanted to be him.

He stops a few feet from me. "Finlandorio Bulgari," he says.

This can't be good.

Unless...

Unless Vi sent him.

"That's right," I say.

"Do you have somewhere we can talk?"

I glance back at the bar. Roger's busy pulling another round for the young group. I catch his eye and thumb toward the outdoors. He nods, not recognizing the Prince. Not unexpected. We're in Brussels and Leopold is completely out of context.

We walk a few steps outside of the door. The guard keeps a respectful distance.

"Can I help you?" I ask.

"My sister Octavia came to visit me in New York," he says, and my heart leaps. So he's seen her.

"How is she?"

The Prince scrunches his face. "I've seen her better. I hear you were one of the new guards I forced my father to hire. So ridiculous that he had none under thirty. Totally killed our vibe in Ibiza."

This conversation is a revelation a minute. The Prince talking about vibes, for one. And he knows I was a guard trainee. And Octavia isn't good?

"Where is she?"

"In the car." He tilts his head toward the Beetle.

I take a step to race for her, but the guard moves to block my path.

"Hold up," the Prince says. "I need to know something before you can go to her."

I refuse to take my eyes off the car. I can't see inside it in the dark. "What's that?"

"Were you fucking with her?"

I definitely didn't expect him to ask that. "No."

"What do you want from her?"

"Nothing. I don't know. Just to know her. To be able to talk to her. They keep separating us." I turn to face him. "Your father keeps separating us. We shouldn't be kept apart. It doesn't matter if we're friends or whatever. We shouldn't have to go through life without each other."

"That's a better answer than I expected." He nods toward the guard, and the man steps aside.

Then I'm racing. Running toward the tiny car. Wrenching open the door.

And she's there. Sitting inside. Until she's not.

She's in my arms.

Vi.

My Vi.

I have her.

CHAPTER 39

Octavia

I want to kiss him. I want to make out with him for a thousand years right here in the street.

I think he does, too. He can't stop looking at me.

"You're okay? You're really okay?" He keeps asking me this.

"I'm fine." I press my palms to his rough cheeks. I don't think he's shaved since I saw him last. I don't mind.

I'd like to tell him I want those whiskers scraping my thighs again, but my brother is too close.

He draws me tightly against him. "What now, Vi?"

"We're going to talk to my father."

"I'm not allowed back."

I rest my head on his shoulder. "Then I guess we'll have to call him."

Leo walks up. "I say we take lover boy to New York. We're not due back in Avalonia for months. He can stay on our floor."

"His mom," I say, and Finley squeezes my hand.

Leo rubs his chin. "Right. She can come, too."

I try not to shiver in the chill, but I do anyway. Finley wraps his arms around me. "We need to get her inside somewhere."

We look at the tiny car idling by the curb.

"I told Leo not to get in the Bug," I say. It was hard enough to squeeze me, my brother, and the guard in the thing.

And now we have Finley.

"I'll call another car for Vi and Finley," Leo says, but his guard Rubin shakes his head.

"You insisted on only one guard. That means both of you ride in the same car." His stern face brooks no argument.

"Okay, bigger car needed." Leo pays the woman driving the Bug and peers up at the awning of the bar. "Is this a good place to hang out?"

"Sure," Finley says. "Let's go inside." He runs his hands up and down the sleeves of my white sweater.

There are only a few people in the pub. Nobody recognizes us, although Rubin gets several curious glances due to his uniform. Finley speaks for a moment with the man behind the bar while we find a booth tucked in the corner and pile inside.

When Finley has returned, Leo asks, "What's the plan?"

"I'm not leaving Finley," I say.

Leo taps the table. "Okay, that's settled. I'll call for another guard so we can separate. I have a feeling whatever you two are about to do, I don't want to be there for."

I sneak a look at Finley. His face doesn't tell me anything, but under the table, he reaches for my hand and squeezes.

Rubin pulls out his phone. "I'll have someone cross the border."

"Don't tip them off," Leo says.

Rubin frowns. "They already are. Pace has to inform the Crown when the Crown Prince leaves the country."

"All right. Only mention me then. Don't bring up Octavia. You'll go with her. I'll take whoever comes."

Rubin nods. "It'll take an hour to get someone."

"Good. That gives us time for a drink."

Finley shifts to the end of the seat. "I'll get them."

Leo holds up a hand. "No, I'll do that. Rubin, come with me. Let's give them a moment."

The two of them move to the end of the bar, their backs to us. I scoot closer to Finley. "Do you have to go back to work?"

"No, it's quiet enough. I told Roger my situation has changed."

I can't seem to get close enough to him. I snuggle in. "I couldn't reach you."

"And I couldn't get to you. How did you know to come here?"

"Your mother. Leo got through to Madam Mariam and had her paged."

"So that's why she said to text her if anything interesting happened."

"She kept the secret. I wanted to surprise you."

He lifts my hand to his lips. "You definitely did that."

I lean my head on his shoulder. I don't want anything to change from this moment. He's here. I'm here. My brother is in charge, not my parents. "Could you go to New York? Would your mother come?"

He hesitates, and my stomach falls. "It's too much, isn't it?"

"It's far. And I don't think I could work there. Mom either. I'm not actually a citizen anywhere."

"You would be with us!"

Another hesitation. "That seems like a lot of pressure to put on us so soon."

He's right. We've barely even begun.

But I know what I feel. Maybe he's second-guessing being with me.

I hold his hand to my cheek. "I understand. Thank you for being my one-night stand, then. I know it cost you everything." Tears squeeze from my eyes.

"Hey." His thumb lifts my chin so he can look at me. "You were not a one-night stand. You're my Vi. I've loved you since we were small. You were the reason every *other* woman was a one-night stand. You are the only one who could never be that."

His gaze holds mine. Beautiful, perfect Finley. Slayer of hearts.

Mine?

"I know we don't know how it will work out," he says. "Remember what you told me in the trees that final night?"

"Live in the now. It's all we have. This very moment."

"Now is pretty good."

"It is."

He leans down to kiss me, and he's everything I remember, all that I've dreamed about. I don't know how long we're there, unwilling to part, our lips getting their reunion, but it must be awfully long because eventually

Rubin stands over us. "The guards came for your brother. Where are we going?"

I look up at Finley. "Where are you sleeping these days?"

"My apartment is a few blocks over. It's not much. Not at all."

I take his hand. "We've been meeting in cemeteries. Anything is a step up."

He laughs as we slide out of the booth. Rubin follows us at the proper pace as we head down the sidewalk.

A light rain starts to fall, and, by the time we arrive at a brick building, we're soaked.

"Sorry, Rubin!" I call. My hair is plastered to my head.

"I've been through worse," he says.

"There's a hall inside," Finley says. "You'll stay dry. Can I get you a towel?"

Rubin points to his cap. "I'm good. That's why we cover our heads."

Finley unlocks a door that looks like it's been painted many times. In the scrapes and nicks there are hints of green, brown, and red. I run my fingers over the imperfections. Even a door can have many lives.

Rubin settles into place in the hall as we enter the small room. I've never been in an apartment like this. The entire living space and kitchen could fit in my closet. Even when Finley turns on a light, it's still dim.

I know nothing about how people live. I whirl around to Finley. "I want a place like this. I want to go to grocery stores. I want to figure out how to make dinner from whatever's in the fridge."

He draws me close. "There's no reason why you have to do that."

"There is! How can any of us do anything for the people of Avalonia if we don't even understand their struggles? How they live?"

"I like it. But your parents won't go for that."

"I'll make them. I don't have to go home. Leo understands. He has a lot of power. He's the reason you were a guard, despite my father's rules."

"What will you do?"

"Get a place in town. It can have a guard. I get that. But let me live like any other young adult making her way. I would volunteer instead of work for pay, but I'd be doing things."

He draws me close. "I love these plans."

He doesn't say the "but" part, but I feel it. "But you're still banished."

"Brussels is only an hour away from the palace."

Father won't relent on this, not right away. But maybe I can chip away at him. If I come to visit Finley here in Belgium, day in and day out, or if I choose to live here rather than home, he'll see.

"You're not in the now," Finley says.

He's right. I've got him back. The future will take care of itself.

"You have a bedroom around here?" I ask.

He leads me to a door beyond the sofa. He doesn't flip on the light, letting the living room lamps create a soft glow over the bed.

It's made up simply with a sheet and a single blanket.

His voice is low. "We should get out of these wet

clothes. Let them dry." He fingers the bottom of my sweater.

"You're right." I push his jacket off his shoulders.

I step out of my shoes, and he lifts my sweater over my head, carefully draping it over a chair near the bed. He sits to untie the laces of his boots.

I stand there for a moment, and he takes me in. "Take off the pants."

My throat tightens. This is different from when we undressed each other in the trees.

I unbutton the top and ease the zipper down.

"Take it slow, so I can see every inch of your skin as it comes."

Heat rises in my body as I push the jeans down my thighs. They catch at my knees, and I step out of them. Now I'm only in a bra and panties.

His voice takes on the huskiness I remember. "Come here."

I get it. Why women come for him. He's impossible to resist.

I step closer. He reaches out to trace a finger along my collarbone, dipping between my breasts in the pale pink bra.

His hand spreads over the cup, and the sudden tightening of my nipple makes my head rush. I suck in a breath.

"A little closer."

I step between his knees. All the things we did before rise in my vision. I get to do them again. Again and again.

He reaches behind me and unhooks the bra.

"Let it fall."

I drop my arms, and the bra slides down my body to hit the floor near our feet.

For a moment, he only looks at me. Then his hands lift, thumbs on both nipples, hands cupping me. I can scarcely take it. I want to move fast, get part of him in me, any part, fingers, mouth, him. Anything.

But he takes his time.

"Turn around."

I do as he says, and his hands capture the back of me, fingers spread, his thumbs sliding down until they ease my thighs apart. He kneads the muscles, sending a vibrating thrill through my body.

Then he teases the panties down until they fall.

His hands on my hips urge me to turn back around. I'm naked, and he's fully dressed, other than his boots. It's titillating, hot. I feel desperate.

He doesn't stop looking, his gaze everywhere. He leans forward and draws a nipple into his mouth. My fingers clasp his head, threading through his hair. One of his hands lifts my knee and sets my foot on the arm of the chair.

Then his hand is there, fingers inside me. I'm slick around them, tightening down. Every moment I missed him, every night I revisited our time together, rushes back. I'm so eager. I want so much.

He works me, the pleasure growing, making me clutch at him until I finally say, "Finley, please."

He stands, shifting me so that I'm carried across the room to the bed.

His sheets are cool and smooth, the blanket folded at the bottom. He moves my knees to his shoulders and down he goes, his mouth where I want it. Fingers join in, and I'm weightless, lost. The stars gather overhead despite us being indoors. I'll always see that night sky, like the first time.

His tongue makes languid strokes along those tender places. His fingers curl inside me. I'm already so in need, so desperate, that I don't have long to wait. Everything quickens below my belly, gathering energy. It's so intense, so tight, like a spring coiling.

Then it reverses and lets go. The tension releases like petals falling, the feel of rain on flowers. It's beautiful and sweet and tears prick my eyes. There's some other emotion there. Something tender. I gasp, sucking in air. It's strong and goes on, pulse after pulse, like paradise stretching into infinity.

Finley moves over me and I feel his skin. He's shucked his clothes. I hear the tear of a package, then he wraps my legs around him and slips inside. Just when the pulses might slow, he coaxes them back, thrusting into me, his fingers between us, too.

This is nothing like before. The softness is gone. Now it's pounding. The tears dry on my skin as I lean toward him, reaching out to hold his neck.

This part is fire and force. He's not afraid this time to really work me. His muscles flex and he stands, bringing him with me. We step to the wall and he turns, pushing my back against it.

I'm pinned against the wallpaper, his body slamming into mine again and again. I clutch at him, each stroke pushing me into a new destination.

I cry out, a long whine forming in my throat. I need

something, feel desperate for it. I understand where we're going, but it's so different. It's all of me, my straining arms, my thighs, holding on tight.

It's every part of my body, moving with him. He's so deep, so strong. He's within me. The edges between us blur.

Then he groans, and my body responds. It's so tight, and clamps down so hard, I wonder how we can be separate anymore. The burst isn't petals at all this time, but pure energy, like a star exploding.

My scream is low, guttural, rising up from somewhere way below the surface. It's us, running over the fields, whistling at the donkeys like the big grown herders around us.

It's the garden path, crunching beneath our feet. The bounce of a tiny ball as we capture jacks with our hands. It's lunches and dinners and naptimes and finally his rugged face in the rose garden, one I should have recognized but still I knew.

It's us.

Both of our bodies pulse like hearts beating against each other. We hold on tight. I sense the condom catching what he could be giving me and long for the feeling of only him. I will work on how to make that happen.

He holds me against the wall for another long moment, our breathing ragged. Then he laughs.

I smack his shoulder. "What."

"That was my first second time. You should have been gentle with me."

"Sorry. This is no country for manwhores."

"Your manwhore."

He walks us back to the bed and we lie quietly, both of our chest rising and falling from the exertion.

He draws me to his shoulder. "I love you Octavia Henrietta Montgomery, Princess of Avalonia, second in line."

I roll onto his chest. "And I love you, Finlandorio Javien Bulgari. Donkey herder. Guard trainee. Bar bouncer. What do you think you want to do with the rest of your life?"

He situates me more squarely over his body, and that bulge that's become familiar starts to press against my belly. "How about that?"

I sit up. "I think I need birth control so we don't have interruptions." We discard one condom and replace it with another.

I slide my knees on either side of him and situate myself so he's positioned in just the right spot. "Now this looks like the perfect way to spend a life." I wiggle my way down, slipping him back inside me.

He closes his eyes, hands on my shoulders. "Till death do us part."

He knocks my knees wider, and I gasp as he slides farther in.

I hold him still. "Wait. Is that what it's referring to? I keep parting my legs until we're both dead?"

His laugh is full-throated as his hands move to my hips. "It can mean anything we want."

"Weddings are ruined forever."

He lifts my body above him, then brings me back down. I suck in another breath.

"I think you mean weddings are suddenly way more fun."

I picture every priest and minister saying the words at all the weddings I've attended, and even as my body moves over him, I have to laugh.

He's right.

Every ceremony from here on out will be tainted by all I've learned from this man. And they'll be so much better.

Till death do us...part.

CHAPTER 40

Finley

Four weeks later.

I pause by the florist's window as I head toward the bar. Mom is in the window, pulling down the display to keep in the fridge for the night. She's enjoying her new job arranging flowers, and she seems to have a knack for it.

Her apartment is above the shop, a small set of rooms the owner kept in hopes her daughter would take over the store. But the girl moved to London to study accounting and got married.

The owner is recovering from a surgery and was so happy to bring Mom on. The two of them have become fast friends and the living arrangement means neither of them is lonely. They can look after each other.

She sees me and waves. I'll have dinner with her tomorrow. It will be Sunday, when the shop is closed.

I head on to the bar. I will only officially work until midnight, when the doors in the front close. Then I'll be the one who opens the door to the back. I get paid extra for the bonus hours.

Luka shouts, "Fin!" when I enter and several of the regulars lift their glasses. I've become a fixture here since Leo reinstated my citizenship. Now I live in a house a few blocks off Town Square with other former herders. The place is a wretched mess, but it's fun. We all get along.

I've barely started stacking empties to carry to the back when Octavia pops in.

"We have a surprise for you," Luka tells her. "I've got your favorite cider on tap. It's proving quite popular."

"Oooh! Yay!" She nods to her guard, who takes a seat near the door as she hurries over to Luka. The guard isn't one of the new trainees, who got their stripes a few weeks ago, and it's not her old one, the stern woman Octavia resented so much.

He's called Pace, and he saw Prince Leo through his travels prior to his wedding. Leo decided he was the best fit as Octavia got more freedom to wander Avalonia.

We never went to New York. Leo immediately visited his father, the very night I spent with Octavia. He said he'd hide his two sisters indefinitely unless the old man changed the way they were treated.

Octavia stayed with me for three days while they hashed things out. Lili hung out with Sunny and Anthony, traipsing around New York and having a fine time meeting influencers and friends from Lili's social media contacts.

I never went back to Roger's bar.

And Octavia and I scarcely got dressed for the whole three days.

Even when we all agreed I could return to Avalonia, Mom didn't change her mind about leaving the washing rooms. Her love of palace life was permanently tarnished.

But now she's at the florist. I'm working at the bar.

And Octavia can leave the palace whenever she likes. She hopes to get permission to rent a house in town soon. Even with fewer restrictions, she longs to be out in the world.

I load the dishwasher below the bar with the glasses and set the cycle to start.

"There's a whole crate of deliveries in the back that need to be unloaded," Luka says. He's enjoying being my boss. It's all right. He's been fine, and if he's not, I pretend to clock him and he laughs and gets rid of his attitude.

It's not a life's work, but it's a life.

"I'm coming to help!" Octavia calls. She rounds the bar and ducks under the opening. We pass through the swinging door to the back.

The boxes and crates are haphazardly stacked. Octavia finds the box cutter and starts slicing the tape. "I saw your mom at the florist. She wants me to come to dinner tomorrow."

I nod. "Good."

"Do your roommates have to work after?" She bites her lip.

I know what she means. "Jake is off to Berlin. Z will be on the night shift. And Luka will be here."

"So an empty house?"

"An empty house."

"Kitchen or bathroom?"

She wants to break in every room. "Both."

"Yes!" She counts on her fingers. "It will be our first seventeenth time."

I wrap my arms around her. "I like having all these firsts with you."

Luka pops his head into the back, so we break apart. "No sex on the job!" he calls with a laugh. "And a group of ten just came in. I could use some help."

"I'll keep opening these," Octavia says. She enjoys doing work like this, and she's gotten to know where we store everything at the bar.

I kiss her head. "I'll be back in a minute."

She lifts her cider and takes a sip. "I'll be here!"

We haven't figured everything out. But we're together. Octavia has her freedom.

It's like she said all along.

We will live for the happiness we have now.

And it's plenty. More than we could have ever seen coming.

Epilogue: Octavia

Six months later.

With each gust of the chilly wind, more rose petals turn loose from their blossoms and spin through the air.

The path is strewn with them — red, white, pink. My favorites are the ones that are white with pink in the center, like the bouquet Finley brought that first night we were together.

I snap a blossom from a stem before it can fall apart. It's not long for this world, anyway. I might as well hold on to it. I tuck it behind my ear.

We're having a formal dinner in half an hour, and Finley's coming. It's the third palace meal he will have attended. The first one last summer didn't go great, with him and Father glowering at each other for six courses.

But the second one was better. They exchanged a few pleasantries about the Avalonian Cricket Team making the semifinals in the European Championship.

Hopefully, this third one will go well. I haven't made

any headway in convincing my parents to allow me to rent a house, but the longer Finley and I are together, the more they will come to understand that my life might be best lived outside the main palace.

These days, I'm allowed to wander the roses alone, but soon I hear whispering footsteps. They can't be a guard. Or Finley.

"Octavia!" Lili's singsong carries through the vines. "Where are you?"

"Near the bench."

She rounds the end of a row, glorious in a fitted sapphire dress. With our brother's return home, we have the good stylist back. Aisha gives us a lot more choices than Mother's stodgy old dressmaker.

"I saw somebody walk in, and he looks fantastic!" Lili hurries forward to take my hands. "Come this way."

Lili leads me to the bench in the far back of the gardens. So many things have happened here in the last year. Sometimes I swear I hear my grandmother's laugh on the wind. She knew exactly how to use the gardens to her advantage.

Finley waits there, and Lili's right, he looks fantastic. This is an official state dinner with a visiting Duke, so he's wearing white-tie formal and a black jacket with tails. My heart flutters. I'm used to his jeans and rolled-up long-sleeved shirts, often smelling faintly of bear and roasted almonds.

I don't mind. He does honest work. So does his mother. Any time I hear that sales are slow in the flower shop, I make a point of having Rosenthal use them for the arrangements at the palace entrance. As long as I have some say, that happy, harmonious place for those two ladies will remain on the square.

But today, Finley smells dreamy, like pine woods and aftershave. He must be anxious about the dinner, because his hands on mine are tighter than usual.

"Tonight will be wonderful," I tell him. "Don't worry."

He doesn't answer, and I'm about to make a light-hearted joke with Lili about how we'll have to create a diversion if Father gets testy.

But she's gone.

The light slants through the vines as the sun sets. We're alone in the rose garden, the palace stretching high above us, including the tower where I used to watch Finley work out. I'm glad he's not a guard. I couldn't have visited him and worked by his side like I sometimes do at the bar.

"Vi...I..." He trails off and takes a deep breath.

"Are you okay, Finley?" His forehead is shiny. I open his coat and extract the extra handkerchief I tucked there myself when I approved the suit and tap it along his hairline.

He takes the handkerchief. "I am."

"Then spit it out!" I want to laugh. "Surely you're not that worried about dinner."

His Adam's apple bobs. He tucks the handkerchief back inside his pocket and extracts a small velvet box. "I already spoke to your father today."

"You did?" Then I realize why. My dad. The box. "Finley..."

He drops to one knee. "He said yes, Vi. He said he knows it's what you want. That you keep asking to live outside the palace. So he asked if it was all right if he purchased the old Farthington estate on the edge of town for us. If that would upset me."

My throat is tight. "And you said?"

"I said that would be all right. I'm not too proud to accept a whole house."

"It's a lovely place. It's been so empty." I glance down at the box.

"But I insisted on buying my own ring. Not some jewel from your vault. I saved for it." He opens the velvet case.

Inside is a simple diamond on a white-gold band. It's modest and lovely, each facet sparkling in the fading light. A princess cut, perfectly square. "I love it," I tell him.

"So, you will?" he asks. More sweat pops on his brow.

I grin. "Will I what?"

He draws in a shaky breath. "Octavia Henrietta Montgomery, Princess of Avalonia, Second in Line, will you marry me?"

I'm about to answer, when bells start tolling. Bells in the towers. Then the abbey. More and more, until they seem to come from everywhere.

"Is that for us?" Finley asks.

I pull him to his feet. "That's for the baby! It means the Crown Prince's child is on the way! Sunny's in labor!"

I grab his hand, and we run through the rose garden to the palace. The guards open the door and we find Lili and Mother in the Grand Foyer.

"Where is she?" I ask.

Mother looks anxious, her mouth tight. "Sunny is getting settled in the birthing room with the nurses and the Royal Physician." She glances at my empty hand. "Didn't you say yes?"

"Oh!" I turn to Finley. "Yes! Yes! I'll marry you!" I hold out my hand, and we both laugh as he slides the ring on my shaking finger.

"Let's go see Sunny!" Lili grabs my arm to lead us through the foyer.

"Wait!" I turn back to my love, my new fiancé. I kiss him hard on the mouth. "We'll celebrate this soon!"

He laughs. "Go to your sister-in-law."

I throw my arms around him. "I will. See you soon! So soon!"

As Lili and I race to the hall to the Crown Prince's wing, I take a moment to look back. This is the now. The right now.

Father approaches Mother and Finley. He shakes Finley's hand. Finley gives him a deep bow.

He looks perfect there in his tux. My Finley. My Dory. He can fit in anywhere. The palace. The back of a bar. The club.

And finally, everywhere he goes, I get to go, too.

Would you like to be present for the birth of the royal baby? Superfans on my email list will be sent this momentous novelette shortly after the release of *Royal Rebel*. Make sure you sign up!

Until then, make sure you have read Prince Leo and Sunny's love story in Royal Pickle! He's the King of Cock, and he only has seven days to convince the girl he met in a Brooklyn deli to be his bride!

CHARACTERS YOU MET

Were you intrigued by Mack and Rory back in New York? Read their second-chance love story after Mack trades his law degree for the big red suit in Second Chance Santa.

And if you missed how Anthony Pickle accidentally poisons a TV show host with his pickle, leading to an enemies-to-lovers romance with the woman everyone thinks may have framed him, grab Spicy Pickle!

The Pickleverse is nine books strong! See the entire reading order!

BOOKS BY JJ KNIGHT

Romantic Comedies

Single Dad on Top

Big Pickle

Hot Pickle

Spicy Pickle

Royal Pickle

Royal Rebel

Tasty Mango

Second Chance Santa

The Accidental Harem

MMA Fighters

Uncaged Love

Fight for Her

Reckless Attraction

Get emails or texts from JJ about her new releases:

JJ Knight's list

About JJ Knight

JJ Knight is one of the pen names of six-time *USA Today* bestselling author Deanna Roy. She lives in Austin, Texas, with her family.

To choose your next read from one of her sixty books, visit the web site **Read Laugh Swoon** to pick by book boyfriend, story line, heat level and more!

facebook.com/jjknightauthor

twitter.com/deannaroy

instagram.com/deannaroyauthor

bookbub.com/profile/jj-knight

tiktok.com/@deannaroy.author